NO GHOSTS

THE COWBOY AND THE DOM
BOOK 3

JODI PAYNE

BA TORTUGA

No Ghosts: The Cowboy and the Dom, Book Three
Copyright © 2020 by Jodi Payne & BA Tortuga

Cover illustration by AJ Corza
http://www.seeingstatic.com/
Cover content is for illustrative purposes only and any person depicted on the cover is a model.

ISBN: 978-1-951011-29-1

Electronic edition published by Tygerseye Publishing, LLC, March 2020
Printed in the USA

CONTENTS

As always, to our wives.

1

"No, Sam can't be alone yet. Can you set up a conference call?" Thomas stared at the Scrabble board. "After three."

"Three thirty?" Thomas's assistant, Ally, was on the phone, being her usual organized self and covering for him while he was out of the office, looking after his lover.

"Yes, that'll work. Put it on my calendar and email me the slide deck?"

"Sure thing, I'm doing that right now." He could hear Ally typing. "Doctor Kinessey called about continuing his sponsorship for next year."

While they were talking, Thomas pulled a handful of Scrabble tiles off his rack and placed them on the board, spelling out C-A-N-D-Y. Not great, but not terrible. He gave Sam a shrug and a smile and paced away from the board, one eye still on his lover, his sub.

"When did he call? Did Kathy call him—"

"Yesterday. She's on it."

"Oh, good. That's promising."

Sam tilted his head, playing Y-O-D-E-L-I-N-G. "You can go in, Mister. I swear."

He shook his head and mouthed the word *No* to Sam.

"So how's the cowboy?"

He stared at the board and sighed. "Jesus."

"That bad?"

"What? No. No that wasn't for you. He's much better. I'm just getting my ass handed to me in Scrabble. Sorry."

"Okay...that's not sexy at all. So...ah. Amanda wants to know if you're planning on making an appeal at the donor gala next month."

"Yes. Tell her I'm interested, and I'll try to get in to see her early next week."

"She goes on vacation Wednesday."

"Oh. Okay, well Monday, then."

"You're sure?"

He had to return to work someday. Sam would be coping by then. "Yes, Monday."

"Okay, Boss. That's all I got. Check in with me later?"

"All right. I'll call you around four." Thomas looked at his watch. He was pretty proud of himself. He was up, showered, shaved, he'd made breakfast, and even gotten dressed today. It was as if he were real.

"Kiss your cowboy!"

He snorted. "Thanks, Ally." He hung up the phone. "You cheated."

"I did not. I'm just brilliant." Sam stuck his tongue out at him and rolled those pretty eyes. Once Sam's stitches had come out, the boy shaved his head, and with the knit caps he wore constantly these days, Sam's eyes seemed huge.

"I liked it better when you still had the concussion and you thought the Hs were Ls and the Vs were Ws." He picked five tiles and stared at his new letters thoughtfully. "Ah." He grinned. Maybe he could keep up after all. He played D-E-V-I-C-E off Sam's D in "yodeling" and replaced the tiles in his rack. "Looks like I'm going back in on Monday."

"I'm more than capable of managing. I've got this. I'll even make you chili." *A-X-E-S and D-E-V-I-C-E-S?* Thomas was about to pinch Sam.

"We'll have to talk about some ground rules while I'm not home." He turned Sam's "axes" into T-A-X-E-S and also put down A-B-L-E off his T.

"Nicely done. What kind of ground rules? I'm just going to work, mostly. I'm still five hundred emails behind." Sam played V-O-L-E.

"Well, for starters, no working out." God, he had impossible tiles. He sighed and used the C in "candy" to make R-I-C-E. *Pathetic.*

"I'll get soft in the middle, you know."

"You can do some crunches when I get home. But no running at all."

"No. Not yet. Maybe in a little while, but...no. Not yet." Sam reached out for him.

He abandoned his letters, moved around the coffee table to sit closer to his boy, and took Sam's hand in his. "Yes. That's right. Not yet."

"Mmm...hey." Sam twined their fingers together, holding on to him.

"Hi." Thomas gave his boy a smile. "It'll be good, won't it? Getting back to our routine." If they could even call it that. Sam had only just moved in when he was attacked and hospitalized, so they hadn't had a routine in place for more than a couple of weeks. But Sam had been happy before all this insanity, working on his book and making progress on his research projects. The focus had been good for his boy.

"You know it. I'm aching for a little normal. Just a little. Maybe a lot."

"Aching, yes." He'd been fine all week. His body had been just as focused on Sam's recovery as his mind. But talking about normal suddenly made him want his lover back.

He reached for Sam and pulled his boy in for a kiss.

Sam's hand was warm on Thomas's cheek, his thumb moving lazily, stroking under his eye.

His boy smelled like Old Spice and tasted a little wild, just like his cowboy should. He slid a hand over Sam's hip and tucked it under one firm ass cheek, giving it a squeeze. The grin he got was pure happiness, Sam leaning hard into his touch.

His boy's energy lit him up and he grinned, catching those hazel eyes, loving the little extra green he saw there this time. "Hey, don't I know you from somewhere, cowboy?"

"That's the rumor. You found me wandering, I hear. All aimless and shit." Sam licked the corner of his lips, the sensation featherlight, intriguing.

"Right, aimless. I remember now." He huffed out a soft laugh. "Well, we can't have that. I'm sure I've got something you can focus on." He nudged Sam's chin up with his own and inhaled against smooth skin, breathing his boy in.

"Mmm..." That satisfied sound settled deep in his balls. "Oh, that's just right."

"Mhm." He licked and kissed his way past Sam's throat, humming as he felt the boy swallow against his lips, and tested the bend near the boy's shoulder with his teeth.

Sam moaned for him, moving sweet and slow against him, almost like he was dancing. It didn't take anything at all to encourage Sam into his lap; then he had that perfect ass rocking into him.

"Yes." That was what he was after. Heat spread up his spine, making him suck in a quick, deep breath. "That's good, sweetheart." He slipped his hands up under Sam's T-shirt and explored the hot skin and hard muscles with knowing fingers.

Sam stared at him, letting him see all the hunger, the love. It could get addictive fast, that open desire.

A piece of him was so ready for a throwdown, but he took a breath and made that wait because his hands needed to feel Sam whole; to feel his lover's strength, make sure it was real, make sure Sam could handle what was building in him.

He reached up and traced the edge of Sam's cap. "Are you sure?"

"I am. I got this." Sam kissed him hard enough that he forgot to breathe. "I need to feel us together, you know?"

He found a breath, thin though it was. "I do. I want you. God, so much." He urged Sam off his lap and stood. "I have to have all of you."

"Yes. Every bit." Sam nodded and led him to the bedroom, hands sweating just a little. Thomas followed eagerly, captivated, recognizing the gesture for what it was. As they moved into the room, he tugged off his T-shirt and tossed it, going for another kiss, chasing down Sam's lips.

Sam opened up, hands sliding down into his sweats, easing them over his ass.

Thomas kicked his jeans off, stepping past them and reaching for Sam's T-shirt. He got hold of the fabric but stopped himself, eyes glancing up at the knit cap on Sam's shaved head. He lifted the shirt off, careful not to bump anything that might still be sore, and dropped it.

"May I?" he asked, catching Sam's eyes, fingers reaching for the hat, the only garment his lover was still wearing.

"I don't want to turn you off, Mister." There was a question in Sam's expression, a test.

Thomas tilted his head, wondering why his lover couldn't see how entirely unnecessary that was, but he gave Sam the only answer he had...and his heart with it. "I want all of you, sweetheart. I love all of you. Every bit. Always."

"All right, then. Yeah." Sam took the hat off, no more hesitation, trusting in his word.

He was continually in awe of the depth of Sam's trust in him. He smiled, gave his boy a nod, and ran his fingers lightly from front to back, across Sam's skull, examining the scars and what was left of the bruises, learning them a little and accepting them as part of who the boy was to him. "Thank you."

He planned to reward that trust tonight for as long as they could stand it. He took a kiss, bumping against Sam as they shuffled toward the bed.

Sam snuggled in, pressing into him, shoulders to hips, holding nothing back.

"Mmm." He got his arms around Sam. "You feel so good. I was missing you like this. I'm so ready to get lost in you, sweetheart. Inside you." He shifted, trapping Sam's cock against his hip and rocking them together.

Sam made the best sound—half moan and half happy yelp—and his eyelids went heavy. Thomas tugged Sam in tighter, giving him more friction, making his boy feel the pressure.

"Good, yes?" He could feel Sam moving...always moving, his boy. One more thing he'd missed. He was aching in earnest now, wanting Sam's attention, his boy's touch. He was patient, though. He'd get what he desired most. For now, he was enjoying watching Sam feel, watching his boy begin to dissolve.

"Oh, Mister. Good don't begin to..." Sam's words trailed off, a low moan taking their place as a deep flush climbed his chest.

Not even close, he knew. "My boy," he said with a growl that started down deep. He moved to the bed, pulling Sam with him by the hand. "Come on, sweetheart, off your feet."

Sam crawled up onto the bed, arms open to him, begging for him. His boy did need so well. It was a beautiful sight. It made him breathless, eroded what was left of his patience. He moved over Sam and into those arms, gliding his stiff prick along hot skin and kissing his boy until they were equally unable to breathe.

He made sure that tender, bruised head was cradled in the pillows, but that was where he let his worry stop. Sam's body would tell him everything he should know.

With his eyes on his boy, he curled his fingers firmly around Sam's cock and stroked, thumb dragging up the back and circling around the head, just to see it in Sam's face. Just to see what he was doing reflected in his boy's eyes.

Sam's lips dropped open and one leg drew up, his knee bending to give him more access.

The knowledge that two weeks ago Thomas might have lost this, that he might not have had his boy in his bed again was present with him as he touched Sam, watched the boy move. It wasn't distracting or even painful, not with the reality of Sam right in front of him, but it made him appreciate this first time together since the incident, made him more acutely aware of what they had, what they were together.

It made some of his other worries feel less significant, less pressing. That was their work. This was their world, and he was more than content in it.

He reached for his nightstand, craving his lover beyond words.

"Damn, you're pretty." Sam reached up, fingers stroking his nipple to hardness, pinching the barest bit, teasing him.

He hissed at the quick little jolt that sent across his chest, raising goose bumps and making him shiver. "Thank you." He was going to accept those words, the same way his lover had accepted his own earlier. Simply. He was trying to be better about that.

He smoothed the rubber over his cock and offered his boy two slippery fingers and a little pressure. "Soon, boy. Need you soon."

Sam pinched again before bearing down, taking his fingers in. Sam was silk inside, tight and heated, and Thomas groaned at the promise Sam's body made.

He twisted his fingers as Sam took them in, slicking and teasing, stretching and making sure his boy relaxed. The last was hardly necessary, as Sam felt loose and ready. That made the corner of his mouth twitch in a knowing grin. His boy wanted everything he did.

He'd never known a man that had so little sexual experience and so much natural instinct, such deep desires. It suited him to be Sam's first and only. It made him just that much more proud, and it was hot as hell. He groaned as that thought settled right into his groin, making his balls tight and his cock stretch. *Fuck.* "Sweetheart…"

"Mister. Please, love me, huh?" Sam spread wide, knees bent in a clear offer.

Damn, it didn't get any hotter than that. "Love you." He lined up, one fist around his cock to guide himself, and sank into his boy to the root with a long sigh. Sam rippled around him, the sensation driving another spike of heat up along his spine.

He stretched over Sam, instinct already driving him. Sam's need was making him high, making it hard to think but easy just to let his body have what it wanted. Sam met his thrusts, gaze dragging over his body like his boy wanted to devour him.

"Fuck, Sam." He leaned down and kissed his boy, hard and deep, thrusting in with his tongue even as his hips went wild. "Feel so good. Perfect."

"Yes." Sam nodded, biting his bottom lip, white teeth just digging in.

Sam's prick pressed into his belly and he reached for it again, giving the boy just enough of a grip to feel it. That soft cast slapped against the sheets, Sam's right hand fisting tight. "Oh, damn. Fuck. Want you so bad."

He ducked his head and shifted his hips a bit, the steeper angle giving him a little more rub. "Fuck!"

Sam wrapped those strong legs around him, adding all that core strength to his, and shit, he was going to lose it. Sam rode him like no one else, frantic, hungry, pushing them both. He grunted and gave in, breathing hard, single-minded, taking everything Sam offered and returning it. He loved the way they worked together, no shame, no boundaries, just giving and getting everything they needed.

"Sam!" He had to let go of Sam's cock to brace himself before he fell over; his boy was so strong, and he had to balance.

Sam bore down, squeezed hard around his cock, and Thomas barked out a sharp cry. Thomas trembled and gulped in air, thrusting uselessly, his cock choked by Sam's body. To his own ears, his shout sounded hoarse as his climax roared through him, just a breath before he was ready, one second before he'd have lost control himself, his own pleasure summoned by his beautifully impatient boy.

"So-so fucking fine," Sam breathed, right hand pulling at his needy cock, clumsy, harsh, awkward.

"I've got you, sweetheart." Jesus, his voice felt blown. He pushed Sam's hand away and took over, strokes solid and steady, Sam's cock gliding through his fist as he watched the pleasure roll over his boy's face in waves.

"Mister!" Sam shuddered and shot for him, ass still clamped tight around his cock.

Thomas groaned as another jolt ran through him, making the blood roar in his ears and his vision blur. He blinked it clear, wanting to see his boy, wanting to watch. "You're stunning, love."

Sam panted for him, blinking up with a purely dazed expression.

Oh, that was adorable.

He leaned down, took a slightly breathless kiss, and smiled at Sam. "That was...you're...fuck, I love you." He had so much to say, but he didn't seem to have words yet, so he hoped that summed it up well enough.

"Love." Sam moaned for him, licking Thomas's lips. "Wow, huh?"

He nodded. That about covered it. "Yes. Wow. Incredible." He kissed Sam again. "The way you drive me out of my mind."

Sam grinned at him. "Good. I'm so glad. I want to make you feel as good as you make me."

"Oh, sweetheart. Without even trying." He put a hand on Sam's hip and shifted, dropped the rubber in the bin by the bed, and stretched out alongside his boy.

"Mmm...that is one of my favorite feelings on Earth." Sam sounded utterly tickled.

He laughed in agreement. It felt good to have this back,

the warmth, his boy so relaxed, nothing between them but skin.

"It feels much better than being crushed at Scrabble."

"Yeah, yeah, yeah." Sam patted his leg, fingers trailing over his skin. "I missed making love with you, Mister."

His chest tightened at Sam's words. "Yes, so much. We needed this, sweetheart. I was craving you." Mindful of the boy's injuries, he pulled Sam to him, helping his lover settle in his arms. Sam didn't hesitate for a second; he snuggled in with a satisfied sigh, resting hard against Thomas's chest.

He held his boy close, grateful to have felt Sam's strength, to know for sure that every bit of Sam was solid and whole. They still had other pieces of their relationship to visit, other aspects of their lives to bring back around to normal, but as far as new beginnings went, this was the perfect start.

2

Sunday would be three weeks since his...accident? Was it an accident? A beating? An attack?

Something.

Whatever.

Sam was getting used to wearing his cap, to not shaving because he didn't want to look in the mirror, to fighting a steady, low-grade headache that the doctor insisted would ease. At least he could sit in front of the screen easier now, right?

Right.

Fuck.

What Sam wasn't used to was the lack of movement, the lack of exercise, so he took the afternoon to walk, taking voice notes on his phone as he enjoyed the early spring sunshine and told himself that he wasn't nervous and, if he was nervous, he needed to fuck right off because he was a cowboy and he got back up on the horse. He didn't look over his shoulder. He didn't think about his head. He didn't let this keep him in the...

He tilted his head as he turned the corner, surprised as

hell to see Buzz from Mike's sitting on a bench across from home. "Buzz? Buzz, is that you? What are you doing out here?"

"Hey, man. What's up?" Buzz gave him a wave and shifted in his seat. "Where are you coming from?"

"Right here. How's it going? It's been forever."

"It has, it's great to see you. We all heard about the attack. How's the recovery going?"

"Fine. I'm all set to normal, thanks." Okay, this was a little strange. More than a little. "See you, buddy."

He couldn't just invite Buzz up to Thomas's apartment. That seemed...well, it seemed like it wasn't really his place.

Buzz raised an eyebrow. "Uh. Sure, man. Take it easy."

"You too....Okay, this is fucking weird. You want to go get a cup of coffee?" There was a coffee shop close by, and he could text Thomas to have him meet them on the way home.

"You good? You don't need to, you know..." Buzz pointed to his head. "Rest?"

"I got to tell you, man. I'm so goddamn tired of taking it easy. Seriously. Come on. I'll buy you a coffee. I'm waiting for Thomas to come home for supper."

Buzz hauled off the bench with a groan, like he'd been sitting there a while. "You're on. I could go for a cup."

"Good deal. What all have you been up to?" He could small talk with the best of them, God knew, and Buzz was a sweetheart for all he looked like a rough bastard.

"Oh, just work. You know, keeping the riffraff in one piece. Bar's been busy since the weather warmed up a little. Lots of people out. Some of them even ask about you." Buzz winked at him.

"Yeah? I need to come for a beer. Let Darla try to boss

me around." Hell, he ought to go next week sometime, see Angel, have a beer with Thomas. They'd have fun.

Buzz laughed darkly. "Try, huh? Watch yourself. You're best to always have a 'yes ma'am' with her, whether you still work there or not." That grin looked like Buzz knew firsthand what he was talking about.

Sam snorted, opening the door. "No shit on that. Let me text Thomas and see where he is. That way I'll know whether to just order his drink or what."

"Sounds good."

Hey. Having coffee w/friend. You want to join us?

Who are you with? Leaving now. Text me where.

Buzz from the bar. Just at the corner. You want caramel?

Sam didn't know if Thomas wanted something sweet before supper. He tended not to.

straight up latte, give me 15

He followed Buzz to a table while he was texting.

"Is he coming?"

"Yeah, he needs fifteen minutes or so. I figure I'll wait a few, then order. What are you drinking?"

Buzz grinned. "You gonna tell anyone if I get a hazelnut mocha?"

"Not a soul."

"Then you have your answer, my friend." Buzz took a seat and pulled out a phone, going quiet for a minute, quick thumbs hammering on the screen. "Sorry, just..." The phone kept chiming softly and Sam assumed the man was having a text conversation. "Okay. Just had to check in, sorry."

"No worries. We all have two lives, huh? One online and one for real." Sam wanted to touch on that in his book.

Buzz glanced at him, that eyebrow going up again. "I suppose."

Shut up, Sam. This guy doesn't want your theory on...well, anything. Save it for Thomas. Maybe for some of the folks on the art history loop. Not Buzz.

"I'll go order the coffees."

"Hang on, one sec." Buzz physically stopped him, tugging on his sleeve. "You're on social media? You need to watch that, you know. People track you that way. People you don't want tracking you, you know?"

"I'm pretty careful about that—not telling where I am, not checking in."

Buzz nodded and let go of him. "Okay. Okay, good."

Okay, that was weird. This whole thing was just...was Buzz following him?

Why the hell would Buzz be following him?

He headed to the counter and ordered two lattes and a hazelnut mocha, worrying his bottom lip as he pondered.

By the time he got back to the table, Thomas had arrived. His lover stood up and gave him a quick kiss. "Hey, I have great timing."

"Perfect! Do y'all remember each other? Thomas, Buzz. Buzz, Thomas." He let his eyes drag over his lover, just for a second. He did love the way his man was put together.

Mister must have noticed, because he got a crooked smile. "I do. We were just catching up. Buzz says you ran into him after a walk? Nice day for it." Thomas helped him hand out coffees.

"Yeah, I was blowing out the cobwebs. I didn't know y'all were friends. That's cool."

"I took a walk at lunch for the same reason, I just felt like I needed the sunshine."

Buzz glanced at his phone. "Oh, hey. I'm sorry, man, I have to run. I guess I'll take this to go." Buzz stood and shook with Thomas, then with him. "Really sorry. Thanks much. Come by the bar soon, Little Sammy."

"Sure. I'll try to come in next week." He gave Buzz a smile before looking at Thomas. "Man, how odd was that?"

"Big city, small world." Thomas took his hand, gave it a squeeze. "How was your walk? Do you feel all right?"

"It was good. I made a lot of notes. I had to get out and wander, you know?" He had been too cooped up, too worried, too everything.

Thomas nodded, smiling. "Feeling shut in? You need to move, I know you. Have you been sleeping all right?"

The concern felt good, and he smiled over. "If I can remember to not sleep on the side with the scars, huh?"

"I know. I try to stay close enough that you can't roll, but even in your sleep, you're a stubborn cowboy." Thomas sipped the tall coffee. "We'll work this weekend and get you out of your head a little. I'll figure out something we can do together that's safe."

"I hate that you're always having to stress about me. I'm not fragile, you know?" He was a damn cowboy. He wasn't any more broken than anyone else, right?

Thomas leaned toward him, arms crossed on the table. "Sweetheart. What would you say if I told you I hated that you have to stress about me?"

Sam didn't know what to say to that. He was going to do it anyway. He worried all the time. *All* the time. He wanted to do right by Thomas. He wanted Thomas to be happy. He wanted to be enough. "I guess I'd tell you it was my job."

Thomas nodded. "Physically, you're not fragile at all. Emotionally, there are things about you that are, but you are still plenty strong. I don't *have* to stress about you. I care about you, so it's my job to care *for* you. I want to care for you. I want...so much for you."

He reached out and squeezed Thomas's hand, feeling flushed and warm and loved. Totally loved. "Thank you. Hey. Happy Friday."

"TGIF, love." Thomas smiled and leaned over to kiss his fingers. "Thank you for the coffee. It was a little boost I didn't know I needed."

"I just was so surprised to see Buzz, I invited him to coffee, and when I smelled it? Yum."

"You should spend more time with friends. From the bar or the club, whatever. It's good to make those connections."

"Yeah. I may run down to Mike's sometime next week." He wasn't sure how he was supposed to make friends at the club, really. He wasn't blaming anyone; he just didn't know how, exactly.

"Wear a helmet." Thomas looked like he was only half-kidding. "You can run over to the club too, you know. You're a member. You can go anytime, see who's hanging out."

"Turd. No helmets." Right now, he wasn't interested in embarrassing Thomas accidentally. No way. He'd stick to the tavern.

"Very well. No fights, then. Do we have a deal?" Mister didn't look like he was kidding at all this time.

"Not unless someone takes a swing first, you got my word."

"It's Mike's. That doesn't make me feel better." Thomas leaned back in his seat. "You can't have another blow to the head. You get that, don't you? If someone takes a swing first, you're already in trouble."

"I know." God, he wanted to say he hadn't gone out looking for trouble. He surely hadn't been, but he didn't know for sure. He couldn't remember.

"That's all I need to hear." Thomas looked at him

thoughtfully. "Do you feel like you're ready to work tomorrow? I'm not talking about your physical recovery."

Part of him immediately said yes; part of him said he was just going to disappoint Thomas again. He told himself that he had to try. If he could just get what Thomas wanted him to do... "No time like the present, I guess."

"We don't have to go to the club, we can just work at home. Keep it simple. Sound good?"

"It does. Baby steps." He went for light and easy, trying not to seem stressed out because he wasn't, right? Right.

"Not baby steps, just uncomplicated ones. Affirmations."

"I do like how you think, Mister. Affirmations." This smile felt easier, more natural. "You have supper thoughts?"

"I'm a little wiped out from the week." Thomas sat up again. "I want pizza, of the everyday, boring, delivery variety. And perhaps a movie. Thoughts?"

"I can't think of anything I'd like better. You, me, comfy pants, wine and pizza."

"Done, then." Thomas stood, offering him an arm and a relaxed smile. "Hey, you. We made it to Friday. I actually think we did pretty well."

"I thought we did great. It only took a week to get through all those emails." He took Thomas's arm and grabbed his half-drunk up coffee. "Now we have our weekend. Together."

It was a nice evening, cool but not chilly, still pretty light out. Thomas actually hummed a little as they left the coffee shop. His Sir was in a really good mood, all relaxed, almost forgetting that stiff suit and the New Yorker walk and just strolling along the sidewalk with him instead.

He sighed softly, his eyelids just a tad heavy. He felt... normal. Just like two lovers walking home.

"It must be spring; all the lovebirds are out."

Thomas stopped them and turned to face the voice behind them. "Scotty! Hey, it's good to see you."

"You too. Great night, isn't it?"

"It's perfect." See him. See him be nice. "How's it going, man?"

"I'm heading in to work. I'm closing today."

"Ah. I know all about that."

Scotty's head tilted slightly, and one eyebrow went up. "I almost didn't recognize you without your hat."

"No? I thought it would have been the beard and mustache that would have been different." His new felt had come, but the scars hurt even with a gimme cap. The knit cap worked best right now.

"Nothing a razor can't fix." He winked at Thomas and Thomas laughed.

"It's definitely taking some getting used to."

He didn't say a word. He had his reasons, and he didn't have to explain them.

Scotty looked at him and when no answer came, the man turned eyes on Thomas. "I guess it'll be a while before you're back at the club, huh? Sam still looks like he's recovering. I guess he can't really handle all of that."

Thomas put an arm around his shoulders. "We're taking our time. Hardly any reason to rush things."

"Well, we miss you, Master. All of us. I hope you'll be back soon." Scotty shot him a slimy little smile. "Both of you, of course."

The temptation to snarl "Fuck off" was so big, his toes curled.

"Thank you, Scotty. Don't let us make you late, boy. Clive will stripe your ass."

Scotty grinned at Thomas, possibly the most sincere

smile he'd ever seen on the bartender. "You know it! Good night, Master Thomas. Sam."

Scotty took the last few steps to the corner and turned down toward the subway.

Lord, he hated that little bastard.

He had to let it go. Seriously. He had pizza and wine, Thomas, couch time, and movies. Scotty was jealous.

Hell, he'd be jealous if he was going to work right now.

"Scotty looks like he needs some sleep, don't you think?"

"Yeah. He looks grumpy. Sucks to feel like that." *No, Mister, we're not going to be buds. Don't go there.*

"I wonder what's up? Maybe he could use a friend too. You...should...what?" Thomas looked at him curiously.

"I'm sorry?" What had he missed?

"Your shoulders got tight all of a sudden; are you okay?" Thomas gave his shoulders a squeeze as if to make the point.

Oh. Oh, damn. So, lie? Tell the truth? It meant a lot to him that Thomas paid attention. It meant a lot to Thomas that he was dead honest. "Scott and I had words a few weeks ago. It wasn't fun."

"What? Words over what? Why didn't you tell me?" Mister seemed genuinely shocked, concerned, but not upset with him at all.

"It was no big deal. I think he might be a little into you, hmm?" A little into Thomas, a little bit of a bitch, and a little mean.

"Into me?" Thomas laughed and shook his head. "That's...what? You're not serious."

"I don't know what to tell you. One way or the other, I don't foresee a blossoming friendship here. Just a polite truce."

Thomas blinked at that and started them walking again,

pulling out his keys. "Huh. I'm sorry. I wish you'd told me sooner."

"I didn't want to cause trouble. It was no big thing."

"Maybe not for you, but I feel pretty foolish not knowing." Thomas shrugged and opened the door to the building. "I know now, I guess."

"I mean, he didn't come up to me and say, 'Oh, I want your man' or anything. It was way more, 'Hey, you suck.'"

Thomas snorted and pulled him onto the elevator. "All right, sweetheart. I get it. He's jealous. That's a first for me."

"Huh. That's hard to believe." Thomas did it for him, all the way to the bone.

"You're good for my ego, stud." He got herded out of the elevator and Thomas let them into the apartment. "Pizza."

"Sausage? Pepperoni?" He shrugged his jacket off.

"Sausage. Mushrooms?" Thomas took his jacket and went to hang it up.

"Sounds good. I'll order." He grabbed Thomas's arm, brought them together. "Hello, Mister. I love you."

Then he kissed Thomas good and hard.

3

Saturday morning, Thomas woke up ready.

He got a shower, thanked his boy for the coffee, and pulled on a pair of soft leather pants. He went bare otherwise—no boots, no shirt, just enough leather to ground him.

When Sam got out of the shower Thomas suggested he dress comfortably, put the boy's cuffs on him to give him something to think about, and sent Sam off to make breakfast. Sam had appeared one morning a few days ago after a shower without his cast on. He'd given Sam a look, the boy looked right back at him, and he'd deemed it best not to ask any questions. Hopefully the boy's wrist could handle the cuffs.

And for all that, he hadn't gotten more than a curious look from his boy. So things weren't off-track so much as unfamiliar, like muscles they hadn't done any heavy lifting with in a while.

He'd promised Sam an affirmation, and they'd have that, but he didn't promise it would be an easy day. Still, they'd start with a good breakfast and some casual comfort to make sure they were both in the right space before he dove into some of the headwork he had planned for his boy.

Before the eggs and toast were brought over, Sam was whistling with his phone, the music muted in his pocket.

George Strait, one of those hundreds of love songs. That made him smile. Maybe he owed his boy a dance tonight.

"This looks great." He grinned at Sam. "Is there more coffee, or have you finished the pot?"

"Would I have finished the pot without making more for you, Mister?" Sam winked at him and held a hand out for his coffee.

He laughed and handed the boy his mug. "Only if you wanted a spanking." They might not be great chefs, but they sure knew how to drink coffee. He'd thought about getting one of those expensive coffeemakers that ground the beans and served up fancy creations with no effort, but he'd decided not to deprive his boy of the simple pleasure of making him a cup of coffee.

In his head, that made perfect sense.

Somehow, he thought it would make sense to his boy, too.

"Here you go, Mister." Sam sat and stretched, wiggling side to side.

"Thank you." He took the mug and took a deep sip before setting it down and digging into his breakfast. "Tell me what you're hoping for today."

"That we're both at peace tomorrow morning."

He nodded. "That's the goal. Is there anything specific that you want? Or, anything you feel you need?" He didn't usually ask questions like this of a sub, but he was curious how the boy would answer.

"You. I want to be together, connected. Sometimes it's so

hard to know—" Sam stopped and shook his head. "I just want you."

Well. That was interesting. He put his fork down and looked at his boy. "Finish what you were going to say. There's no reason not to say it, boy. This is our space."

"Sure, there is." Sam winked at him, body language relaxed, open, letting him know that Sam was here with him —right now, not stressing. "I say, 'It's hard to know what you need from me.' Then you tell me, 'I have no expectations of you,' and you end up down because I didn't give you what you needed."

He grinned slowly, picking up his coffee. "Ah. *Touché*. But, we discussed that. We're not at the club for one thing, so there's a layer there you don't have to be concerned with today, and further, I was wrong if I used those exact words. I do have the expectation that you try, and that you're truthful."

He sipped his coffee and put it down on the table. "In fact, my expectations, and my needs are not the same thing. But discussing semantics doesn't help you. The better answer is that I appreciate your concern, I will try to be...no, I *will* be clearer about my needs. But I also expect that if you don't know, you'll ask. In the moment. Not tomorrow. Not in retrospect next weekend after you've lost sleep over it. The moment you feel you've lost sight of what I'm asking for, I want to know."

"That's fair."

The words made him smile, because wasn't that important to his boy? In that, he could see all three O'Reilly boys. They were all hyperaware of balance, of what was right and what was wrong.

Sam took his coffee cup and sipped. "The week before my...thing—I don't even know what to call it, you know? It wasn't an accident, but attack makes me feel like a victim, and I don't like that, but that week that was so hard? I wanted to ask you for...I don't know, I was all caught up in my head, but you were too, so I felt shitty about even thinking about it, but I was. Needing you, I mean. Bad."

When his boy could breathe, when Sam just let go, found words, and trusted he was listening, it was always breathtaking, and it was always important. This moment was no exception, and not surprisingly, what was on his mind for today as well.

"We lost sight of each other that week. I want as much as you to figure out why, and to make sure we don't disconnect like that again. I know some of it is habit and some of it is perhaps not wanting to admit we need help." It wasn't only Sam that needed to trust, that needed to ask.

"I'll admit to being conflicted. You're my lover, my best friend; I should have explained to you the stress I was under that week. But I didn't know what was in your head, and as your Dom I felt like you shouldn't..." He sighed, trying to find the right words. "Like you shouldn't have to hold me up. Like that was...my job." That wasn't quite right, not quite everything, but he couldn't put his finger on what he was missing.

"Holding you up is my honor, my privilege." The words were so sure, ringing with truth.

He reached over and took Sam's hand. "Thank you, sweetheart. I'm still learning to see things with different eyes." And suddenly it came to him, what was missing, and it was embarrassing really, in light of everything. "I know what it was. As your Dom, I didn't want to let you down." He grinned a little ruefully, realizing that his boy didn't have a corner on the market for insecurity.

"Well, sure. Nobody wants to let somebody they love

down. I get that, bone-deep. Sometimes I want to do something right so bad that...that I fuck it ten ways to Sunday from worrying." Sam reached up and stroked his lips. "I think sometimes y'all have way too much pressure on you to be perfect."

"I think that's something we have in common, boy." He stood and gave Sam a quick kiss. "Clear the table and come back. I need to show you something; leave my coffee." He took off for the bedroom.

He heard Sam doing as he'd asked, rinsing dishes and putting them in the dishwasher, the happy whistle sounding again.

He came in from the bedroom and sat at the table, sipping his coffee while he waited on his boy, hoping they could continue this open communication through the next few minutes.

Sam came to him, a glass of ice water in his hands. "We moving to the table?"

"No, we don't have to. I just sat here so I could watch you in the kitchen." He grinned and got up, took his boy by the hand, and pulled him down on the couch. Then he handed Sam the note the boy had left him that insane Sunday afternoon. " 'Mister, if you're going to tell somebody all about the things I do wrong,' " he said, reciting the note from memory because he'd read it that many times. " 'At least let me know to go out so I can pretend that I'm not totally fucking this up.' "

He waited a moment, watching Sam, and rested a hand on his boy's knee. "Do you remember writing that?"

Sam read it, a puzzled frown on his face that slowly deepened into something much less confused and much more subdued, Sam drawing into himself. "I...you were on the phone. I could hear you. I needed some air. I was going to bring back lunch."

"That's what you said, yes." He nodded. "I was talking to Clint, getting his advice about something I thought we needed to work on."

Sam nodded once. "You need this, or can I throw it away?"

"You can keep it in your hands until I understand what you were feeling. I never said you were fucking anything up. I've never felt that. What made you feel that way?"

He'd already come a long way since that moment he called Clint; he didn't feel the same way about those issues that he did now. But Sam might, and he wanted to clear the air.

"I don't know what I remember, but I know you weren't happy with me, with why I did things, and you were telling someone else about it instead of just talking to me." Sam wouldn't meet his eyes. "I'm not used to that."

He turned on the couch to face his boy and drew a finger along Sam's bearded jaw. "That's fair. Clint is a mentor. I am very used to going to him with things I'm having trouble working out on my own. I'm not defending that stance; I'm just explaining that it's what I'm used to."

Sam nodded for him but didn't say a word. God, he wanted to know what was in there, what wild worries his boy was filing away to pull out and stress over in the darkness.

"I don't know what's worse, me talking to someone else, or you not talking at all."

"I don't have a whole hell of a lot to say. You have the right to talk to whoever you want to. I'd like that to be me, but I get it." Sam smiled for him, the expression self-deprecating, bittersweet. "It's not the first time I've been the troubled thing that someone needs help working out, and I seriously doubt it'll be the last."

"Whoa, Sam. That conversation I had with Clint wasn't about you—it was really about me. You only heard half of it. We weren't connecting that week. We were in a strange place. You're not troubled, sweetheart. There's nothing wrong with you. You're learning. We're learning. I will come to you first from now on, all right?" He sighed. This shouldn't be so difficult. They should have... "I think we need some rules, sweetheart."

Sam closed his eyes for a second, took a deep breath, and leaned into Thomas, demanding connection, touch. "So, obviously that's a sore spot for me, huh? Way more than I thought it was. I'd appreciate it if you would talk to me first, and I'll try to remember that none of us comes without old shit we're carrying."

He tucked an arm over his boy's shoulders, not realizing the extent to which he was craving Sam's warmth too. "Okay, first rule, we don't go to other people until we've tried to work whatever it is out between us first. Yes? First stop, each other."

"That works for me, down to the bone. Thank you." Sam rested against him, beginning to breathe with him, syncing them together.

"All right, so let's talk about how we keep that week from ever happening again. We...held things in, didn't ask for what we needed, right? Either one of us."

"Right. I didn't know whether I could. Hell, whether I should."

"And I didn't think you should have to deal with it." He snorted. "All right. So, where does that leave us? What's the rule? Because you should have, and next time I want you to. We need to share those things."

"We do." Sam nodded. "I will, next time. Now that I know."

"Good. So, first stop, each other, and...speak up. Those are pretty straightforward. Is that enough?"

Simple, perhaps, but he felt lighter having distilled those things down to something actionable.

"Yes. First stop, each other. Speak up. I'm all over that."

Thomas felt like he'd removed an obstacle. Sam would say they'd learned more of each other's language.

"Excellent. Now, I heard you earlier; you want to connect." He slipped free of Sam and stood, pulling his boy up off the couch with him.

Sam followed easily, staying close, hand on his arm. He led the boy into their bedroom and stopped just inside the door. "Strip, please, sweetheart, and bring your chair over."

"Yes, Sir." Sam grabbed the chair before stripping off his shirt, his sweats, that little knit cap.

"Good boy." Thomas had to smile at the little fire that lit under Sam's feet, and he picked up the boy's flogger. He glanced at the blindfold, but he didn't think he'd be able to tie it on and avoid all of Sam's scars, and the heavy chain was out until he was convinced that wrist was strong enough. That was all fine. There were other ways to accomplish the same thing.

He stopped a couple of feet away and looked his boy over, frankly admiring. "A few weeks without a heavy workout hasn't hurt you one bit, boy. You're as stunning as ever."

Sam blushed but offered him a happy little grin. "Thank you, Sir. I'm ready to start again, but I'm glad you don't think I'm getting soft."

He grinned and moved to the chair, stopping close enough to whisper. "Nothing soft about you, boy." He handed Sam the flogger. "Sit, facing the back. Hold on to that."

Sam sat, the motion grateful, easy. Sam let his arms fall to the sides of the chair, holding the flogger between them.

He laid his hands on Sam's shoulders, let them take some weight, and breathed with his boy for a minute. Then, under the guise of a massage, he ran his fingers over every bit of skin he could reach from shoulders to ass, digging into muscle, following the line of Sam's spine and shoulder blades, smoothing a hand over Sam's ink and the scarred skin underneath it.

Sam began to moan for him, his boy melting, relaxing beautifully for him. All the time, Sam breathed, following him, the act natural as, well, breathing.

He hadn't found any hot spots, nothing that made Sam flinch or even twitch. When he was satisfied Sam was free of injury, he slid his fingers higher, working them into the boy's upper arms, and finally and more gently, Sam's neck.

"Oh, God." Sam gasped out the words, and he found the muscles there were hard, almost hot under his fingers. "Please. That feels so good."

"Of course, sweetheart." How had he not noticed all the stiffness and tension? Sam was a master at covering discomfort. He might consider a rule about that as well.

He worked on the muscles and tendons in Sam's neck carefully and deliberately, taking his time, feeling Sam's breathing settle, even and shallow, like sleeping, only his boy was most certainly awake.

He reached down with one hand and slipped the flogger from Sam's slack fingers.

Sam didn't move, trusting Thomas completely. "I love you, Mister."

That was beautiful, love offered in return for something

as easy as a massage. He knew it wasn't quite that simple though; it was bigger than a back rub. Sam craved touch, physical presence. "I love you, my boy."

He rolled his wrist and let the leather tails fall gently on one shoulder, then the other, keeping it gentle and slow, fitting the energy in the room.

Sam lifted his hands to the top rail of the chair and let his head rest down. "Is this okay, Sir? I've got baby head."

He smiled. "Of course. Anything that's comfortable, boy." He hadn't wanted to interrupt while Sam was quiet, but as long as the boy was speaking now, he went with his customary ritual. "What are your words, boy?"

"Yellow and revolver, Mister." Sam took a deep breath and exhaled, relaxing even further.

"Yellow and revolver." He drew each word out, liking how familiar they were on his tongue, how easily they fit into their work. "Good boy."

He started with the flogger again, light and slow, consistent as a metronome, covering the whole of Sam's back. He even covered the ink, which was in an area he wouldn't touch with a real blow, watching Sam's skin blush.

Sam responded beautifully, melting into the chair, soft moans filling the air. It was lovely, the ease. He would remember this, know how to see when the tension ratcheted up.

Interestingly, though, in his concern for his boy's physical well-being, he'd managed to absorb a lot of that tension rather than let it dissipate. Concentrating on the fall of his flogger was helping; channeling that energy down his arm was a sure bet most of the time.

"One moment, boy. You just breathe." He pulled away, stepping clear of the chair and letting it go for a second, the force in his arm and the sound of his flogger slicing through the air enough to satisfy him and blow out some of the tension.

Sam hummed softly, the sound deep and low. "So fine, Mister. You're so fine to me."

Feeling much more in control now, he looked at his boy, eyes focused on the places he knew could take his arm, the places Sam responded to best. "If you're not comfortable, if you need to move, I expect you to tell me. Just ask, or use your words if you need to." He rolled his shoulders, admiring the way the boy's back was offered to him, a smooth canvas waiting for his attention. "Harder now, boy. And I need to hear you count. I won't go full out."

Not full out, no. Not today. But barring a safe word, he would go until he tired or his boy lost count.

"Yes, Sir." It suited him, how there was no tension in Sam's voice, no worry, just trust.

"That's my boy. So proud of you. Breathe."

He took a breath himself and raised his arm, starting high on Sam's shoulders and working his way lower, allowing every fifth blow to wrap a little so the tips of the flogger could nip at Sam's sides.

Each of those strikes earned him a wiggle, a gasp, those numbers husky, rough.

When Sam reached twenty-five, he paused and approached his boy, ghosting a hand across reddening skin just to feel the heat, and because he knew his boy liked the burn. Sam arched, the motion slow and sensuous, his hips tucking under to curve closer.

"How do you feel, boy?" His voice was low but confident, and he let himself smile slightly, knowing he was feeling good, that his boy was feeling good.

"Warm. It's good, to be here with you like this." Sam chuckled softly. "It's good to be here with you, all the way."

That was exactly right. Here, together, period. And a hundred percent open to one another. He leaned over Sam's back and slid a hand over the boy's hip, to cradle Sam's cock in his fingers.

Sam gasped softly, and his head lifted as he rocked into Thomas's touch. The motion was natural as breathing, Sam's body responding eagerly.

"My beautiful boy." He let Sam move a little more, kissed the boy's cheek, and stepped away again. "Counting again. Ready?"

"Yes, Sir." Sam stayed upright this time, hands on his thighs.

"Start again with one." He shook his arm out, realizing he had a lot left and reconsidering how heavy he should go. He started off at the same pace but allowed himself a little more strength in his blows.

Sam took another set, then stopped him with a murmured "Yellow."

"Boy?" He tucked the flogger under his arm.

"I need a drink, Mister, please. I'm dry as a bone."

"Of course. Good boy." He got Sam a bottle of water and pressed it into the boy's hands. He got one for himself as well while they were stopped.

It was interesting how self-aware his boy had become, given the relatively short time they'd been working together. He gave his arm another shake. "Your back is gorgeous, boy. The color." He illustrated his words with one finger, drawing it across the lines on Sam's skin. "And these through here stand out beautifully."

Sam shuddered and cried out softly, goose bumps popping up under his fingertip.

"Mmm. Good, yes? Finish that water." He needed to blow out his arm. *So much for not going full out.* "Sam, I want to try..." He stopped himself and sighed. Maybe his boy needed it too. *Speak up, Thomas.* "I need a few hard ones; are you up for it?"

"Yes, Sir." No hesitation. No worry. Just a simple agreement. *Yes, Sir.*

"Thank you, boy." He leaned close again, resting a heavy hand on Sam's hip. "Do you want me to touch you? Ask me."

"Oh, God. Mister, I want nothing more. Please? I crave you."

His boy. A simple please would have been enough for him, but Sam gave him everything. It made him groan, made his balls ache. He was gratified by the heft of his boy's cock in his hand and stroked it slowly, exploring the head with his thumb. Sam began to pant, eyes wide. When he pressed in, working the slit, his boy started to leak for him, and the groan he was gifted was pure hunger.

Fuck, that was a beautiful sound. He wanted, but the flogger in his other hand called to him. He replaced his hand with Sam's own and stroked around Sam's fingers, giving the boy permission, before letting go and stepping up to a measured distance, working the handle of the flogger in his fingers. "Full out, boy. Just a few."

"Yes, Sir." Sam nodded, arm beginning to work that heavy cock, proving how badly they both needed this.

"No need to count. Remember your words." He didn't give Sam another second to think. He hauled back with his arm and laid down four heavy blows, two on each side, with only enough time in between for a breath.

"Mister!" Sam tossed his head, the scent of his boy's seed sharp on the air.

"Boy." The word held everything he was feeling, all his pride and need, somewhere between praise and possession.

He dropped the flogger and tore at his fly. "Need you, sweetheart. Knees. Now."

"God, yes. Please." Sam spun and hit his knees, that mouth burning around his cock immediately, the suction wild, fierce.

He cried out, instantly lightheaded and half-blind with want. He arched over Sam, bracing a hand on the boy's shoulder so he didn't lose his balance. "Fuck!"

Sam took him to the root, swallowing over and over, throat squeezing the tip of his prick.

"Yes. So good." He was shaking and he couldn't breathe. Finally he groaned heavily and shoved his cock deep once more, only pulling away when his hips tensed and balls drew up, emptying into his boy's mouth. "Sam. Fuck!"

Sam took him down, every drop, tongue sliding along his shaft, adoring him. *Jesus.* Eyes riveted on his boy, he watched as long as he could stand it. Then he knelt with Sam and kissed him, tongues tangling, tasting himself on his boy's lips. Sam pressed close to Thomas, rubbing them together, kissing him with a deep, raw hunger.

He got his hands on Sam's ass, the only thing he could really get hold of and not injure the boy, and returned the kiss, trying to listen to Sam's body, gauge the boy's strength. Sam wasn't holding back from him, not a bit, hips rocking into his hands.

Christ, he'd never be twenty-six again. But his boy was beautiful and wild; he was more than willing to watch. He tugged hard with both hands, pinning Sam's rejuvenated erection against his hip, giving his boy some fight and some friction. "Want that, boy?"

"I can't imagine not wanting you." Sam's eyes went heavy-lidded, and he licked his lips. Thomas kissed them again, loving the way Sam made him feel.

"That prick feels good. It's hot, you needing more already. Are you close, you need more? Tell me what you want."

"I am." Sam moaned, lips right at his ear. "Love sucking you. Makes me hard, all over. Touch me. Please."

He moaned, feeling those words down deep. He made some room between them and got hold of Sam, stroking firmly, the boy's stiff cock on fire and solid as steel in his fingers.

"Yes. God, Mister. I need you so." Sam humped up, driving into his touch. He squeezed, slowing Sam down a bit, reminding his boy who was in control here, even now.

"Watch yourself. I have boots that need polishing; you could do that for me instead." He thought about that. "Mm. Boots, that flogger we just used. You know the coffeemaker needs a little TLC."

Sam groaned. "It's mean to tease."

He let his voice sink low. "Then slow down and appreciate your Master's hand around your prick, boy."

He loved the shiver, the soft moan. "Yes, Sir."

"Good boy. I'm watching. Show me." He started stroking again, eyes on Sam, shamelessly enjoying his boy's pleasure.

Sam arched for him, following his touch, a dark flush climbing his boy's abs. Fuck, that was open, exposed, Sam holding nothing in reserve.

"Lovely, boy. You look amazing." And fuck if his cock wasn't trying to play along. "Close? Feeling that rush?"

Sam nodded, lips parted. "Mister. Oh, fuck."

Mmm. Incoherence.

He moved his fist a little quicker, a little shallower, leaning in with his body and giving the head something solid to rub against. "Good. Good boy. Come on."

Sam mouthed *Good boy*, then shot into his hand, face going slack. He kept sliding his fingers lightly along the shaft, took Sam's jaw in his other hand, and covered the boy's mouth with a kiss. Sam moaned for him, returning the kiss lazily.

"All right, sweetheart. Let's get you on your tummy. I need to look at your back." He helped Sam to the bed a little wistfully. That...all that had been so wonderful.

This was good too, though. Sam liked the attention, and he liked caring for the boy, soothing all that lovely red skin. He slid his leather pants the rest of the way off and pulled out his kit as Sam got comfortable.

Sam hummed softly, still and relaxed, a soft smile on his lips.

Thomas grinned; that little love-drunk look made his boy more adorable than ever. "Sleep if you like, sweetheart. Plenty of time left in our day for a nap." Hard to believe it was just afternoon, given how long they'd been working. But he'd woken up impatient to get started, and their work began early today.

He spent a good while tending to the welts left by those final blows and a few spots on Sam's sides where the flogger had bitten into the skin.

"Love how your hands feel, Mister." Sam was floating, and Thomas had to admit, he was too.

"Your skin, boy. Make sure you get a look when you get up again. My fingers can hardly get enough." When he was done with his kit he set it aside, then climbed into bed alongside his boy. Such a big day. A really...big day.

Sam smiled at him, one hand coming to rest on his stomach. "You look happy."

He laughed lightly and covered Sam's hand with his own. "So happy. Elated. High." There hadn't been a single thing he'd needed that he hadn't gotten from that scene, not a thing. He was wholly satisfied. "You're magnificent."

"I'm yours. Thank you for everything."

"I know." He knew it so deeply, he hadn't once felt the need to say it. "And...you're welcome." He had to grin; this was one of those odd moments that snuck up on him, where for his lover he'd return the thanks, but there was no need to thank his boy. It was hard to know which way to go. He went with the latter.

Sam smiled, fingers moving in lazy patterns on his skin, his boy not just easy in his skin, but in his soul.

"Connected? You got what you needed?" He knew the answer, but he liked that smile.

"Yes, Sir. I feel like we got the same heartbeat, damn near."

He nodded, letting Sam know he felt the same way. "Let's rest a bit, and we'll decide what to do with the rest of the day, hm?"

"Yes, Sir." Sam kissed his cheek, the caress soft as silk.

4

Sam floated. There wasn't another word for it. He wasn't asleep, but he wasn't worrying. He was warm and happy, tired, but in the best way.

Hell, there was nothing as good as knowing that all his aches came from being well-loved. Even his headache was gone.

Thomas was still, his eyes closed, and Sam watched for a second, loving the way the lines at his Sir's eyes and mouth had eased.

Sam let his eyes close, let his breath match Thomas's. He'd felt wild today, almost out of control with need, but Thomas had been there, taken everything he'd offered and given him everything he needed.

When he opened them again, the shadows in the room had shifted and he figured it had to be late afternoon. Plenty of Saturday left for them to enjoy, and they'd still have Sunday to snuggle.

He felt fingers on his shoulder and looked up to find Mister smiling at him, brown eyes warm and thoughtful.

"Hey."

"Hey." He grinned back, happy as the proverbial pig in slop.

"I love you." Simple words, though they didn't feel simple when Mister said them. Truthful, happy, but complicated somehow.

"Thank God for that." He would hate to be in this alone.

Mister shrugged, that smile changing. "I was actually just thanking James."

"I can see that." James was up there, looking out for him; Sam had no doubt. "He loves us both."

"He did. You're a real gift to me, Sam. I don't usually waste my time on the concept of fate or why things happen, but for some reason, that's where my mind went when I woke up thinking about James. I'm way out of my comfort zone with this one." Mister winked at him. "The emotions are...quite complicated."

"Well, sure they are. How often does this happen like this? I know it probably sounds naïve, but I believe that God has a plan, whether or not we understand it, and I believe James is still with us, still loving us. Energy can't be destroyed, right? So his soul is still moving around. That love that y'all had, it's still a real thing." It made perfect sense to him, but he was a man of faith.

"I'm glad you have that. I'm glad it helps." Gentle fingers played over his skin. "How is your back feeling?"

"Like you love me." He searched Thomas's eyes. "You can talk to me about him, you know? You're not going to hurt my feelings, and he's part of us."

"I want to. I would, I just don't really...have words. Imagine that." Thomas snorted. "I just keep thinking that I'm sad it wasn't like this, and I don't know whether I'm mad at him because he wasn't open enough with me, or at myself for not looking hard enough to see what he was doing. On the other hand, I didn't know this was possible until you."

"I read that journal you showed me. James got what he needed from you. What he needed and what I do aren't the same, huh? You got to be special, to give us both so much."

"I wasn't thinking about me, but thank you. I was thinking more about you. How it took your depth to help me find mine. I wish I could sit down with James and say, 'Can you believe this? I had no idea, did you? Look what we were missing.' You know? It's strange, because we were happy." Thomas huffed, laughing softly.

Sam liked that Thomas was talking about it, letting himself open up and feel. He didn't know how to say what he was feeling, but he sort of thought Thomas didn't know how to believe in what he felt.

"It was so hard, right after he died, because I felt so small, so much like I was this shiftless redneck. I think James would laugh like a loon, seeing me here."

"He might. But I also think he'd be proud of you." Thomas sighed, his eyes losing focus for a second. "I can't even describe how I felt right after he died. Everywhere I looked, there was this void. It was awful. And suddenly there was this cowboy with James's eyes stepping on the same sidewalk where he was killed, and everything tilted... shifted sideways. They'd only just taken down the police tape. Like two minutes before you arrived. Seriously. I don't believe that you showing up at that exact moment was just a coincidence. I don't. I was leaving. Another thirty seconds and we'd have just walked right by one another. I don't know what it was, but it wasn't an accident."

"No. No, it wasn't." And that was that, wasn't it? They were meant to meet, to find solace in each other, then to find more.

Thomas nodded. "You knew that. God's plan is enough explanation for you? I think that's great, that you can be content with that. I respect that, honestly. But the God I grew up with hates me. That was, and still is on occasion, made very clear to me. So I'll figure out what to call it. Maybe it's all the same thing anyway."

"I'm sorry, honey. That sucks. I know my people are disappointed that I'm gay, but it's because they want me home and making babies. Mostly it's the babies." Never once did Momma or Daddy make him believe that God wasn't about love and forgiveness. Faith, hope, and love.

Thomas snorted, grinning. "No babies. I'll explain it to your mother when I meet her. It'll be fine because she is going to love me."

"No babies, and she will. Two of her sons do; she doesn't have a choice."

"I dress well, I'm polite, and mommas are always right. I'm good at this. Did you get us plane tickets?"

"I did." He was tickled shitless, actually, that Thomas could still take time off to see his world. Not only that, but his lover really seemed to be looking forward to the trip.

"Good. Thank you." Thomas ran a warm hand lightly over his back, probably checking the rougher spots. Mister always liked to be sure he was okay. "So. There's one more thing I'd planned for us today, sweetheart."

"Yes, Sir?" Whatever it was, he could handle it.

"It's time you shaved."

He blinked. That was absolutely out of the blue. "What?"

"The beard. It's time to get out a razor."

"You don't like it? I was considering growing it out so that it reaches my chest like I'm some great big lumberjack."

Mister laughed. "Sure. Then I'll restrain you and shave it myself."

"You're no fun." He rubbed his chin against his lover's shoulder. "It's a little weird to look in the mirror, still."

"I know. I figured that out when you started brushing your teeth with your back to it. I understand it's disconcerting, but it's time. Past time." Thomas tugged on his scruff. "I have a reward for you when it's done."

"Yeah? I like rewards." He would shave for Thomas. It had been easier to just...not. "I'm hoping my hair comes in okay at some point."

"It will. Or it won't. You're just as mine one way or the other." Thomas kissed his forehead. "Let's get you up."

Together they stood, the little rush of dizziness like that first cigarette after you've been quit for a while. He stretched up tall, his cock giving a little jerk at the pull and burn.

Thomas looked at him, eyes twinkling. "My boy."

"You know it. You're sure about the beard?" He sighed dramatically at Thomas's nod and headed for the bathroom. He trimmed everything close, then started the process of shaving. There was something about it, he had to admit— the shaving cream, the towels, the sound.

Thomas leaned in the doorway and smiled. He'd pulled on sweat pants and a black T-shirt instead of his leather. "Looking better."

"I don't know. I look awful young like this." He winked over in the mirror and got a washrag steamy and cleaned his face off, checking for missed spots.

"You don't look a day under twenty-six. And I look like the dirty old man I am. Where's my walker? Thirty-one is a bear." Thomas came in and kissed his newly smooth cheek.

"Dirty old man, bah. Five years is nothing." He leaned

into the kiss before he cleaned up his mess. "Better?" He held up his face for inspection.

"Are you upset I prefer you with a clean shave? I missed your stubborn, handsome chin." He got a real kiss then, a sweet one, Thomas's fingers snaking around the nape of his neck.

"Mmm...no. I wasn't ready to stare at myself is all." *More kisses, please. Those were heady as all get out.*

"I am." He got his wish, another kiss as sweet as the last, followed by one that wasn't sweet at all. "Mmm. I could stare at you just like this. I better get you your reward before I get sidetracked."

He hummed deep in his chest, more interested in the way Thomas felt against him than any reward.

"Not to worry, we'll come back to this." Thomas traced his lower lip with a gentle thumb. "Find something loose to wear, and we'll go sit in the living room."

"Give me two shakes of a dead lamb's tail and I'll be right there." He kissed Thomas's thumb.

"Dead lamb's tail," Thomas muttered, heading for the hall. "Texans. What kind of an expression is that? What does that even mean?" His lover disappeared, headed toward the living room.

He started chuckling on the way to the bedroom, and by the time he had his rainbow heart pajama pants on—thank you, Momma—he was laughing his ass off.

"What's so funny, boy?" Thomas called from the living room; it sounded like his lover might be laughing too. "Are you coming or what?"

"Coming. Yes. You. You're funny as all get out." He grabbed a T-shirt and tugged it over his head as he headed to the front room.

"Mhm." Thomas went to him. "Oh, you got a shirt on.

Doesn't that..." Mister grinned at him. "You like the sting, hm?"

His cheeks went red-hot and burning, but how was he going to deny it? "I do. It turns me on."

"I like knowing that." Thomas laughed softly. "Would you like some coffee before we sit? Water?"

"Water for me. You want something?" He rubbed his smooth, sensitive skin, his toes curling a little with the buzz.

"I'm fine, boy. Thank you." Thomas reached out and did the same. "Feel good?"

"I do." He cuddled right into his Sir's hand. God, that was fine.

"Sit. I've got it." Thomas ducked into the kitchen and was back in a second with his water. He set it on the coffee table next to an envelope addressed to Thomas. The handwriting was familiar; it took him another second to realize it was Momma's.

Thomas pushed the envelope toward him. "I texted Bowie."

He blinked and looked at the envelope, then opened it. He wasn't sure what he was going to find, but when he pulled out the photo of the three of them—Bowie, James, and him standing there, Bowie in his uniform, his breath caught in his chest.

Oh.

Oh, God.

"Bowie got in touch with your mom. She remembered the picture, and she found one like it in James's things. There's a short letter in there where she tells me about the day it was taken. I thought you'd like that too."

Sam felt Thomas's hand on his leg, then another on his shoulder. "Sam?"

Come on. Come on. Don't make him think you don't appreciate this. Come on, Sam.

"It's perfect."

He couldn't breathe.

"Are you all right, sweetheart? Should I have told you I asked Bowie? I didn't want to get your hopes up if they didn't have anything similar." Thomas squeezed his thigh. "Boy. Breathe."

He stared at Thomas, terrified he was going to burst into tears.

Thomas held his eyes and cradled his jaw in one hand. "It's all right, sweetheart. I'm right here. Just you and me. Speak up, remember? Just be honest."

One single hot tear escaped, sliding down his cheek, burning all the way down.

"Oh, my boy." Thomas leaned close and kissed the trail, under his eye, the hollow of his cheek, then softly on his lips. "So difficult, I know. Let it out. You're safe with me."

"I miss him."

He wanted to turn and run, but Thomas was right there, so close, and he pushed in, hiding in the curve of his Mister's shoulder. His chest felt like it was cracked open, the pain curled around his bones.

Thomas pulled him in, one hand around the nape of his neck. "That's it. It's just me, Sam. I miss him too. So much." Mister's voice was soft but strong, his words flowing smoothly. "I know that feeling, like you'll never get a deep breath again. Just let the tears out, boy. Give them to me. I've got you."

The tension holding him loosened, and he sobbed, trusting that Thomas's arms were the safest space on earth.

Thomas kept him close, the embrace steady as Mister whispered softly to him. He didn't catch it all, but it didn't matter. His lover's tone was present and soothing, keeping him from falling too far. "Good boy," he did hear Thomas say, and, "love you."

The storm passed, leaving him empty and a little embarrassed, but Thomas held him close, refusing to let him pull away.

"Breathe, boy. Deep breaths now." Thomas loosened his grip and gave him a little more room. "Just breathe. You're all right."

"I'm sorry. I didn't mean to." He let himself stay, let Thomas hold him.

"Sweetheart. There's no need to apologize for your needs, for being truthful. For grief. Isn't that what I am here for? I know that was hard for you, but they're just tears. You loved James, you miss him, that pain is real, and it's nothing to be ashamed of."

He didn't know what to say. Cowboys weren't supposed to cry. Ever. "Thank you for my picture."

It was the dearest thing anyone had done for him in a long time.

"You're welcome. I hope it helps." Thomas kissed his temple, then tilted his chin up and kissed his lips. "Breathe. Just breathe."

"I never...not since I was a little boy."

"James either. I can tell you, I've cried a lot over him, though. I don't think I could have held it in if I wanted to. How do you feel?"

"Empty. A little embarrassed." He wanted to stay where he was. Close. "Exposed, huh?"

Thomas nodded. "Sure. Raw, right? All that emotion burns on the way out. It's a truth from deep down, it's hard to let anyone see that, but I'll keep it close, I promise."

"I believe you." He never questioned that. Not once.

Thomas loved him. Thomas knew. "I know you have my back."

Thomas reached for his water and opened the bottle, handing it to him. "This has been a good day, sweetheart."

He drank deep, letting the water cool the heat inside him, ease his headache. Then he took off his T-shirt and settled against Thomas with a sigh, seeking contact and comfort. "It has been."

Thomas got it, tugging that black T-shirt off and dropping it with his, folding comforting arms around him. "It's good to feel solid again. Whole."

"Love you." He rested his cheek on Thomas's chest.

"Mmm. My boy."

5

Thomas had dressed for all kinds of occasions: weddings, galas, work, the club, a football game, cocktail parties, dinner out with friends. He had a wardrobe that covered it all.

But never, not once in his entire life, had he dressed to meet someone else's parents, let alone his lover's parents. Sam's parents—James's parents—people he wanted to meet more than anyone else in the world. He was anxious to make a good impression. Not that he'd admit that out loud. He was going for the perfect picture of confidence.

He was no dummy, though. He knew he might have a hill to climb. He was the last man with James before he died; then he stole their youngest boy out from under them. That alone could cast him in a bad light, never mind the realization that they'd never be grandparents.

So he was nervous but excited as he and Sam made their way to baggage claim to collect their suitcases and hat boxes. He schmoozed with people for a living; he could have a conversation with anyone. But in the end, he couldn't be anything but himself. He'd been looking forward to this trip.

"We'll call once we get our stuff. DFW takes forever. Aunt Linda is waiting in the cell lot." Sam had a ball cap on; the cowboy hats came on for special occasions, but they were still uncomfortable on that scarred head.

Aunt Linda. Had Sam told him anything about Linda? "Sounds good." He started to hook an arm behind Sam's back while they waited and realized they hadn't discussed public conduct and decided against it for now. "Feeling all right?"

He watched the carousel, waiting for the bags to appear.

"I am. I have to admit that I'm looking forward to showing you where we grew up. It's about an hour, hour and a half drive home from here, and we'll have my truck to tool around in once we get there."

He gave his boy a smile. This whole thing made him happy, in fact: the visit, the way Sam's shoulders were set like the man belonged here, the idea of Sam driving him around in a truck. It made him think of the first time he saw that rodeo cowboy swagger, Sam coming up out of the subway in a hat and wranglers, heading toward him on the sidewalk through a sea of people with cell phones, black jeans, and messenger bags.

He'd fallen deep in lust with the cowboy that evening.

"Ah, that's yours." He stepped up and pulled Sam's suitcase off the carousel.

Sam snatched the hatbox and his suitcase, then grabbed his phone, texting one-handed. "She's on her way."

"Great. There's mine." He grabbed his suitcase, always relieved when his bag appeared at his destination. It made him strangely anxious when a bag got lost.

He followed Sam out to the curb, shocked by the warm air that hit them as the sliding doors opened and glad he took Sam's suggestion to wear short sleeves. "Wow. We're not in Kansas anymore, are we?"

"No, Sir. We're in Texas." Sam lifted his face to the sky and smiled. "Man, I hope Momma made brisket."

Oh, he could watch his boy out in this sun all day. He took a deep breath, but he didn't appreciate the airport air as much as he did the warmth.

A huge cherry-red pickup pulled up, a handsome woman with a long auburn ponytail and a shirt that read *Hey y'all, watch this* hopping out. "Baby boy! Oh, look at you!"

"Aunt Linda." Sam stepped forward and they embraced, Sam almost disappearing in her arms.

"Oh, honey. You had us worried near to death. Thank God you're home where we can pet you for a while. Your folks are so ready."

"Good deal. I want to introduce you to Thomas now. Linda, Thomas. Mister, this is Daddy's sister, Linda."

He put his hand out, trying not to do more than blink at Sam's use of that respectful term in front of family. He supposed Sam's personal take on "Master" passed well enough, but it didn't stop the little zing up his spine. Clever boy. "Very good to meet you, Linda. Thank you for the ride."

"Anytime. I'm tickled to meet you." She shook his hand, smiled at him. "Are y'all hungry? I'm fixin' to starve to death, and I know you haven't had good Tex-Mex, baby boy."

"No, ma'am. I mean, yes, ma'am I could eat, and no, ma'am, this is the place to have Tex-Mex. I'm going to feed Thomas everything from here to Corpus." Sam beamed at him. "Let me get the bags in the back. Mister, you can have the front seat. I've seen everything."

"I guess we'll be running every morning if you plan to feed me that much." Despite the offer, he helped Sam with the luggage, but he took the boy up on sitting in the front. He definitely wanted to see everything, and he already liked Linda.

His stomach growled not one minute after Linda pulled away from the curb, and he laughed. "I'm hungry too. I don't like to eat before a flight."

"We'll head out and stop at the El Chicos in Rockwall, if that's good with you, Sam?"

"Perfect. Guac and tacos al carbon. I'm all in." Sam leaned into the seat, making the leather creak as he stretched out in the back. "Lord, woman. When is the last time you had your damn truck detailed?"

"Shut up, or I'll have your happy ass out washing it. Little shit." She grinned at Sam in the rearview mirror.

"Linda, what do you do when you're not hauling family around in your truck?"

"I'm a hospice nurse. Sammy says you work at a museum? You must meet amazing people too."

He liked how she did that. "That's good work. And yes, I meet all kinds of people. Some are truly amazing individuals, some are eccentric and interesting, some have too much time on their hands. I imagine you know what I'm talking about." He grinned at her.

"Indeed I do." Linda smiled at him. "So, I'm going to get it right out in the open, because that's me—"

"Aunt Linda, don't."

"Hush, boy." She changed lanes like she was lunging for meat. "Are you trying to replace James? Because Sam and James are as different as night and day."

"Aunt Linda!"

"What? Everyone wants to know. Once it's out, it's out."

Ah. Excellent. He appreciated the direct approach. And

if ever there was a question he was ready to answer, it was that one. Moreover, he'd already answered it for Bowie.

"It's quite all right, Sam." He turned slightly in his seat and looked at her, even though she was driving and could only glance his way. "The short answer is no. It would be impossible to replace James."

That was the simplest place to start and the most respectful of James's memory. He took a breath, smiled at his boy, and told Linda what she really wanted to know. "I wouldn't want to try, and if I did, Sam would be the wrong choice. They have very similar eyes, which of course I noticed, and I'd be lying if I said it didn't draw me to him at first. Otherwise, I can't imagine two men whose approach to life, to love, to pretty much everything but food, could be more divergent."

He shifted in his seat again, grinning. "Sam's eyes actually have more green and a little gold in them, and he's also a hair shorter, in case you hadn't noticed."

"A hair." Her laugh was loud, boisterous. Pure joy. "And Bowie is a hair taller. Right?"

"Yes. A hair taller and easily ten times the man I am. It was quite an honor to meet him." He wasn't blowing smoke; he meant that. He was smart, but Bowie was brave.

"He's a good guy. We've all decided to keep him, huh Sammy?"

"Aunt Linda, you pulled a gun on us the last time you saw us together."

"You two deserved it."

He raised an eyebrow. "I believe that. Linda, I think you and I are going to get along very well. I almost feel sorry for Sam." He laughed. "So, tell me. Now that I've answered that for you, you'll go ahead and spread that around so no one else has to have the *chutzpah*, right? Let them know I'm happy to back up my thesis with specific examples if they require further evidence."

He was playing with her now. He liked her, and if she was asking direct questions like that, he could only imagine the things that Sam's parents would be thinking and *not* asking. He might need the ally.

"Fair enough. Remember, I'm a nurse. Nothing grosses me out."

Sam groaned from the back seat.

"I think he's hungry. Also, you're safe, Annie Oakley, but I better watch it because he could kick my ass if he wanted to."

"He's a bull rider. He can take more blows and stay standing than anyone I know."

No more. No, that poor skull didn't need any more blows. Not now, not ever.

He was getting a little cross-eyed with all the travel until Linda crossed over a huge lake and almost immediately made a series of turns like a bat out of hell, ending in a parking lot. That woke him up. Things like highway speeds and parking lots were practically foreign to him these days.

"Lunch?" He grinned over his shoulder at his boy. "Are you ready to eat half of Texas?"

"God, yes. Lord, this place has been here forever." The place seemed like it would work, the restaurant older but clean, and the smell was like spicy heaven.

Lunch was fantastic. So good, he wondered if he'd ever want another New York taco. Hell, he might never eat again in this lifetime. He leaned back in his chair with a groan. "Oh, I am stuffed."

"Does that mean no skillet apple pie with cinnamon ice cream, boys?"

"Momma's going to be cooking already. We'll come back up in a few days, hit Target. Fair?"

"Fair."

"Linda, not that I don't trust that Sam's mother has been completely and totally honest with Sam, but how is Mister O'Reilly faring?" He didn't trust. At all. It certainly was possible he was paranoid, but if there was something to know, he'd rather Sam know now than be surprised.

"Dan's got a bit of a slur, and his left hand isn't a hundred percent, but he's managing pretty well. He's been driving, been out on the barns working. He'll make it, y'all. He's hired that friend of yours from high school...Bradley Counter?"

"Ah. Cool."

"Y'all talked since—"

"No, ma'am." Oh. Oh, what was that?

The question was whether to ask for details here and now, or later when they were alone. He looked over at Sam, deciding to feel him out. "Bradley Counter is...?"

"Guy I used to be friends with."

Huh. Interesting.

"Used to be?" Linda looked at Sam in the rearview. "Y'all boys fight?"

"No, ma'am."

"Well, then? He's going to be at the house; you'd best fess up."

"He and I got nothing to say to each other, that's all." Sam held her gaze, and Thomas began to worry about the other trucks on the road.

"This about you coming out of the closet, about James dying, or about you coming out of the closet by hooking up with James's man?"

"I don't know, and to be honest, I don't give a shit. People let you know whether they got your back or not."

"I beg your pardon, but I wasn't James's any longer when Sam and I got together, and I think that remains an important distinction." It was to him, anyway. "Sam, if you're saying it's not going to matter, I'll let it go for now. But if this is going to involve me, I'd appreciate it if you considered telling me what's going on."

"It's not going to matter. It's none of yours. This is all about me and him."

"None of mine?"

Everything about you is mine.

He wanted to growl at his boy. If they'd been alone, that comment, especially with that tone, would have landed Sam on his knees. As it was, he had to be a bit more discreet. "I'm the first stop, Sam."

Sam blinked up at him, then offered him a half smile, a nod. "I mean that it's not about you, Mister. Lots of people decided they didn't want nothing to do with me once things weren't easy anymore."

"Oh, good Lord and butter, that's not uncommon, even though it ought to be." Linda shook her head. "I see it in my line of work a lot, baby boy."

"I lost a lot of people, too. It doesn't make it easier to lose people just because it happens everywhere. I'm glad you told me, so at least I understand if things feel tense. I've got your back, sweetheart."

Just please don't get into a fight.

"Aren't y'all dear as all get out."

"That's us. Dear. Cute, too." Sam grinned at him, the expression purely evil.

"Mm. Adorable. *Baby boy.*" He looked at Linda. "How

did he get that name? Is it because he's the youngest? Or is there a better story?"

"He is the youngest, and he was premature and tiny. Bowie weighed fourteen pounds and was twenty-three inches long. James weighed nine-nine and was nineteen inches long. Little Sammy here weighed four and a half and was sixteen and a half inches long. The boys thought he was a baby doll, a toy, their baby boy."

"Aw. Little Sammy." He grinned. If he were more into babies, that would probably be truly adorable. As it was, it was something to file away to tease his boy about later. "Well, I'm glad everyone ended up healthy. I love that the name stuck."

"He proved himself to be the toughest little shit on earth. I swear to God, Thomas; James and Bowie damn near killed him about a hundred times before he was in school. Those two could be evil."

"That explains a few things. Although the way Sam tells it, James was his fiercest defender. Right, Sam?"

"That's how it worked. They could be evil to me, but no one else had that right."

So that was how brothers were supposed to work. Shame his own didn't get that memo. Although Peter did haul him out of the creek that time Billy Ames knocked him out and dumped him there. Dragged him all the way home too. Maybe that was love.

"So how far from your folks are we?"

"Fifteen minutes to Greenville, another fifteen to the ranch." Sam grinned and leaned forward over the back of the seat. "Aunt Linda owns the ranch next door to ours."

"Really? Are we staying with you, Linda?" He laughed. "You know I never did ask about sleeping arrangements. Do we get twin beds like Lucy and Ricky?"

"You'll be lucky if Steph doesn't make Sam sleep at the house and you over at mine."

"I got a queen-sized bed in my room," Sam muttered.

"That could be fun. I can come by and help you sneak out and we can make out in your truck." Making out in Sam's truck was already on his agenda.

"Or we can just sleep on the sofas in the front room like we all used to when we had friends over."

He looked out the windshield with a perfectly bland expression. "I don't know what you were doing with your friends during sleepovers, but I don't think the front room is a great idea. Your mom might go blind."

"Oh ho!" Linda cackled like a huge bird. "Oh, sweet Jesus, y'all'd best lock your door, and I pray to God neither one of you are screamers."

"Thomas likes to sing opera during sex, Auntie. Me? I prefer chicken sounds."

He broke out into the first several bars of Figaro's "*Largo al factotum*" in Italian, then grinned at Linda.

"Oh, I like you. I like you a lot." Linda hooted and nodded for him. "You should keep him, baby boy."

"Yes, ma'am. I intend to."

"I'll just make sure to keep the chicken feed stocked for him." This was bad. This was bad because he was very relaxed and enjoying himself, and now he had to meet Momma and Daddy O'Reilly and be polite and be a gentleman to Sam and...oh. He was in trouble. It was too bad he couldn't stop grinning.

They were all still laughing all the way through the town, then out into rural land—he saw horses, cattle, buffalo, llamas, all this grass, fences, barns, blue sky.

And a big smile on his lover's face that was more beautiful than any of it.

He looked out the windows like a kid in Disneyland, taking in everything new, picturing his boy growing up in a place like this.

"Llama. I don't think I've ever seen a live llama."

"No? I'll take you to see Momma's. She loves them. They're tame as all get out." Sam pointed out different places. "That's BK's place, this one up here is Mister Ernie's. Joe and Sara live here. We all went to school together."

"I remember knowing my neighbors once." He had no idea who they were anymore. Occasionally he'd recognize one of them and nod.

"Everyone knows me here. Knows who I am, anyway."

"Well, sure. You're the mini rodeo cowboy with the heart of a Rottweiler." He snorted, grinning. "I'm sure there are other things you're known for too."

"Besides his hot bod cowboy modeling career and his penchant for sleeping naked in his hammock?"

"Aunt Linda!"

"Modeling?" He looked at Sam, utterly unable to control the laughter. "You were a model? You? Mister Don't Mind Me, I'm Going to Hide in My Hat?"

"One calendar."

"He had the hat on."

"Just one calendar!"

"Not much more than the hat," Linda added.

"It's a good look on him." He and Linda were laughing so hard, it was a wonder Sam hadn't grabbed the steering wheel. "Where do I get a copy of this calendar?"

"I have a case of them."

"I'm going to beat you, woman."

Linda snorted. "You'll try, short stuff."

"She's armed, don't forget." Oh God, laughing again. And on a full stomach. He took a deep breath. "Linda, you're a bad, bad influence. Slip me a calendar when Sam's not looking. I have to see this."

"No problem, my friend. I'll make sure you get two."

Sam groaned. "It was for charity, y'all."

"Modeling is modeling. Doesn't matter where the money went. But if it's a good cause, I could arrange for a few dozen more to be printed up and sell them to our friends. Mike would hang one behind the bar, I'm sure."

"You're totally sleeping in the front room on the sofa, Mister."

"I'll bring him over to my place, and we'll make margaritas." Linda winked over. "So, this is my place here."

The little stone ranch house was neat, well-kept, pink roses blooming everywhere around the white porch.

"The big house is about a quarter of a mile down this road." Sam pointed to a house about three times as big, sprawling out in the back of pastureland.

The road was rough as hell, six pickup trucks parked in a row along the side of the fence.

"My goodness. How much land?" He looked around, the aesthetic somewhat familiar but the view completely different. He climbed out of the truck as soon as Linda came to a stop, and waited for Sam.

"Three hundred and eighty acres." Sam pointed. "The black truck is Bowie's. The burnt-orange Dodge is mine. Momma's is the red Toyota, Daddy's is the GMC. The Ford POS is a work truck, and the white one is Bradley's."

He wondered briefly what had happened to the blue one James had shown him pictures of, but he didn't ask. "Burnt orange seems about right. Does it have gas in it? Where do you keep the keys, in case I need to make a quick getaway?" He grinned at Sam and helped the boy haul their bags out of the bed of Linda's truck.

"I'll show you where all the keys go. It's right by the door." Sam met his eyes, pretty eyes steady as stones. "You ready for this?"

"I am. It's important to me and I'm a little nervous, but not in a bad way. I want to meet them." He had a feeling he might play back seat for a bit to the scars on Sam's fuzzy head anyway.

"You'll be fine." Sam led him around the house. "Hey, y'all. I'm home."

A huge, slow-moving man turned to face them, along with a lean woman that he recognized from photographs.

"Well, I'll be damned." Dan O'Reilly smiled, one corner of the man's mouth dipped. "Howdy, baby boy. Glad to see you."

He pretended like he didn't know Stephanie was staring at him, and when it took more than a second for Sam to answer, he gave the boy a discreet nudge.

"Momma, Daddy, this is Thomas. Thomas, Dan and Stephanie." Sam stared at his mother and opened his arms.

He gave Sam and his mother a second to work that out without too much scrutiny and offered a hand to Dan. "Sir. It's very good to meet you."

Dan shook his hand, then motioned to a set of chairs. "Pleased. Are you a Thomas or a Tommy? You want a beer? Come have a sit."

He started to answer reflexively, but something he'd have a look at later changed his mind. "I'm Tho...mmy. Tommy's fine." That was the strangest impulse. "I would love a beer. Tell me where to find them, and I'll bring you one."

"I have them right here in the cooler. Momma filled it up for me today."

Sam's momma and Linda had Sam moving, bringing the

luggage inside. He was torn between helping and letting the boy find his own way over. Sooner or later he'd have to say hello to Stephanie.

"Well, that's convenient." He took a seat with Dan—it felt like the right move, and he had an arsenal of appropriate topics of conversation with Dan. Stephanie would be more challenging. "Great drive getting here. Sam says you have over three hundred acres?"

"Yessir, I do. We run cattle on most of it, cut hay. And there are the horses and goats, chickens, llamas." Dan leaned deeper in his chair. "It's been in our family for three generations."

"That's impressive. Your side of the family, I assume?"

"Yessir. I caught my girl at a dance hall, believe it or not. Her people were fancy-assed folks from Dallas, and back then, Dallas might have been the moon."

He smiled, liking the way Dan referred to Sam's mother as "my girl." So endearing. "Was it a scandal? Or did you win them over?"

"Oh, they never quite forgave me for being a cowboy and knocking her up, but after three grandbabies, they came around."

He laughed. "It took all three? They were pretty hardheaded. She seems like a good catch, though. Sam speaks of her fondly."

"She's my lady. I wouldn't give for her." Dan nodded once, like that was that.

He caught Sam looking his way and smiled, raising his beer so Sam would know he was doing fine. "So cattle is your main business?"

"Cattle, hay, meat goats." Dan smiled, the look of pride on the man's face eerily familiar.

"It couldn't be more different from our seventeen-hundred-square-foot apartment on the fourteenth floor. There's a little bit of a view." He winked and sipped his beer.

"Yeah, one day I want to come out and visit y'all. Take pictures." There was a long, pregnant pause. "Y'all ever figure out who beat up Sammy?"

Oh. He hadn't expected that one. Not right out of the gate. "No. The one security camera nearby was pretty useless, and Sam doesn't remember any of it. He's all right otherwise, though, healing well, has most of his energy back."

"Good deal. He's a tough little shit. Always has been." Dan's eyes followed his son. "Never thought he'd leave the ranch, I got to admit."

"Honestly, sir? I don't think he did either." He was fairly sure Sam would have kept on his path. It took a strong force to change his boy's trajectory. "He's happy, though."

"He seems to be. He says he's writing a book, thinking about getting his doctorate. My son. My roughstock son."

"All true. Your son has a keen, curious mind. He likes asking questions and digging up the answers." His boy loved the research. Loved to put pieces together. "I think his book is really going to be something."

"I've no doubt. I told him he ought to write a western for me after he's done this. I'd like to read that." Dan smiled, the look fond. "His momma, now? She'd understand the book he's writing on now. She was a schoolteacher until she retired."

He nodded. That he knew. "James told me that. He said it's why he wanted to teach."

"Yeah. James was the most like her. Bowie and Sammy are my boys, through and through. Sammy is smarter than me and Bowie, though. Maybe smarter than all of us, for all we despaired getting him through high school."

"I can only imagine. Was it getting him to sit still and stay in class, or were you just afraid he wouldn't live long enough to graduate?" Even he'd been a little reckless in high school. He didn't want to think about what trouble Sam might have gotten himself into—or found himself in.

"He couldn't sit still to save his damn fool life. We tried everything, but it was rodeoing that did it. All he had to do was hold on for eight seconds. He could do that."

"Well, and it's more than that, right? Nobody gets one over on Sam, not even a bull. He probably felt like he had a little something to prove." Eight seconds. He shook his head, feeling a little a smug that he could keep his boy plenty focused for...well, a whole afternoon if he wanted to. And had.

Sam came over to him and sat next to him. "Hey, Daddy."

"Sammy. Beer?"

"Yessir."

Thomas did love that he knew the difference between Sam's "Yes, Sir" and "Yessir" now.

"Should I go say hello to your mother, or does she need a minute?" There were many layers to that question, and he knew Sam would hear them all.

"She said she's going to come out and sit with Linda here in a minute. She had to change her shirt. She got something on it."

He nodded. That might be true, or it might be code. Either way, he understood. He grinned. "Your dad and I were just talking about you in high school, and the value of eight seconds."

"Yeah. Sitting still is hard. I didn't have to sit long on a bronc or bull, so at least I wasn't fu-screwing that up."

Oh, parent language. Good catch, boy; he might have

forgotten that himself. He thought about talking about the land a little, but it occurred to him that the farm that had been in the family for three generations was going to pass to Bowie and that was a complicated conversation, so he didn't go there.

"I haven't been on a plane in over a year. I forgot what a hassle the whole thing can be. I'm very glad to be sitting here instead and enjoying the view."

"It's something else, isn't it?" Sam looked over the pasture, and Thomas wasn't sure whether it was peace or longing on his face. "I might have to go see the horses this evening, take one of them out. Have you ever ridden, Mister?"

"I grew up with horses. Obviously it's been a while, but James and I rode on the beach sometimes on our winter vacations. I should be able to keep up." He grinned at Sam. He could ride. He might be sore in the morning, but he could keep his seat.

"Put him on Sugar. She's a good girl."

"I know, Daddy. Even Bowie can ride her." Sam grinned at his father and got a matching smile in return. "It's good to be home, sir. I missed y'all."

"You know you're welcome, anytime, as long as you want."

"I know."

Stephanie came out carrying a pitcher and a stack of red Solo cups, Linda trailing behind. "Hey, y'all. I made margaritas."

He set what was left of his beer on the deck by his chair and stood up. "I love a margarita. Can I help?" He reached out and lifted the tray from her so she could hand them out.

"Thank you, sir." She offered him a smile, and it didn't

feel fake or forced. "I'm pleased to be able to meet you in the flesh."

He gave her a similar smile. "It's very good to meet you, too. I've really been looking forward to this visit, to the opportunity to get to know you both a little. Sam speaks highly of you." That was the truth. For all their issues, Sam respected them. And who didn't have some kind of issue with their parents?

"I would hope so. I'd hate to have to beat his butt for lying." The little flash of wicked humor surprised the hell out of him.

"Everyone's all about the beatings, man..." Sam leaned back in his chair, feet crossed at the ankle.

Thomas laughed. "It's easy to pick on the little guy." He offered his seat next to Dan to Stephanie and took one between Sam and Linda, doing pretty much the same and sipping his margarita. Much better than the beer, which hadn't really been to his taste, but he didn't want to be impolite. "This is an excellent margarita, Stephanie. Thank you."

"You're more than welcome. I bought some of that wine you like too, baby boy."

Sam beamed over at his mom, obviously tickled. "Thank you, Momma. When I open my suitcase, I've got goodies for y'all too. Things to tempt you to come visit me next."

That sounded nerve-wracking, but he'd do it. He could be a good host and a decent tour guide. "I can get you museum passes, you could see a show...we could keep you well entertained, I think."

It was probably the margarita, but his fingers itched to reach out and take Sam's hand, and he knew if he was that impatient, his sensual boy was probably craving by now.

Maybe once they'd finished their drinks, they could find a need to go unpack.

"We'll see. I'm sure we can manage something. Did Daddy tell you Bradley was working for us now?"

"Aunt Linda did. Good deal."

"He's a good boy. He's getting married in October."

"Him and Ginny have been an item for a long time." Sam's voice was perfectly neutral.

"Ginny broke up with him. He's marrying Angela Beecaves after the baby gets here and all, so she looks pretty in her dress. I'm surprised he didn't tell you."

"Nope."

"Momma, men don't gossip like you ladies." Dan shot Stephanie a look.

He was grateful for the download on Bradley that he'd gotten out of Sam in the car, or he might well have said something stupid and played into Stephanie's hands. He decided to let his boy laugh instead.

"I hear you have a snake museum nearby."

Dan frowned, but Sam cracked up. "Out on 35 South, Daddy, right outside of New Braunfels."

"Y'all heading that far?" Stephanie asked.

"We're going through Hillsboro to Austin, then down to see San Antonio and then Corpus."

"You taking your truck?"

"Yes, ma'am. My buddy, Win, he's going to buy it from me. I'm meeting him down there."

He didn't know Sam had plans to sell the truck. That was more than a gesture—that meant Sam was a real New Yorker now. Not that he'd had any doubt, but it was meaningful that Sam felt ready to let go of it.

He hid a grin behind his margarita. Now he *really*

wanted to hold Sam's hand. He wanted to kiss the breath out of his boy too.

"Austin sounds like fun; I'm looking forward to that trip."

"It's going to be beautiful. The bluebonnets are everywhere." Stephanie smiled. "I remember when I used to take you boys out for pictures in the bluebonnets."

"Sounds lovely. I'll get you a current picture of Sam in the bluebonnets, shall I?" He wasn't kidding, though Sam might not appreciate he'd offered.

"Well, we ought to get one of both of you together, don't you think?" Stephanie's words surprised him, honored him.

"I...would appreciate that. We don't have any pictures of us together yet. Do we, Sam?" He had a couple of the pictures of him and James together but nothing suitable to show Stephanie. Too much leather. In fact, he didn't know that he'd want to show them to Sam either.

"I doubt it. We're not the selfie types."

"No? Hand me your phone." Aunt Linda held out her hand to Sam. "Unlocked, please."

This woman could be a Domme that would make grown men sob.

He watched Sam do exactly as she asked, though the boy's eyes were on her and the look wasn't exactly what he'd call trusting.

"Now, you two lean together and smile. You deserve proof you were here."

He leaned closer and looked at Sam, looping an arm around his boy's shoulders. "Is this okay, sweetheart?"

He could feel Sam relaxing against him, breathing and leaning toward him. "Fine. Smile."

"Cheese." He wanted to tell his boy that yes, that did feel good, that he needed a little of that contact himself, but the best he could manage just then was to squeeze Sam's upper arm with his fingers. He smiled, though, and Linda must have taken a series of pictures before handing Sam back the phone. "Let me see?"

Sam passed the phone over, and there were a half dozen better than decent pictures of them. Most had them looking at the camera, but in one Sam was looking at him, dead on.

God, he wanted that on his wall.

"Thank you, Linda. Those are great." He took a second to text himself that picture and two others that he liked and grinned at Sam as he handed the boy the phone back. "I just wanted a couple of those on my phone."

"We'll get more. Our whole trip, huh?" Sam slipped his phone in his holder. "I promise."

Sam's folks were staring at them, and Sam looked right back, daring them to complain. That was Sam's job. His job was to make them see that he was someone Sam could be proud of. So far, he thought he was doing fine.

He smiled around his boy at Stephanie. "Would you mind terribly if I got a picture of the two of you with Sam?"

"Of course not." Stephanie stood, then held her hand out to Sam, who took it and tugged her into his lap all of a sudden, hugging her tight. "Love you, Momma."

Oh, he snapped that one fast. A couple of different ones as she pretended to be annoyed with the boy, smiled, rolled her eyes, and kissed Sam on the cheek. His boy was going to like those. He smiled with them. "Come on, Dan, get in here."

Stephanie and Sam stood, perching on either side of Dan's chair, the big man's arms wrapping around their waists.

Once they were done, Linda had him join the family, and by the time Stephanie went to check the brisket, pronouncing it smoked, they were all goofing around and laughing.

Nothing like laughter to break the ice.

"Brisket, Sam." He rested his hands on his boy's waist for just the slightest moment. "I'm going to like this aren't I?" He was going to go home ten pounds heavier. They were definitely going running. He could take it slow for Sam.

"You are so totally going to like this." Sam grinned at him. "Come help me grab the rest—potato salad, pickles, coleslaw, and bread."

"There's nanner pudding for you too, baby boy."

Sam made a sound he'd only ever heard during sex.

He followed Sam inside. "Well. I guess I am going to like this." *Damn.* He might have to learn to cook.

They helped get the food on the table; then he sat exactly where Sam's mother told him he should. "This smells amazing, Stephanie."

"Well, thank you, sir. I hope you enjoy it."

They filled their plates and Sam took his hand, Dan's. Stephanie took his other hand and Linda's, then they all bowed their heads as Dan said a short, simple prayer of thanks for the food, for safe travels, and for meeting him.

He gave Sam's hand a squeeze and said "Amen" with everyone else to be polite but also because he did feel grateful. He hadn't been to a family dinner since the day he turned eighteen, and he recognized that this was special. He was happy his boy had this, and he was hopeful he would be able to call a corner of it his as well.

6

Sam sat on the edge of his bed, looking around his room. God, he needed to ship some stuff home.

It hadn't changed a bit. Seriously. Not one bit.

He had lived in this same room for twenty-five years. From rocket ships to dinosaurs to video games to the current brown everything—what was Thomas going to think?

Thomas had done beautifully over dinner. Hell, he'd even done the dishes, which had made Momma beam, and they'd foregone the riding for more beer and margaritas and a fierce game of Spades.

Now everyone had gone to bed, Thomas was in the shower, and he was...wigged and pleased and fucked-up and here, but for the first time ever *here* wasn't *home*.

He heard the water shut off, and Thomas came out a few minutes later in a towel, hair neatly combed, and a tired but happy smile on a newly-shaved face. "When's your mother coming in to sew me into my bundle?"

"They crashed without asking where we were sleeping. We should be able to fit in here, right?" And with the door locked.

"If not, I'll just chain you to the foot of the bed, and you can sleep on the floor." Thomas winked and gave him a light kiss.

"That would totally suck." He reached out, hands sliding on Thomas's stomach. "You having fun?"

"I am. Your parents are very kind. Linda is hilarious. It's beautiful here. The little shamrocks all over your pajamas are adorable." Thomas winked at him and moved away, opening a suitcase.

Sam chuckled and pulled down the covers, shaking them a little, just in case. Scorpions sucked.

Thomas pulled on much less festive bottoms and climbed into bed with him. "Your father and I had a nice talk, I thought. I just felt like...one of the guys. We talked about how much James was like your mother."

"Yeah. He was. Me and Bowie, not so much." They were their daddy's.

"That's what he said. The two of you were just like him." Mister slipped an arm under him and pulled him closer, and he felt the deep, open breath of Thomas's relieved sigh. "I've wanted to do this all day."

Sam curled in, his eyelids going heavy. "I hear you. I'm spoiled to touch."

"How does it feel to be home, boy?"

"Weird. I'm excited to show you everything, but...it's a little weird."

Thomas huffed. "Weird. Can you elaborate?"

"I don't know. I mean, this has been my room for a long time, and this is the first time I've been here that it wasn't really my room." He'd expected it all to be easy—well, okay, not the parent meeting part. That had gone well except for the tears from Momma when he first showed up; he'd expected that to suck—but it wasn't.

"Your perspective has changed. This isn't your house anymore; it's your parents' house. You don't live here, you're just visiting. How does that make you feel?"

The temptation to tell Thomas he was a cowboy and they didn't have feelings was huge, but he didn't. "Weird. Uncomfortable, but it's not bad either. Is it weird to you, knowing this was my room for so long?"

Thomas seemed to think about that. "No. I didn't know the kid that used to sleep here. I just feel...too big for it." Mister laughed. "That's not a comment on your size, I swear. I mean I feel like you've outgrown this."

"I have." He loved this, when Thomas and he were connected, speaking the same language, hearing each other. It made him feel solid, somehow.

"Are you feeling sentimental? Sad? Do you miss it?" Thomas was drawing slow circles on his skin.

"I'm glad to show it to you, so you can see where I came from. So you get to meet my people." He felt himself relaxing, deeper and deeper. "I will be glad to get home too, at the end of our vacation."

"I feel the same way. I feel like I know you more fully already." Mister kissed his forehead. "How is your mother?"

"I think she likes you way more than she wanted to." She'd been all teary over his head, over the scars. "She wants me to go see James's stone tomorrow. You want to come?"

He wasn't sure, exactly, how Thomas felt about cemeteries, but he needed to stop by.

"Yes, I do." Well, that was pretty clear. It would be good to go together. "I told you she'd like me. How'd you like the dishes thing, hm? Nice move, right?"

"That was exceptional. Pure class act. Seriously. You got hard-core points." Momma had been over the moon.

Thomas took another breath. "Truthfully, I was nervous, boy. I felt like this was an important day for you. For me too. But I'm not nervous anymore."

"I appreciate you letting me show you this." He wanted Thomas to know where he'd come from. He didn't understand why James had hidden them all away, but Sam wouldn't do that. He wouldn't hide his roots, and he wouldn't hide his lover.

"It means a lot to me that you want to." Sam knew Thomas meant that; he had been invested all day, thrown himself into the family, was polite and respectful but had made himself a presence they couldn't just ignore.

"I do." Sam knew his lover wanted to care about the people he cared about, wanted to know about this part of his past. He sighed because part of him felt a little disrespectful of James, like he was passing judgment on James's choices.

"What are you going to do when you run into Bradley?"

He'd like to believe that was just small talk, but he knew a loaded question when he heard one.

"He's going to give me the cold shoulder and pretend that he doesn't know me. I'm going to snark at him and wish him luck in the 'replace me' attempt."

"Suppose you don't, and you just say it's good to see him?"

"Then that would be a lie. He turned his back on me when James died. I don't need that shit." The straw that had broken the friendship had been Thomas, but he wasn't going to tell Thomas that. They had been cracked before that.

"Mm. When James died or when you came out? I thought Linda said the latter." Thomas wasn't letting it go.

Sam shrugged, feeling his muscles creak. He didn't want

to think about it. He'd been in New York for months and no one called him, emailed him. No one missed him. *Fuck them.* He figured shit out, right?

Thomas hugged him for a minute, long arms wrapping all the way around him. "I know you're used to a fight, sweetheart, but sometimes you come out on top by not giving them something to be mad at you for. I'd guess he'd be expecting you to give him some snarky comeback. Why give him what he wants?"

"You're just worried about me breaking my head again." Bradley had been his best friend for his whole life. His best motherfucking friend.

"Can you blame me? If you tell him he'll never be enough to replace you, is he going to throw a punch?"

"I wouldn't. You have to know I wouldn't do that, Mister. Not really. Not in so many words. Hell, if I'm lucky, I'll just avoid him altogether."

Thomas sighed. "Who is he to you, boy?"

"He was my best friend. I mean, we must have spent four nights a week at each other's houses our whole lives. We met in the nursery at church. I was there when he got his heart broke the first time. He was there when I lost my first tooth." And all it had taken was a single email for it to disappear.

"I'm sorry, Sam. I don't suppose it's possible he's more upset that you didn't tell him sooner? That he feels like you should have trusted him? Can you talk to him at all?"

"I don't know, Mister." He wasn't sure what to do. He wasn't sure he wanted to do anything. He felt like everyone had deserted him when he went up East and let him swim or sink. He'd managed to stay afloat, and now he was happy. Why should he talk to anyone?

"All right, boy. He was your friend; you'll figure it out. I just think you should know what you want to say in case he does speak to you. And remember what it feels like when people give up on you. Maybe you don't want to do that to someone else."

He lifted his head, staring at Thomas. He loved the man to death, but really? Moralizing? "Seriously? Does that ever work? Your job is to be on my side, remember?" He made sure to soften the words with a kiss and a wink.

Thomas grinned at him. "That's all you need from me, hm? Just hush up and be on your side?" He got a long sigh. "I'm always on your side. In public, you know I'll stand with you. But in private? I'm your friend, and I'm going to tell you what I see. I'd expect no less of you. Are you really saying you don't want me to challenge your thinking?"

"No. I'm saying that he hurt me when I needed a friend, and I'm petty enough to want him to know that he doesn't get to replace me here like I never existed." He blinked, his anger surprising him.

Thomas nodded, making no effort to calm him. "And if it weren't for that head, you'd be looking for him, not avoiding him, wouldn't you?"

"I don't know." And that didn't matter, did it? Just like with James. It didn't matter because some things were just what they were.

"You're going to have to find some way to deal with these people without your fists, Sam. And without running. Whatever choice you make, I've got your back. But make a choice; don't just maneuver around them."

Thomas kept an arm around him, thumb massaging his upper arm, digging into the muscle, making sure Sam felt him.

"I'm tired, Mister. Sometimes..." He looked at the art tacked up on the wall—cowboys and bulls, horses and boots. Sometimes he missed the simple; then he remembered how fucking bored he had been, so restless.

"Sometimes what? Sometimes you want to return to this? To what's easy? That's understandable. You lived under a comfortable cover. Lonely, I'd bet, but comfortable. If you decide you're going to let it go, fine. But think about it, decide what you want, what you can live with."

Sam didn't know what to say to any of that. What could he say? He didn't want to come back here. He wanted to fit in somewhere, but he was beginning to suspect that wasn't in his cards. He wanted to be okay, and he thought he basically was. He wasn't sure how he felt about the fact that Thomas thought he only fought or ran. He didn't feel that was all of him, but obviously it wasn't reading.

Maybe he was just genuinely tired.

Maybe he just needed to sleep and go visit James tomorrow.

Hell, maybe he'd eaten too much pudding with his beer.

Thomas kissed his forehead, tangled their fingers. "Mm. I've said something to upset you, misread your reticence somehow. I'm sorry. We're...out of context here. Maybe I should have waited a couple of days before interpreting things."

"I think I'm just overwhelmed a little. I'm glad you're here with me. We laughed a lot today." That gentle apology went miles toward making him feel less off-center. "And, yeah, totally out of context, which is part of the deal, huh? I should feel less like a stranger."

"You're not the same person you were when you lived here. We all change. I think you'll figure out how the new you fits in here after a few days. In the meantime, we'll just keep laughing and enjoying ourselves."

"Works for me." The best part was the together part. He was addicted to Thomas's laugh.

"Would you like to try a run in the morning? I ate too much banana pudding."

"Sounds good to me. We can head down to the pond, even." The dogs would love that.

"You're the tour guide. My feet will just follow. Let you think you're in charge." Thomas's laugh was soft but dark.

"I love that sound." It made his balls ache, just right.

Thomas nodded, and he realized his lover knew. "You make some good sounds too. That one you made over the pudding made me wish I could cook."

His cheeks burned. "I do love me some nanner pudding. You were all over Momma's potato salad, too."

"Oh, that was pure potato heaven, my boy. The brisket was outstanding, but that potato salad could make me love her." Thomas shifted them, pressing him into the pillows with a hard kiss. His eyes flew open and he gasped, his lips parting, his world focusing down to his Sir in a dizzying rush.

Mister kissed him until he thought he might need to use a safe word just to get air, then grinned down at him. "That, is how I feel about you selling your truck, by the way." Thomas took a breath. "Thank you."

"We don't need it, right? And we can use the money for... whatever we need to." He clung to Thomas, the world off-center. "God. Love you."

"Love you too, boy." Thomas moved down his body, lips leaving damp, cooling skin behind on his neck, his shoulders, one nipple. "Will I be the first person to blow you in your big-boy bed?" There was that laugh again, Mister pushing at his pajamas.

"Ass. You know you are. You know you have damn near all my firsts."

"I do. It's just such a rush to hear you say it." Thomas finally just sat up and yanked his pajamas off, sliding them down his legs and tossing them off the bed. "Mm. Better."

Sam moaned softly, reminding himself to be quiet as a mouse, because Thomas made him ache. This felt daring as fuck, illicit and exciting as hell.

Mister laughed again and reached up, tossing a pillow over his face. "Can't let Stephanie hear. Or Dan. Not sure which would be worse."

He chuckled at the pillow and started to remove it when Thomas went after the head of his cock with a hot tongue, looping around in a circle and tracing the length of the slit.

His abs went tight and he gasped, fingers digging into the pillow instinctively. He was lit up, one of his knees drawing up.

Thomas hooked an arm around his raised thigh, then took him in, tongue pressing against his shaft all the way down, fingers curled around the base. He threw the pillow and pushed up on his elbows, staring down at the sight of his Sir, lips around his cock.

Mister was busy, attentive, fingers and tongue working him like there was nothing in the world Sir would rather be doing than making him feel good, making him fly.

"Love," he croaked out. He was surrounded by sensation, Thomas playing him like a guitar, making his body sing.

Thomas hardly missed a beat getting naked too, before his lover tugged him lower down on the bed and growled out, "Want your mouth." Mister shifted and was suddenly straddling his head, that heavy prick slapping him in the chin as Thomas swallowed him down again. He muffled his cry with Thomas's cock, his focus on the thick shaft spreading his lips, the way his entire world was his Mister—around him, inside him, against him.

They sucked and teased each other, and Sir didn't let up at all, didn't give him a chance to figure out how to breathe and suck while he was trying not to lose his mind. His cock kept alternately hitting the roof of Mister's mouth and sliding down his throat.

He arched up as he grabbed Mister's ass and pulled him in deep, trying to wrench his control back.

Mister's head flew up, releasing him with a loud pop, and his Sir muffled a cry on the inside of his thigh, teeth digging into skin and muscle. Sam swallowed convulsively, his feet drumming on the mattress, his balls tight and aching.

"Fuck." Mister released his thigh, leaving hot skin behind and swore, voice rough and intense, though barely above a whisper. Thomas arched, hips driving downward into his throat, thighs trembling.

Mine. Fuck. He needed this—Thomas's hunger, his cock, his flavor.

No sooner had he thought that than he had it. Thomas's hips stuttered and went stiff and Sam's mouth filled with bitter, salty seed, his lover actually smothering a cry with a white-knuckled fist. Sam swallowed over and over, undulating under Thomas, one hand on Thomas's ass.

Thomas finally relaxed and leaned down, running a tongue over his balls. "Such a naughty boy."

"Mmm..." He groaned softly, that touch threatening to light him on fire. "Not."

"Oh, yes. Naughty." His cock was suddenly surrounded by heat and pressure, Thomas's tongue sliding against his shaft. One hand worked his balls, rolling and pushing, giving him a delicious ache that kept him off-balance, off-center.

Thomas was moving again, this time stretching out long beside him, fingers playing only lightly on his thigh. "What do you want, Sam?" His lover's tone was heated but playful. "If you can say it, you can have it...albeit quietly."

"Mister..." He spread wider, groaning softly. "Please."

The man was asking him to think? With that mouth on his dick?

"Hm? Oh. This?" His cock disappeared into Thomas's mouth and was buried in Mister's throat.

Oh, sweet Jesus, please. He arched and shot, his fucking world spinning wildly.

Mister spoiled him, sucking and licking him, kissing and nuzzling, bringing him down slowly enough that he could actually think by the time he was breathing deep again.

"That was...wow, Mister." *Wow. Also, yay.*

Thomas laughed and flipped around, pulling him in and kissing him. "It's always wow with you, boy. You drive me out of my mind."

"Uh-huh. You make me lose all my words." He found all the ways they fit together.

"Thanks for that. I didn't realize how much I needed you."

"Couldn't hardly touch all day, huh?" That wasn't even Texas; that was family.

Thomas nodded. "Yes. It was making me crazy. I've gotten so used to being physical, having you close, reaching out anytime. My fingers itched."

He grabbed Thomas's hand and kissed his fingers, one by one. He heard that.

"My boy. I'll get used to it I'm sure. I just hadn't

considered it would be that tough." Mister gave him a smile. "I am going to hold you all night to get my fill. That's all."

"Thank you." He snuggled in with a sigh. "Love you, Mister. Glad you're here with me."

"Me too, boy. We're in for a good week. Sleep now, love."

7

Sam's momma made a respectable cup of coffee. Thomas finished his second cup and his last bite of breakfast, watching his boy move easily around a kitchen he was clearly comfortable in, helping clean up. He'd gotten up late—well, not late by New York standards but late by Texas farm standards—and Dan had given him a little shit about it, which he decided meant the man liked him. You didn't waste your energy on people you didn't like, right?

"Thank you for breakfast, Stephanie. The coffee hit the spot too."

"Of course. What do y'all have planned today, baby boy?"

"I'm taking a ride out to see James and Mamaw and Papaw; then I thought I'd just take a drive, maybe Molina's for lunch. You want to meet us there?"

Oh, he did like how Sam managed that—making it clear that the parents were not invited and making a lunch date at the same time.

"Sure. What time?"

"I'll call. I'm thinking a late lunch, though."

He took his dishes over to Sam at the sink. He liked Sam's parents, but he was ready to get out of the house, see what there was to see. He was a little anxious for this cemetery visit. He was looking forward to seeing where James was buried, having context, saying a proper good-bye. But he was also dreading it and ready to just get it over with. He'd decided in this instance that those contradictions could exist at the same time—it didn't have to make sense.

"I'm ready when you are."

"Let me grab my boots and my wallet." Sam disappeared for a second and returned with a filthy ball cap on. He was handed one that was...somewhat cleaner. "You'll need this today."

"Thanks." He took the cap and tucked it under his arm. When was the last time he'd worn a ball cap? College? "Oh, right. Sunglasses. Give me...two shakes." He laughed and elbowed Sam on his way to the bedroom and hurried back with his sunglasses. He gave Stephanie a smile on their way out the door. "Looking forward to lunch."

"So is Sammy. Molina's is his favorite restaurant in all the world. Y'all have a good morning. Tell James I said good morning and I'll be to visit next week."

Thomas caught both Dan and Sam rolling their eyes. He decided to stay on Stephanie's good side.

"Happy to. Enjoy your morning." He was going to have to scrub the brown off his nose with Brillo after this trip.

Sam's truck was...a little bit of a revelation when he got in. The back seat was filled with camping gear, clothes, bits of riding gear, books, dozens of notebooks—not a bit of trash, but somehow this was his boy distilled down into leather and dust and paper.

Thomas understood Sam had spent a lot of time moving around and defined himself in a lot of different ways. Unlike James, who took all the different pieces of a diverse life and compartmentalized them, it looked like Sam had been trying to find a way to integrate all his pieces into something that made sense. There must have been very few people who took that journey with him, because it was obvious he'd never quite figured out where he fit in.

And having left and come home again, his boy clearly didn't know now. That was something Thomas was going to have to take more time to think about.

"We should get some boxes while we're out so we can ship your things home."

"Yeah, I'd like to have some of them at home, especially my Jack Wells." Sam turned the radio down and pulled out. "I spent a lot of time in this truck."

"I see that. It looks like you had a busy life here. We'll have to clean it out before we head to Austin." He was careful not to sound judgmental. He wasn't, but knew it would be easy for Sam to feel that way.

"Yeah. Most of it can be thrown away, saved for Bowie, or sold. Some of it I'd like to keep." Sam drove confidently, his boy sure and steady. "Like these." He flicked the mass of stuff hanging from the rearview. "They're my tassels, high school, undergrad, and grad school."

Tassels. Fuzzy dice. A weird stuffed bull...

He reached up and ran his fingers through the tassels, just because he knew how they would feel. He like that silky feeling, and he also like the feeling of accomplishment they represented. "I like the bull. Where's the glass crystal and the air fresh...oh. Found it." He laughed. "I don't think it's working, though."

"Probably not, no." Sam laughed. "I bought this truck for cash, did you know that? My first big purse."

"I didn't. You must be proud of it, then. I've never owned a car. If I hadn't needed the ID, I might not even have bothered with a license." He actually assumed he'd be better at riding than driving.

"I mean, I was at twenty-one. Now it's just a truck. A good truck, but a truck. There's no room for her where we are, so I decided to get some cash for her."

"There's certainly no need for a truck in the city, no." And keeping a truck in a lot would cost a fortune even if there were. "You should do something fun with the money."

"I figured we could talk about it. Maybe put a good chunk in savings, huh? Then use the rest for something cool together."

"That sounds reasonable." It also sounded like another financial discussion because if Sam wanted to save the money, they'd have to discuss how and where. Did Sam have his own account? Were they at the point of discussing whether to combine finances? With Sam's recovery, they hadn't really done much beyond talk in suppositions about money, but he knew it was important to the boy. "What do you define as 'something cool'?"

"I'd like to travel. I'm getting twenty-five for the truck. We ought to be able to save fifteen for emergencies, right? I'm pretty good at saving money and all."

He nodded. That was an impressive sum. He propped a hand on Sam's headrest, then thought better of it and moved it to the boy's thigh. "I would love to travel with you. Tell me where we're going."

"I'd like to do a cruise, I think, but I love going and doing, seeing new things. I've been to all the big rodeos—

Calgary, Cheyenne, Houston, Denver. I even rode in Hawaii once."

"So we'll do a cruise, and you'll take me to the rodeo... somewhere." He paid more attention as Sam took a tight turn. "Oh. Are we here?"

"Yeah. Momma wanted him in the family plot. She bought one for me and Bowie too. I don't want it, though. I want to be cremated. I don't want to be stuck in the ground. I have a will. It's in there."

"I also want to be cremated. You'll find my wishes in my will as well." A sudden chill went down his spine as a simple thought about whether they should keep copies of their wills in the office twisted into a worry that one of them might need such information, especially with James's killer still lurking somewhere. And that grim thought reminded him that he needed to have James removed from his paperwork.

God, this wasn't the way he wanted to begin his visit to his late lover's gravesite.

He'd better pull it together. Sam didn't need that stress. He looked out the passenger-side window and took a breath.

Sam reached out and took his hand, just held it, and it reminded him that Sam might be the one of the two of them that was solid this time, well-adjusted. That Sam was here and willing to take him at his less-than-perfect.

He gave Sam's hand a squeeze and nodded to him. Strange how often he had to remind himself that Sam deserved all the same trust his lover gave him so unconditionally. He promised himself he wouldn't be anything less than truthful today.

"It's a pretty site. So green."

"Yeah. It's all peaceful and shit. I guess that's better for folks who come to visit. Come on with me, and I'll show you where the stone is. I want to make sure it's all spelled right."

Make sure it's all spelled right. *Fuck, really?*

He hated cemeteries. They were pretentious and obligatory. When he died, he wasn't going to make anyone worry over a typo or feel guilty for not visiting enough. But the only good-bye he'd had with James was a bloody chalk outline on the sidewalk. He'd never shake that image, but this was at least more peaceful.

He followed Sam along a gravel path and stuck close when his lover turned off onto the grass.

There were three low stones, all with bright fake roses in the built-in vases. "Mamaw and Papaw are there. This one's James."

Sam looked at the stone, which read simply *James Fannin O'Reilly, Held in Our Father's Hands*, and the dates, a dove carved into one corner. "Everything's good. I'll let you have your time."

"Thanks," he said automatically. But as Sam turned away he wondered if he needed time. He didn't really want to be alone. He reached for Sam's hand, stopping the boy. "Actually, stay?"

He didn't know why, but he had strange questions. A gravestone wasn't going to answer them.

"Of course." Sam grabbed on, held his hand, twining their fingers together.

"What was he wearing?" He knew it had to have been a closed casket, but surely Stephanie had someone dress James.

"We put him in his jeans, the blue shirt he wore the day he graduated. No one saw him but me and Bowie. Daddy wouldn't let Momma. His boots rode in on Old Red with me in the front and Bowie following up." Sam chuckled softly.

"He probably...no, he wouldn't have cared about that, but we didn't know. We were just doing it the old way."

"Old Red?" He didn't know this tradition; he was picturing all kinds of crazy things.

"One of the horses. Cowboy funerals. You turn the boots backward in the stirrups and ride them in. It's our way."

"I had no idea." Sam was right. James wouldn't have cared about that, but he supposed what mattered to the family was more important. "Was it a nice day? Were there a lot of people?"

"It was beautiful. Hot like it is in September, sunny. There were a couple hundred people here, maybe more. Me and Bowie, my cousins Charles and Adam, my uncle Jim, and Chris Stamp were pallbearers."

He looked out over the expanse of green grass and tried to picture it, all these people that James had so deliberately left behind, gathering to support Sam's family. "That's incredible, all those people. Who is Chris Stamp?" That was the only name that wasn't family.

"James's best friend. He's a soldier too. He's stationed at Fort Bragg with the 82nd. Good man. You'd like him a lot. He wants to open his own restaurant one day."

"His best friend." He snorted and shook his head. "And I didn't know the name. I was thinking I might want to spend the rest of my life with someone that didn't trust me. With someone I didn't even know."

"Oh. Oh, I swear to God, I wouldn't ever try to hurt your feelings."

"I asked the question, sweetheart. All you did was answer it." He squeezed Sam's hand to make sure the boy knew it was all right. He went quiet, though; he didn't know if he wanted to ask any more questions.

"I will tell you anything. He was a good man, but he...he

hid a lot." Sam rubbed his palm. "He was scared of making people disappointed, maybe. Or maybe...maybe it was him, just built-in. All the boxes."

"I have to assume that he didn't think any one person could love all of him at once, so he had a box for family and another for work, one for his own anxieties—money and the like, and...one for me. I'm sure it wasn't personal. He loved me; I believe that."

"I do too. I believe he loved you. I believe you loved him." Sam squeezed. "I know I love you."

He looked at Sam, turned to face his boy, and smiled. "I know you do. And I love you. You're mine."

"Yep. Every bit of me. I swear." Sam never looked away from him, never hid a bit away from him.

"I know, love. You're not your brother, you're nothing like him. You are your own man. My man." He took a deep breath. "And I'm yours."

He didn't know if this was what closure felt like, but he felt like he'd turned a corner in the last few minutes. He was all right with leaving James here with his family, in one of several worlds that James understood.

"Thank you, Lord, yes. You want to go ride around, get a coffee and just fuck off in the truck? I can show you all the weird little things about here."

"Yes. That sounds like fun. I could use some fun." He took another look at James's headstone, tracing the name with his eyes, then crouching to do the same with his fingers. "I miss you, pet. Be good." He stood up and took Sam's hand again. "Oh. Your mother says good morning, and she'll be by to visit next week." He grinned at Sam.

Sam nodded. "She will. I think his soul is in the city with you, with the kids he loved, with his apartment. His body, though, it's in a nice place. Let's go play, Mister. I want to show you everything."

He agreed. He didn't need to come back here again, but he was glad he came today. "I can't wait. Can I get caramel in my coffee?" He bumped shoulders with Sam, leaving James to rest easy. He wanted to goof off with his boy.

8

"Oh, man. If I eat anything else, you'll have to roll me out of here." Sam had eaten chips and salsa, queso compuesto, beef enchiladas, two margaritas—he was fixin' to die.

Boom.

Momma laughed at him. "I swear to God, you love Tex-Mex better than any of my babies."

"Yes, ma'am." He was going to have to walk around the pasture for a month of Sundays just so he could fit in his jeans.

"This salsa is hot as fu—ire. It's on *fire*." Thomas cleared his throat. "What was that thing I ordered called again, Stephanie?"

"That was the chicken fajita queso chimichanga."

Sam chuckled under his breath. The look on Thomas's face when the platter of food came out was amazing.

He'd even taken a picture.

"Chicken fajita queso chimichanga. That's a lot of words. I'm stuffed." Thomas dipped another chip into the hot-as-fuck salsa.

Note to self: Don't give the man that rarely has more than one glass of wine two margaritas. Or do, and laugh a lot.

"Your son took me on quite the tour this morning."

"Where all did y'all go?"

"We went to the park, down the drag, and I took him out to Tawakoni to see the lake. We wandered down there, then headed back. I'm going to take him to the Walmart next, so we can buy road trip food and some T-shirts for him." Sam couldn't wait to take drunk Thomas to the Walmart.

"Really? I've never been to a Walmart."

The only thing funnier than drunk Thomas was the look on his mother's face just then.

"Is he fucking with me, son?"

"Probably not, Momma." He winked at her. "You're not his type."

Thomas's eyes went wide. "Oh, the pair of you. Swearing and innuendo? I'm shocked. Also, I think it's been fairly well established that I don't have a type."

"Of course you do, son." That was Daddy. "Obviously you're into O'Reillys. Bowie and I should be worried."

Butter wouldn't melt in Daddy's mouth and Sam lost it, laughing hysterically.

Thomas leaned back in his chair. "Bowie, maybe. I'm scared of you. Especially right now."

"Smart man. My Dan is taken, and I'd totally fight for him." Momma winked over at Thomas, the look on her face wicked as hell.

He wanted to crow because not only did Thomas get to see this, but Momma and Daddy were starting to heal up, to recover some from losing one of their own.

He'd been terrified he'd lost them forever.

"Oh, you'd win. Just ask Sam. I have a lot of skills, but

fighting isn't one of them." Thomas's hand landed on his thigh under the table and gave it a squeeze.

"I got enough fight for all of us." Enough for the whole family. Even Bowie.

"He's like a chihuahua that thinks it's a wolf...but is really a little fuzzy puppy." He looked at Sam. "Or something."

"A little fuzzy puppy..." Oh, he was going to pinch Thomas. Hard.

"Oh, Sammy's like a baby pit bull—bouncy and stubborn, but cute as all get out." Momma winked at him. "Tons of energy."

"Tons. It's a challenge to exhaust him." Thomas winked right back. "But I manage all right."

Daddy put his hands over his ears. "La la la, I can't hear y'all..."

"Oh, nicely done." Sam nodded to Thomas. "Very nicely done."

"Point to Tommy," Momma conceded. "I think I'm still three up on all y'all."

"Thank you." Thomas leaned forward again, bowing in his chair. "Do I get a handicap for not knowing we were playing for points until now?"

"Oh, Tommy..." Momma shook her head, all over-the-top drama. "The O'Reillys are always playing for points."

Sam couldn't wait to tell Angel about this.

Thomas reached over and patted her hand. "Good to know, Momma. I guess I'm one of yours now. All I need is that trip to Walmart, and it'll be official, right?"

"That and the Sonic to grab burgers and limeades for supper later on tonight."

"Momma! Don't talk about food right now!" Although limeades were so good...

Thomas's laugh was relaxed and playful. Happy. "Perfect. Dinner is on me. Sam doesn't have to eat if he doesn't want to."

"He'll eat. He loves their foot-longs."

Thomas gaped at Momma, then looked at him and burst out laughing. "There is no keeping up with this woman."

"No. No, Sir. There is not." He stood and stretched, then went to kiss Momma on the cheek. "You got a list for me?"

"I'll text it to you. It's not much. Sausage and toilet paper mostly."

"Oh, biscuits and gravy for breakfast?" Momma was good to him.

"You know it."

Thomas stood as well. "Lovely lunch, thank you for joining us. *Whoa.* Good thing I'm not driving."

"Yeah. You good, son?"

"I got this." He was more full than tipsy, and the Walmart was damn near close enough to walk it. "Come on, Mister. Walmart ho!"

Thomas looked a little embarrassed. "I'm fine, sir. Thank you. I just hadn't expected the head rush. Have a lovely afternoon." Thomas followed him out of the restaurant. "They know how to make a margarita in Texas."

"Yes, Sir, they most certainly do. You'll walk it off." The sun was blazing, and it was gorgeous—warm and pretty, the breeze cutting the humidity. Perfect weather.

"Oh, the sun." Thomas stopped walking for a second and took a deep breath. "So warm. I knew I'd miss my vacation with James this winter, but I thought it was just about James. I think I missed the beach too."

"We'll be there in a few days. Fort Worth, Austin, San Antonio, then the beach." He wanted to take Thomas to Billy Bob's, to the Bullock Museum and Deep Eddy, to the

Riverwalk. Hell, to the Czech Stop for kolaches and to the Oasis to ring the bell at sunset. Texas was beautiful in the springtime and no matter what, it would always be where his soul called home.

"Sounds fantastic. Why are we going to Walmart again? Oh. Munchies and T-shirts. Right. Your parents are good people."

Sam nodded. "I told you they were. Last year was hard on them, but they're coming back. They are."

He didn't know what they'd do if they found out about the bullshit at the apartment. Hell, he didn't know what they'd do if the cops ever found the guy. They were starting to find a new normal; what if there had to be court and shit?

What if it got ugly?

What if...

Stop it. Walmart. Traveling. Worry on your work time.

"It's good that we came, and that we didn't wait forever to do it. And now that I know they're reasonably accepting of me, we should make sure to keep you close. They need it, and you do too." Thomas followed him through the sliding doors. "You're figuring it out here, I can see it."

"Figuring what out, Mister?" He grabbed a buggy and his phone to see Momma's text.

"Where your place is now. What your role is, how you fit. You're steadier even just this morning." Thomas grabbed the handle and steered the buggy away. "I got this. You shop."

"Yes, Sir." Sausage, milk, toilet paper, Doritos. Momma's list was short and sure. "What is on your road trip snack list?"

He wanted Funyuns, grapes, and peanut M&M's.

"Uh. Chex Mix. Raisins. You."

He looked over, his cheeks burning with pleasure. "I can manage that."

Thomas winked at him. "So this is Walmart, hm? It's huge."

"Yep. I have spent a lot of time in one, waiting on Momma, wandering around aimlessly trying to think of somewhere else to go." He started at the shirts. He wanted to pick up a pair of cheap flip-flops too, for the hotels.

Thomas followed along and let Sam pick shirts out for him, saying yes to everything with a smile. The only thing he insisted on was the Chex Mix.

Every so often someone would walk up to him, greet him, and they'd have a little chat. Some wanted to ask after Momma and Daddy, some wanted to offer their condolences, some just wanted to say hi. He introduced every single one of them to Thomas, from Miz Lucy to Bambi from high school, who was the size of the broad side of a barn, pregnant, and dragging three little ones with her.

He shouldn't have been surprised when Bradley walked up to him while he was grabbing Dr Peppers and waters, but he was, a little.

"Sammy."

"Bradley. How goes?"

"Been working hard. You?"

"I came to see Momma before I took Thomas around." He didn't blush, didn't back down, but no one could accuse him of nasty.

"Bradley, was it?" Thomas stepped right up to Sam's shoulder and offered Bradley a hand to shake. "Thomas. Nice to meet you."

"Pleased. When are y'all leaving?"

"Tomorrow morning." Lord, how could you be friends with someone for so long and then it just disappeared with a pop? A tragedy, a move, a secret exposed and bang, you were staring at a relative stranger. Weird.

"Good deal. Tell your folks I'll be at work by noon."

"I'll do that." He had a shitload that he wanted to say—from "Fuck off" to "I miss you" to "I hear you switched girls and there's a baby on the way"—but Bradley walked off without so much as a screw you, and he grabbed a case of water.

Thomas's hands landed on his shoulders and gave them a quick squeeze. "Breathe."

"I got it." He figured he'd just said his good-byes. Sometimes they came as fistfights; sometimes they came as a silence that couldn't be broke. Shit happened. "So, that was Bradley."

He managed a half grin, a wink.

"Not much to look at." Thomas grinned back.

He shrugged, lowering his voice. "Believe it or not, I never once thought about him like that. He was my best friend, but...yeah. No."

"I believe you." Thomas pushed the buggy down the aisle. "You've outgrown him along with your bedroom."

"I guess so." Sad, but true. "What's your position on Swiss Cake Rolls?"

"Is there any position other than yes? I hope you still love me after I've gained ten pounds." Thomas pulled a box off the shelf and tossed it into the buggy.

"Vacation calories don't count. That's a law." Sam figured he'd just have to crunch a lot in the mornings.

"I'm more concerned about the old man belly. But I'm up to three hundred crunches now at the gym, so I figure you're keeping me young." Thomas laughed. "Did I forget my cane again?"

"Old, my ass. You're fine as frog hair and I know it." He was damn lucky.

"You know I wanted to push Bradley's buttons a little, right? I was a good boy."

"I'll reward you later." Damn, that felt daring as hell, flirting with Thomas here in the store.

"Mm. Snacks!" Thomas slipped a credit card into the chip reader and picked up the tab before Sam could protest.

They were laughing together as they loaded the truck. God, he needed to clean out his cab before tomorrow. There was some crazy shit in there.

"You know what we didn't get? Have you got water... whoa." Thomas opened up the rear door of the cab and started catching things as they fell out.

"Oh, Lord. I got a whole case, Mister. Is it in the bottom of the cart? Don't...let me get that." *Fuck a doodle god damn do.*

"Jesus, boy. What the hell have you got—" Thomas got his hands on an envelope, pictures falling out everywhere. "See? I got this. They didn't even hit the...oh. Hello."

"Oh, God. Go get the water." He tried to get them all back in their envelope. He knew exactly what they were— stupid pictures of him trying to be all sexy and shit. He looked ridiculous. Well, maybe some were okay, but...

"Oh, no. I'll take those." Thomas snatched the envelope from him and hopped into the passenger seat, grinning and pulling out the pictures with one hand, while keeping him at arm's length with the other. "Do I know this hottie?"

"Nope. It was for charity. I just..." He'd been flattered to be asked, even if it had been goofy as fuck. "I'm going to rescue the water. Those are going in the trash."

"Under no circumstances. These are priceless." Thomas was laughing, but his tone sounded somewhere between amused and impressed. "This was the calendar shoot? Has your mother seen these? Oh my God, look at this one!"

"She has not, and she'd better not." His cheeks were burning—partly from embarrassment and partly from pleasure. Thomas was sort of allowed to admire them, right?

He loaded the water that they'd damn near forgot into the truck, thanking God that Thomas hadn't found the few magazines he had in there, or the journals...Lord.

"You look so serious. And young...er. Younger." Thomas called out to him. "How long ago was this?"

"I was twenty-one." Lord have mercy. "I was riding good then."

"You ride well now." Thomas let that drop without even looking at him, eyes on the pictures. "I'm keeping these. I will never show another soul as long as I live, and I still like you."

"Yeah? I—okay. I guess you've seen all of me, huh?" So long as Thomas didn't think he was some asshole for doing it.

"And I can't wait to see what else you've got in this truck." Thomas put the pictures back into the envelope.

"We're going to the car wash to dump ninety percent of it." His cheeks were on fire, and he couldn't decide why. Was he pleased that Thomas wanted to know? He sort of thought so. It made him feel important, desired, like Thomas wanted to know him everywhere.

Thomas smiled at him. Not the teasing grin from a minute ago, but a real smile. "That blush. You look gorgeous right now."

"I want to kiss you, but it's a bad idea here. I still want to, though."

Thomas nodded and took his hand, down below the dashboard. "It's killing me that I can't. Surely we can find somewhere soon."

"We'll head toward home. There are places to park for a

minute." He pulled out, headed through town and down around the loop. There was nothing out here but quiet roads, land for sale, and pull-offs.

"I have that anxious feeling, like I'm back in high school, sneaking around with Grant, taking a risk and hoping not to get caught. Strange how that horrible-wonderful feeling is still so familiar."

"Was he your boyfriend?" Sam had a couple of firsts—first hand job, first blowjob, first time a guy tried to beat him up after—but the rest belonged to Thomas.

"He was the boy I told you about. The one that wouldn't kiss me until I pinned him? I don't think I'd call us boyfriends. Or...maybe. I don't know. We were trying so hard not to be."

"Right. I get that. I just had guys I jacked off about. I was twenty before I had my first hand job." Hank was a married roper that had been four beers in and willing in the dark.

"It's hard to believe that hot little cowboy in those pictures was a virgin." Thomas grinned at him. "Actually, at this point it's rather hard to believe you were ever a virgin."

"I'm like a savant, that's all." He looked over and winked.

Thomas shook his head. "Or it's me. It could be me. Would you pull the fuck over somewhere already?"

Sam cracked up, pulling into a little deserted ranch road, far enough no one would bother them. "This work?"

"Yes. It works." Thomas took his seat belt off, grinning. "Come over here and make out with me."

Sam slipped off his seat belt and pushed up the console so he could scoot over and offer Thomas his lips.

"There you are." Thomas leaned in slow and kissed him gently. He knew that kiss; it felt familiar. It was the way Thomas had kissed him when they were new. Sam reached up and cupped Thomas's cheek, stroking gently as he sank into the kiss.

Thomas kept it a nice, long make-out session. Kisses and whispers, not ramping up to anything, not asking for more. Just tangled fingers and tongues.

He felt drunk all over again, but on Thomas and this wonderful little fantasy that had come to life.

"Mmm." Thomas smiled against his lips. "That is so much better."

"This is delicious. Seriously." He'd never realized how much they got to touch at home, how lucky he was.

"You're like a star. I'm just...drawn in. All the time. And it wasn't until today that I realized how hard it is to defy gravity. I'm not used to this, and it gets maddening."

No one had ever said anything about him so fine. No one. "I hear you. I miss being able to reach for you when I need you."

And he did need. Often.

"So, we need to build a little time for this into our touristing days. All right? That will help." Thomas put a little more room between them. "That, and a hotel room will help."

"Yes. A little real privacy. Tomorrow night we'll be in Fort Worth." Then Austin and San Antonio. He was over the moon. "I'm tickled shitless you got to meet my people, but I want our vacation."

"I'm excited you wanted the vacation. I'm looking forward to you showing me everything. I'd gotten the impression you were more about family. I was on board either way, though."

"I love them. I do, but there's so much I want to show you." Thomas had been able to show him everything; he wanted a little of his own back. A little bit of sharing something new to his Mister.

"I'm in." Thomas gave him another kiss. "Mmm. James told me that Sonic has amazing milkshakes. And tater tots." He got a laugh and a big smile. "God, he used to go on and on about their tater tots."

"Oh, my God. The tater tots. The limeades. The foot-longs..."

"Right, the *foot-longs*. Should I be jealous?"

Oh, good Lord and butter.

He grinned, nice and slow. "Well...you are thicker, Mister..."

"All right, well, that's something, I guess." Thomas held his gaze, one eyebrow creeping up. "Tastier? Hotter?"

He licked his lips, his toes curling. "Well, the foot-long's got chili and cheese, but...I think you win, hands down."

Thomas cracked up, falling back in his seat. "I'm thrilled that I can compete with chili and cheese. If you have a sweet tooth, there's also whipped cream, or maybe strawberry-flavored lube?"

"Caramel sauce?" He was trying too hard to stop blushing, to keep up. "That goes good with salt."

"Maybe a little dark-chocolate drizzle?" Thomas leaned in again, blinking slowly. "I am so not into food." He got a slow grin, a lot like the one he'd given Thomas a moment ago, and Mister reached out and tugged lightly on his collar. "It does give me an idea, though."

"That sounds dangerous." He was having more fun than was probably legal.

"It is, actually. And it will have to wait until we get home, boy. Something to look forward to. In the meantime," Thomas said, voice gravelly, "I'm so looking forward to watching you eat that foot-long."

His nipples were tight, his cock was hard as nails, and he wanted Thomas more than breathing. The anticipation was heady too, though, the excitement making him feel fucking alive.

"Oh, look at you, boy. I haven't even touched you yet. You seem a little breathless." Mister didn't touch him then either; all he got was words.

"Just a little. You—I blame you. You make me hungry." He stretched up, trying to make room in his jeans.

"Hungry, hm? I'll take that blame. You look a little flushed too. Very flushed, actually." Thomas didn't so much as twitch in his direction. "Your cheeks are burning. So pretty. What about that? Are you burning, boy?"

"Mister..." He was hot enough that he was going to melt the seat. "I'm...damn. You're...*argh*!"

How did Thomas do that? Just make him nuts with a couple words? It was hot as hell and totally unfair.

"What was that, boy? Jeans choking you?" There was no goddamn way Mister could be as cool as that husky voice sounded. He glanced over and sure enough, Thomas had a hand cupped over impressively stretched denim.

"Yes, Sir. I want you. Bad." It was wonderful to share this. For this to be exciting and not shameful. He felt weirdly free.

"Mm. I want you too, boy." He watched as Mister freed his rigid cock and stroked it with knowing fingers.

He whimpered softly, caught between begging for that heavy prick or watching the way Mister touched himself.

"See what you do to me?" Thomas let him watch, encouraged him even. He paid attention to the way Mister's hand glided along underneath, palmed and circled the head, then smoothed down the top, fingers unhurried, the grip light. Sensual. So patient.

"You're beautiful," he moaned, licking his lips to wet them. Thomas made his mouth dry.

"Thank you. You're just aglow, boy. How do you feel?" Thomas smiled at him and he realized that was a real question, not a tease.

"Turned-on. Happy. Aching in a good way." He grinned right back. "We just ticked a couple three fantasy boxes, you and me."

"You're not kidding. I just made out with a hot rodeo cowboy in his truck. What were yours?"

"I just made out with a hot stud in my truck. Hell, I got to have supper with my lover and my folks together." That was fucking epic.

Thomas tucked that pretty cock away. "I have hot photographs of my partner, and I got to meet my in-laws."

He shifted on his seat, mourning the loss of the sight of Thomas's need, but feeling good, revved up and excited, happy. "And see a Walmart, don't forget."

"Oh, of course. How could I forget Walmart? I was tipsy in Walmart. Very high on my bucket list." That grin was adorable, and Thomas's mood seemed totally in line with his own.

"Tomorrow we'll do Billy Bob's and Cattlemen's, watch a canned bull riding. I can even ride, if you want to see. I still have my card."

Thomas reached over and tapped his forehead with one finger. "No riding. I wish, but no. Sounds like a great day, though."

"We'll have a ball." He had no doubt. He had box seats for Rodeo Austin, tickets for the boat on the Riverwalk, and then they had the beach.

Thomas moved closer and kissed him again, gentle and slow like last time, but this time he felt what was simmering beneath the surface: an invitation, a need, a promise.

He inhaled deep, the world a brighter place than it had been even this morning. Then he put his truck in drive and headed back to his folks'.

9

It seemed like every day of their vacation built on the wonder of the one before, but Austin and San Antonio had truly been fantastic. Great food, nice hotels, a boat ride, sightseeing, nightlife, and his first rodeo, which he enjoyed more than he thought he would. A lot more. He knew that was a little bittersweet for Sam; it had to be hard to be told you couldn't do something you knew you were good at, even if it was something you'd decided on your own you weren't going to do anymore. He felt his boy would have liked to have shown off a little for him, and truthfully, he would have liked to have seen it too.

But Sam didn't seem too terribly down about it, especially once Thomas had a chance to prove to the boy how much he was wanted just as he was.

They'd sold the truck in Austin and rented a convertible, and he was surprised by how anxious he was to feel the sand in his toes. He knew he was a little revved up by all the sunshine and blue sky, but it was all he could do not to start asking how long before they could park and hit the beach.

"I can smell the water."

Sam chuckled at him, the sound fond, merry. "You've been raring to go since the Causeway. Let's get into the condo and we'll go for a walk, huh? The condo has a nice little setup, and I want to get out of these jeans. Time for a little saltwater cowboy time."

"That sounds perfectly reasonable and does not mesh well with my impatience at all." He laughed. Of course his boy was on to him; this trip, this handful of days roaming Texas together had only made them more in tune than they already were. "But changing out of the jeans and into some beachwear sounds good to me."

"Good deal. Keep an eye out for the Villa Del Sol for me. We got a condo with a balcony on the third floor so we could see the fireworks." Sam's grin was absolutely thrilled, and he felt the same rush of joy. "I was thinking you, me, pizza, wine, balcony."

Watching fireworks from their balcony.

He wanted to take Sam's hand, wanted to kiss Sam until the boy couldn't breathe. But all he could do for now was hope Sam could hear the gratitude in his voice. "Perfect, sweetheart. That sounds absolutely perfect."

The boy, after all, was the best part of this vacation. Sam took on all the planning, all the reservations, paid for it all somehow, and did it all for Thomas. To share all the best parts of his Texas.

Thomas could honestly say that no one had ever done this, or anything for him, with so much love. He had never been happier in his life.

Sam pulled into the parking lot and they hopped out, stopping by the management office to get their keys. One quick elevator ride up and they were in a tiny condo with a couch, a bed, a kitchenette, and a balcony that looked out over the water.

He dropped everything he'd been carrying and went right to the sliding glass door. "Sam. Look at this view."

"That's why I picked it." Sam's arm wrapped around his waist. "And *ta-da*. Beachfront."

"*Ta-da*. I love you." He turned in Sam's arm, hooked his fingers under his boy's chin and traced the silky line of Sam's lips with his thumb.

"I love you, Mister." Sam sucked the tip of his thumb, just hard enough to make his eyes cross, before Sam backed off. "Shorts and flip-flops?"

He stole a quick kiss because he could. "Flip-flops. I even like the sound of that. I can't wait to get my toes wet."

"Let's do this." Sam pulled the suitcase open and passed over swim trunks and a T-shirt. His boy started stripping down, baring that fine belly, that tight little ass.

Do this, then do Sam later. God, he loved this vacation.

He pulled on his trunks, the first T-shirt he'd ever owned from Walmart, and his Tevas, before he dug around for the cap he'd bought in Austin. "Beach."

"Beach," Sam agreed, pulling on a pair of loose trunks and an open white button-down, along with a battered straw hat and his flip-flops.

"You look like a man who's been here a few times." That open shirt was delicious. He grabbed the sunscreen and ducked out on the balcony to bathe in it.

"I do love coming down here, yessir." Sam took the tube and got the nape of his neck, his ears, the backs of his legs. The touch was gentle, thorough, and it made him smile.

"Thank you. I don't really want to go home to New York fried to a crisp. Would you like some help with yours? Or are you permanently immune to the Gulf sun?" Sam always had a slightly tanned look, even in the city.

"I bet I am." Sam put a little on his belly, down near his waist. "Just in case."

He laughed. "Bullshit. You just wanted me to watch that." He took Sam's hand and pulled him inside, closing the slider.

"It was a bonus." Sam had found some confidence that Thomas wasn't sure either of them had expected. It wasn't cockiness—more that Sam had discovered his own sensuality, a happiness that wasn't constantly bombarded with tension.

He couldn't be more relieved about that. So much of what he wanted for Sam depended on letting go of some of that incessant worry. "Lucky, lucky me." He herded Sam toward the door. "Beach. Sand. Water. Go."

Sam laughed, grabbing keys and a little cash, along with both their sunglasses. "You got it, Mister. I got to get my merman in the water."

"Ha!" He swam at the gym, but he'd hardly call himself a merman. He straightened up in the hall, took his sunglasses from Sam and put them on, and tugged his cap down a little. The glare out there was probably evil.

They went out the door and across the narrow parking lot, and in no time at all he had hot sand in his flip-flops and a grin he couldn't have contained if he'd wanted to. "Oh, that feels so good." He stuffed his hands into the pockets of his trunks so he didn't reach for his lover's hand, but he wanted to. "Is the water cold?"

Sam let the surf pour over his toes before shooting him a smile. "Lord, no. It's bathwater nice. You want to come in?"

"Damn right, I do." He tugged his T-shirt off and kicked off his flip-flops at the same time, leaving them in a pile with his hat and sunglasses. "Oh, I have been looking forward to this." He grinned at Sam and started wading out. "Coming?"

"I am." Sam lost the shoes and shirt, but left on the hat and his sunglasses, before following him in. "Oh, this is just right, isn't it?"

"It's weirdly warm, but that sure makes it easy to get in." As soon as the water was hip height he dove under and swam out as far as his lungs would take him, popping up a good distance from Sam. He waved. "Beautiful!"

Sam chuckled and waved back, staying where he was, bobbing gently.

He swam out farther, marveling at the color of the water and the wide expanse of beach, almost completely undivided by jetties or piers. "Come on out!" He shouted and waved again.

Sam laughed for him but shook his head. "I'm cool! I've got my eye on you!"

All right, his boy wasn't a swimmer? He would get his fill out here in a minute and head back in. He dove down again, checking out how deep it was and thinking he might look for some goggles or a mask while they wandered later.

He got one more look at the view of the shoreline and swam to his boy. Past him, actually, climbing out for a second to grab his hat and sunglasses. "I'm sorry. Do you forgive me for taking off without you?"

"You're totally cool. I'm just not that strong of a swimmer. I sort of sink. You aren't hurting my feelings at all."

"Maybe you'll let me drag you out there for the view sometime before we head home. It's beautiful." There was something to just floating around right here too. "Thank you for this. The beach, Austin, all your haunts, your parents—the whole thing. It's so thoughtful, and I'm having so much fun."

"Good. I am having a ball. And sure, if you make sure I

don't get pulled away, I would love to go out with you." Sam dared to touch him under the water, stroke his thigh.

"There's a pretty good current, but we won't go out that far. What's the worst that could happen? We get caught in a current and end up in Louisiana?" He laughed but Sam looked a little horrified. "I'm kidding."

"I know. We'd end up on Padre Island anyway. That's what's over there."

"Oh. Well, that could be fun." He grinned at his boy and tangled his fingers with Sam's for a second, giving them a squeeze.

"You want to go out a little farther? I'm cool. I just couldn't make it all the way out there to you, I didn't think."

He did, and he had an excuse to be close since Sam needed some support. "Come on. We'll go easy, you can hold on to my shoulder."

"Okay. I'm in." Sam grabbed his shoulder, holding on, and there it was again—that trust. *Don't let me drown.*

He gave Sam's hand a solid pat, hoping to be reassuring, and started with a slow breaststroke away from the beach. "Kick your feet a little, that'll get us floating better. You make sure to speak up if you're nervous."

Nervous. Between the level of trust and the way his boy crashed through most of life, he couldn't imagine Sam being nervous. But then again, a completely standard restraint collar had made the boy panicky, so anything was possible.

"I'm good. I love how the water is cool in spots, huh?"

"Yes, and as you get farther out, just the top layer of the water is warm, and it's actually chilly down by your feet. I dove down a pretty good way out there; it gets pretty cold maybe twelve or fifteen feet down."

"Fifteen feet. Jesus. That's deep."

He laughed, but he didn't argue. Five feet probably

seemed deep for someone that wasn't a big swimmer. "Right here...you have maybe eight or nine feet under you. We'll hang here for a bit, see how you feel."

"This is good." Sam was still, holding on to him like he was a lifeline.

He treaded water and turned around to face the shoreline so Sam could get a look. "See? Isn't that a great view?" He gave the boy's hand another pat. He didn't know how long Sam could tread water, so he paid close attention to his lover and the weight on his shoulder. "We won't stay out here long; I just wanted you to see how neat it was."

"It's gorgeous. I bet it's something else at night with things lit up." Sam chuckled softly as they bobbed. "We'll have to come for a walk early one morning, huh? Look around for shells."

"I'd love that. I wonder if we can grab a tide chart somewhere. James always found us one, so we'd know when it was low tide and we'd show up to hunt." He and James had hunted for shells at all hours on their holiday vacations.

It was so strange not really knowing the plan. He was so used to being the one in control. When were the fireworks? What else was on their agenda while they were here? He was just following Sam's lead.

"I have no idea, but I have a phone and Google. I can find out." Sam chuckled softly. "We have three whole days of surf and sunshine and nowhere we have to be."

"That is amazing." He felt them starting to drift farther out and began making his way slowly back toward shore. "So, what's next? Sunbathing or exploring?"

"I'm easy, honey. Do you know how to ride a bike?" Well, that came out of the blue.

"Does stationary count?" He laughed. "I haven't ridden a

bike since high school. Can you forget how to ride a bike? If you can, I have."

"I don't know, but they have these neat fat-tire bikes for the beach. I wouldn't mind trying that. It looks fun."

He glanced over his shoulder at Sam and grinned. What the hell, right? "Let's do it." He put his feet down, and the water only came up to his ribs. "You can stand here."

"Ah, I sort of liked holding on." Sam stood up and stepped away, stumbling a little as he got his feet under him. "Whoa. Jelly knees!"

He definitely liked it, but he didn't want to get tired or let Sam get tired. "Treading water is real work. Weird, right?" He grinned. "It's not fifteen hundred crunches or whatever you're up to now, but it's work."

"You mock, but I've had to work back up to my three hundred. If I do too many too fast, it hurts my head."

He sighed, feeling terrible for joking. "Oh, sweetheart. I'm sorry, I know how hard you're working."

Sam snorted, then shot a handful of water at him, hitting him right in the chest, with a wicked look. "New rule. No sighing."

"Oh, sure." He splashed right back. "Shall we make a no worrying rule while we're at it? That would be about as likely to hold up."

Sam started laughing for him, the taut, hard body shining in the sun. "No worrying sounds like heaven. I like it."

He opened his mouth to answer, and Sam got him with another splash.

"Gah." He spit out the salty water. "You play dirty." Then he grinned and dove under, going after Sam's ankles.

Sam tried to run, but his boy had no chance, and he

went down with a splash. They both bobbed up, laughing and sputtering. "Damn, I lost my hat! Grab it!"

He scooped it up and plopped it on Sam's head, making sure it was as full of water as the ratty old thing could be.

That set them both off again, their laughter ringing out.

"Aw, Sam. You're all wet." He sucked in a breath, a dry one this time, and wrung out his ball cap.

"That's me. Come on. I'll buy you a Coke." Sam started wading out, the weight of the water drawing those shorts down to where they were just clinging for life on the top of that tight little ass.

"Mm. The view from here is fantastic." The temptation to yank them the rest of the way down was almost irresistible. Almost. Vacation hadn't deprived him of all his common sense. A Coke and a walk sounded good. Or maybe a Coke and a nap. Actually, they had time for all three.

"Hmm?" Sam turned toward him. "The water goes on and on, huh? Come on. I'm so thirsty. I bet one of these little places has limeades, even."

"Limeades! Yes, please." He blamed his newfound love of limeade on Stephanie and her Sonic order. He scooped up his T-shirt and tucked it into the back of his trunks, then stepped into his Tevas. "Wow, I'm thirsty too. We'll have to watch that with this sun."

"Yeah. We'll need to reapply your sunscreen too. We don't want you all hurting." Sam shrugged on his shirt, leaving it open.

"Yes." He pitched his voice deep. "I much prefer pink skin on you, and from my flogger, not the sun." He adjusted his hat, grinning.

"It's too bad you don't have one here, isn't it?" Sam shot him a warm smile, the mixture of tease and hunger absolutely delicious.

"I have other things." He'd almost brought Sam's flogger, but he just couldn't imagine they'd be anywhere they could use it without alarming neighbors. But he brought quieter, sensual things.

Just in case.

Even if they never got used, he couldn't imagine traveling without *something*.

Sam shot him a glance, and the hunger was stronger than the tease this time. "Yeah?"

"Of course. I had to be prepared if you needed me." He raised an eyebrow. "Didn't you say something about limeades, boy?"

"That's where we're going, Mister. Limeades and curly fries." Sam tromped across the sand with a grin to a goofy, ancient shack.

He loved that grin. And Sam's "Mister" just then was everything. Everything but curly fries.

10

S am moaned as the shower pounded down on him. His skin was tingling from salt and sand, and the hot water made him half-hard and happy as a pig in shit.

"You want to come in, Mister? The water pressure's grand."

They had played all day, going in and out of the ocean, in and out of the sun. They'd bought boogie boards and more sunscreen and stupid shot glasses and shirts. They'd eaten ice cream and burgers, had walked for miles, talking about nothing of any importance.

"Will you chisel all this salt and sunscreen off me? I feel like if I move too fast, I might crack." Sir poked his head in. "Is there room in here for the both of us?"

"There is. Come on in. I'm not scared of snuggling." He opened the shower curtain, the steam billowing out.

"I should hope not." Mister smiled and stepped right in, and he watched the steam settle instantly on Thomas's skin and make it shine. "Ah. Very nice. Warm."

"Mmhmm." He soaped up his hands and started

washing his Mister. This was one of his favorite luxuries—
Thomas and him and hot water and no hurry.

Thomas was an appreciative subject, sighing and
stretching under his hands. Despite the sunscreen, Mister
had picked up a little pink near the hairline, and the tops of
those broad shoulders looked a little tender. He got a soft
moan as he ran his fingers over the skin there.

"I have some aloe in my ditty bag. I'll doctor you up
after." He smoothed the soap away, then kissed one
shoulder. "You can get the small of my back."

"Got a little burn too? I can't even complain about it, the
sun felt so good just soaking into my skin, settling into my
bones. It's been another A-plus day, sweetheart. We are
going to be so disappointed when our days are just normal
again. Let me see that burn."

Thomas laughed, but Sam knew his Mister craved their
normal and was happy when they had a routine.

"We'll just have to spend Sundays planning our next
trip." He turned, hissing softly as the hot water hit his burn.

"Ooh. Yes, the sun got to you for sure." Mister started in
on his shoulders with soapy fingers, taking time, washing
and also massaging him down each arm and across his
shoulder blades.

"Mmm...that feels so good, Mister." He was happy, right
where he wanted to be, and with his lover.

"My hedonistic boy." Thomas chuckled behind him.
Slippery fingers explored his chest, his ribs, his abs. "You're
right, by the way. The pressure in here is just perfect."

"Isn't it? Just buzzes all the sand and salt off." Thomas
cupped his balls, squeezed gently, and slid up to pinch one
of his nipples. He moaned; what else could he do?

Mister bent and kissed his neck, then up behind his ear,
a hot sigh blowing audibly down the line of his jaw. Then

his Sir drew a thumb slowly from one hip to the other, across the sunburn on his lower back, pressure and friction making the sensitive skin sting. He went up on tiptoe, bracing himself on the tile as his whole body rocked into that touch.

"That's my boy." Thomas pinched his earlobe, rolling it between merciless teeth, and did that again, thumb moving in the other direction.

A deep sound tore out of him, surprising him with how needy it was, how raw. He pushed his ass toward Thomas, his focus on feeling each sensation, each one of his Mister's touches.

Mister answered by leaning into him, nesting hard need in the cleft of his ass. One hand pressed into the tile alongside his own, and the other took him carefully but firmly by the throat. "Mine."

"Yours." He lifted his chin, his eyelids going heavy. Thomas's hand was solid, real, warm against him when he swallowed.

Thomas's hand slid higher, tilting his head enough that Mister could kiss him. Once their lips met, that hand released him and dove downward to squeeze and stroke his cock.

He whimpered into their kiss and began to rock toward his Mister's need. Jesus, Thomas burned against him, the temptation and promise of that thick cock perfect. They drove together—hands and ass and tongues all moving together.

Mister shifted and took him by the hips, gliding that hot head across his hole, his Sir's groan amplified by the tile.

"Damn, I want you." He panted softly, his eyes rolling back in his head.

Thomas leaned over him, pressing a damp forehead

against his temple. "I have...in my suitcase but..." Those hips rocked against him again. "Fuck. Sam."

Sam nodded and spread wider. "Yes. Neither one of us shares." And he knew James hadn't either. "Want you, Mister."

Thomas reached past him, going for the little bottle of hotel conditioner. "Stings a little, works well enough." Mister worked fast, skipping the warmup and hauling his hips back before lining up. "Breathe. I've got you."

Thomas's mantra for him.

"Yes, Sir." He inhaled and arched, making a clear offer, his balls swinging between his spread legs.

"Fuck, boy. Look at you." Mister breached him slow with a throaty groan, pulling on his hips, letting him decide how fast, how deep.

He rolled his hips like he was riding in slow motion. This was another first, and he was going to feel every bit of it. Mister's fingers dug into his skin, and the hot water rained down on his shoulders. His hand slipped and squeaked against the tile, which stubbornly stayed cold under his hands despite his touch.

His ass was suddenly pressing right into Mister's hips and Thomas grunted, shifting to hold on to his shoulders, the grip strong and solid as they ground together.

They found a rhythm, steady as a train on a track, and he burned, his untouched cock so hard a cat couldn't scratch it.

"You feel so good." Mister's breath was hot and the words rough in his ear. "Want you like I never...anything. Ever."

Thomas moaned for him, fingers slipping on his wet skin and urgently trying to get a grip on his arms or his hips instead, anywhere.

"Love." *Fuck.* He arched and rocked, adding his strength to Thomas's, both of them pushing so hard they were either going to fly apart or die trying.

"Love." Thomas grunted again, this time hot and frustrated. Mister's arm wrapped tightly around his middle and his lover's other hand strangled his prick, stroking fast.

"Mister!" He barked out the word, bearing down, squeezing Thomas as tight as he could as he shot, his entire world going white-hot and bright.

Sir's hips jerked, and his lover froze, breathing hard but almost silent, and he felt the pulsing and a searing heat as Thomas's balls emptied inside him. "Boy."

Sam panted, resting his forehead against the tile, the world swinging in slow, lazy arcs. Thomas was inside him, all the way, so deep.

Thomas ran a hand over his back, still panting as well, fighting for air. They stayed like that until they were breathing together, until Thomas's cock jerked inside him again, making them both moan.

"Jesus." Mister pushed on his hips and slipped free, the hotel shower still hot, the water driving between them.

He moaned softly, just resting for a second, breath easing up. *Damn.* He was just...*damn.* "You with me, Mister?"

"Yes. Every single nerve in my body." Thomas leaned close again and kissed his shoulder, then reached past him and shut the water off. "Should grab towels."

"I'm on it." *Come on. Move, Sam. Move. Towels. Towels are important.* He managed to reach out and keep his feet at the same time.

Mister caught the towels from him in one arm and tucked the other arm around his waist. "Slippery. Out."

Huh. That was a good idea.

Thomas wrapped him up in a huge, soft towel and they

left the bathroom, his lover heading straight for the bed. Sam followed, the sun fading over the ocean as they dried each other off. He wanted the snuggling, the napping, the closeness that was coming. He needed it.

"Such a great view." Thomas tugged the covers down and hustled him into bed. "That was...you are incredible. Your trust is humbling."

They settled together, his back to Thomas's chest so they could watch the water. "You're mine and you got all of me."

Every inch of him, he thought, and some he didn't know he had.

"We're lucky, Sam. I've been reminding myself of that all week. I'm not sure I entirely understand the journey that got us here, but everything we have, and this moment, that view...? I think we worked hard for a lot of it and we deserve it, but we're lucky."

"Lord, yes." And he gave thanks for it, every damn day. He held Thomas's hand on his belly, tracing the fingers, one by one.

Thomas was dropping light kisses on his shoulder, nosing his neck, and he could feel the relaxation and the content in his lover's body. "When are the fireworks?"

"Nineish. We have time. I was thinking of ordering in and opening that bottle of wine we bought."

"Yes. Staying in is perfect. I would like to take the next few days nice and easy." Thomas laughed, vibrating against his spine. "The real world is looming."

"It is, but we'll make it." He kissed Thomas's hand. "Nice and easy, though, that sounds perfect."

"We will. This has been so good for us. You'll get back to your book, I'll get back to work, everything will be on track, and that will also feel good. We'll find our equilibrium again. Get into our groove."

"I like our groove, Mister." Sam liked their life, and he wasn't reluctant to get into it again.

11

The last day in Corpus Christi, Thomas had decided to let himself get a little sun on the beach. He wanted to come home looking tan and rested and make everyone at work as jealous as he had been when they'd come back from whatever tropical, beachy, warm and sunny location they'd been to in February while he was trudging around in three inches of snow in thick boots and dodging the icy wind.

He probably could have thought that through a little better.

He probably ought to have listened to Sam when the boy warned him he'd had enough sun. It would have saved him both the agony on the plane ride home and also the agony of listening to Sam sigh and shake that closely trimmed head while wordlessly coating him in lidocaine-laced aloe morning and night for the last four days.

But it got better, and because of his boy's diligence, he didn't even peel.

On the bright side, they'd come home to real spring. Even though the evenings were still coolish, the wind didn't have a bite to it anymore, the sun was actually warm when it hit his face, and he hadn't worn gloves or a winter hat, or even a jacket all week. He'd enjoyed his walk home from work today. He stepped off the elevator and pulled out his keys, letting himself into their apartment.

He heard the familiar sound of music, the keyboard clacking, and Sam's soft singing. There was a little bill of groceries on the table. Spaghetti noodles, a jar of sauce, a huge loaf of bread—obviously his boy intended to make supper.

He'd have to see if he remembered how to turn on the oven so they could warm up the bread.

He wandered down the hall toward the office, the music getting louder as he approached the door and poked his head in, grinning. "Quittin' time?"

Sam jumped, looking over his shoulder; then he got a warm grin. "Hey! I didn't hear you. I was deep in my own head."

"I like to see you working hard. But maybe I should start calling you before I leave the office." He cocked his head thoughtfully, as images of the many ways Sam could be waiting for him when he got home flashed through his mind. He might have to try a few of those.

Sam smiled at him; then he had an armful of boy, a warm, happy welcome-home kiss.

He returned the kiss, thinking that a welcome home like that almost made it worth the nine-to-five grind. "Tell me. How was your day? I see you got some pasta and bread. You're trying to put me in a carb-coma."

"I got a salad too." Sam started working his tie off. "And meatballs."

"Mmm. Meatballs. And I wasn't complaining." He held still for his boy and popped the top button of his dress shirt once Sam's fingers were clear.

"I know." Sam kissed his chin, his jaw, beneath his ear.

He huffed a laugh. Adorable. Sam must have missed him a little. "You didn't tell me how your day went. Did you make some progress?"

"I did, yes. I had a bunch of research projects that came in over the last few days. I've been having fun looking things up." Sam sounded pleased, one cheek resting on his chest for a minute. "You have a good day, Mister?"

"I did. Productive. I've been busy catching up from vacation, but so far nothing so urgent that I feel stressed about it." He slid his hands down Sam's arms and around the contour of the boy's waist, giving Sam the warmth of his fingers, and the touch he knew his boy needed. "I'm glad it's fun. That's how you do your best work, staying engaged, soaking up the details."

Sam hummed deep in his chest. "Feels good."

Someone was happy and appreciative, glad to have him home. It felt amazing, honestly.

"Coming home to you..." He didn't even have words to finish his sentence. He just shook his head and smiled at Sam. "So good. I need to change. Do you need to wrap up in here?"

"I'm good. All saved." Sam grinned at him, winked. "I'll come admire as you lose the work clothes."

"Be my guest."

One of the more remarkable aspects of this love affair was the way Sam had changed how he envisioned himself. His boy had a way of making him feel...desirable. He never had an issue feeling intelligent, or correct, or strong, or powerful. But physically he'd never had that confidence. Sam liked to look, to touch. Sam made him feel sexy.

He untucked his shirt as he went into the bedroom and started unbuttoning. He wasn't going to put on a show, but he wouldn't rush either. Sam leaned against the doorframe, watching him eagerly. His boy was in a pair of ancient jeans, an equally old T-shirt, and the visual was...inspiring—a little softcore porn, a little mussed, a lot interested in him.

He dropped his shirt into his dry-cleaner bin, smiled at his boy, and slipped out of his trousers, hanging them carefully in the closet. He'd only worn them once, but he already knew the next time he pulled them out, they'd be pressed. The little things Sam did for him, without request and without comment, had become more and more apparent now that he was paying close attention.

He made his way to the dresser, letting Sam get a good view of his backside.

The soft moan at the sight made him smile, pleased the hell out of him, warmed him up and made his cock start to fill.

He bent to pull a pair of gym shorts out of a drawer and without so much as a glance in Sam's direction, he tossed some kindling on the fire. "You wear those jeans like you're asking me to tear them off you."

"There's not much left to them anymore, is there?" Husky and happy, Sam's voice floated on the air, and Thomas swore he felt a touch to his ass.

"Barely enough to reasonably call them pants." He straightened up and pulled on his shorts, knowing they'd do nothing to hide his interest. He loved this dynamic; it was one of the best souvenirs from their vacation. How his lover had come to appreciate the wait, to enjoy the buzz.

He took out an ancient T-shirt, soft and comfortable from wear, and pulled it on over his head, letting his newly earned ghost of a six-pack disappear underneath.

"Mmm. So pretty." Sam hummed for him. "Love those shorts on you."

He stepped into Sam's space, tipped his boy's chin up, and kissed him. "Me too. They're nice and loose."

Sam smiled at him, hand heavy and hot on his belly. "They show you off real nice."

"Thank you. Wine?" He hooked his fingers into Sam's and headed for the kitchen.

"Sounds like a plan." Sam kissed his cheek and pulled out two glasses. "Merlot or Cab? I think that making supper should be pretty easy without messing it up."

"Cab, please." He handed Sam the opener. "I'm fairly confident that I can boil water." He dug around for a big pot and headed for the sink. "Maybe we should take a cooking class together. Is that weird?"

"I think we'd have a ball. We work together well, and neither one of us is squeamish or picky."

Well, that was a happy answer and no hesitation to it either.

He set the water on the stove and turned it on high. It had to be high to boil. Right? "Great. I'll look into it. Maybe they have a Cooking for Total Idiots class." He laughed.

"I like it. Hey, Mister—where do you go to grill here? I can cook a burger on a grill." Sam poured the wine, handed him a glass, then got the meatballs and box of salad from the fridge.

"Ah. That's tricky." He took a sip of the wine. "Oh, that's good. So, there's a little picnic area and small electric grills stored on the roof. If you want to do charcoal, you have to buy all the equipment and lug it over to Riverside Park. That's the only place I know of, though there may be others."

"Huh. I may look into one of those Weber Q grills. They take the little propane bottles." Sam put the meatballs and the sauce in a pan and turned them on low. Then his boy grabbed his ass and squeezed.

"Mm. No propane, pyro-boy. It's illegal in the city."

"You're kidding. I'll have to talk to Bowie. He'll have ideas."

"Oh, God. No. No C-4. You've just healed up." He put a hand up next to his face, miming a telephone. "Yes, he's fine, Momma. I'm just waiting for Homeland Security to release him and take him off the terror watch list. What? We were grilling burgers. It might be a tad longer than two shakes of a dead lamb's tail..."

"She would totally understand."

The bad part? His boy was right. He looked at his own personal crazy Texan and began to laugh, Sam laughing right along with him.

He reached for the stove display and started pushing buttons. "Oven...um. Bake? What should I set this at for the bread? Hm." He decided on three hundred and hit start, and the oven light turned on. "Oh. Hey, I did it."

"Very nice. We just need to not burn it. That includes setting it on fire, just FYI."

He gave the boy a thoughtful look. "Well...if we set it on fire, we can throw it in the sink and roast some marshmallows over it." He pointed to the ceiling. "No smoke detector. James beat the shit out of it like two years ago."

"He hated them. Smoke detectors. Hated them." Sam grinned over, the look fond, happy, and Thomas smiled back, sharing the memory.

The toaster hadn't survived that morning either. "Reminds me of a certain cowboy and door buzzers."

"Yeah. That was a challenge, huh? I learned quick. The noodles can go in now."

Together, they managed to make a fairly decent meal, and the wine helped to make it just right.

"So, tomorrow is Saturday." He had plans. Plans he suspected would ruffle his boy's feathers a little. Maybe even a lot. But there was one more piece to the puzzle he needed to put in place, and he decided there was only one way to know what he needed to know.

"It is." Sam leaned against his side, wineglass held loosely. "Do we have plans?"

He let himself grin. "I do. So, you do."

"Good to know." Sam looked up at him. "You want to share, or is it a surprise?"

He thought about that. Most of it had to be a surprise. But it might be kind to prepare his boy for one thing at least. "Most of the day, time will be your own. But we'll eat early, we'll spend a couple of hours here preparing; then we're going to the club."

"It's been a while. I bet you miss it."

He did. That was exactly what his plans for tomorrow were about. "I do. I miss the club, I miss a number of things, and that's what I need you to help me get past tomorrow. It starts with something you might need to think about, which is the reason I'm warning you in advance." He tangled their fingers and took a sip of wine. "I'm going to ask you to leave your hat at home."

"Oh." Sam lifted his hand to his scars, which were mostly invisible to the eye. He knew to Sam they felt huge— hell, when he touched them, they always surprised him with how he could still feel where the stitches once were— but no one that wasn't touching would see them. "I don't know how I feel about that, Mister. I...that's hard."

"I know it will be hard. It won't be the only hard thing I require of you tomorrow, but it might be one of the toughest." He turned to face his boy. "I have spent a lot of time, months really, thinking hard about what you need from me. That is as it should be. But this week I've been focusing on what I need from you. Not all the time, boy. Just what I need tomorrow. And I've discovered it's very specific and simple in concept, but in practice, for you, it won't be simple or easy."

"You know I'll do my best to take care of you. I always try my best for you." Sam kissed the corner of Thomas's mouth, soft and quick, then gathered the dishes.

And having said that, his intention tonight was to make sure his boy felt steady in the morning. He stood up with Sam and followed him into the kitchen. "I do know that. I wouldn't ever set you up to fail, boy. I will only make demands that I believe you are capable of handling." Granted, he wasn't always right, and sometimes his boy surprised him. He was still trying to understand everything that had happened with that collar and why he hadn't seen the issue coming. But that turned out well in the end. Every misstep was an opportunity to learn.

He didn't mention the hat again. Sam had heard him; if the boy had questions, they would come out eventually. "I'll grab a dish towel."

"Cool. Thank you." Sam bumped shoulders with him. "Hey, I love you, Mister."

He knew that too. Deep down in his bones. He turned his head and kissed the side of Sam's head. "I love you, boy." Above all else.

12

S am was doing crossword puzzles on his tablet, sitting on a cushion in front of the coffee table. He had coffee, he was leaning on Thomas's legs, and there was weird-assed TV on.

Totally normal day.

Barring the whole tension of probably fucking things up again at the damned club, which he was actively trying to ignore. That part was a bit of a bitch.

A folded newspaper flew by him and landed on the coffee table, and Thomas smoothed a hand over his head, down his neck to his shoulder. "I don't know why I feel the need to read the paper; it's so disheartening. Let's work, hm? It's time."

"Masochism. Pure masochism." He leaned into Thomas's hand, smiling up with a wink and a nod. He didn't want to wait and worry anymore. Whatever Thomas had planned, the doing of it would be better than wondering.

"I should just hand you a flogger. It would be more fun." Mister shot him a look, grinning, and crossed to the middle of the room. "Don't get any ideas. Right here, boy. On your knees."

Sam got up easily and settled in front of his Mister, the temptation to nuzzle in huge. He waited though, to see what he was supposed to do.

"Good boy." Mister squeezed his shoulder and left him there, disappearing down the hall.

He rolled his shoulders and waited. He was feeling good —whole, healthy, not sore. He'd had to admit that his body was appreciating the easier workout schedule, his world still at rights after their vacation.

Mister returned pretty fast. Sam wasn't sure what he'd been expecting, but Sir walked right past him and ducked into the kitchen, then came with two waters, heading right back down the hall. "Come, boy."

Someone must be nervous. He thought about reassuring Thomas that he wouldn't do anything to embarrass him, but at this point, his Mister had to know that. So, he stood and followed Thomas down the hall.

In the bedroom, Mister had laid out clothing. But instead of one pair of leather pants, there were two. His cuffs were also there, chain detached, and a couple of other leather things he couldn't quite figure out by the way they were lying on the bed.

"Strip, boy."

"Yes, Sir." That was an easy task because he was only dressed in the most marginal way. The T-shirt and old jeans came off, his briefs, and he folded them up.

Mister stepped close, smiling, and smoothed warm hands over his shoulders. "You're beautiful just the way you are, but I can't present you at the club like this, sadly. I'm dressing you for me today, asking you to follow a few traditional rules, and yes, I will have a couple of expectations. But they each build on skills you already have."

Those hands traveled around to his back as Mister circled him, speaking his instructions softly. "My first expectation is that you will make a mistake or two. That's fine. If you do, just correct it when you realize it, don't apologize, and move beyond it. I might remind you, but I won't embarrass you, and I'm not handing out punishments or keeping score. I know you'll do your very best, you always do."

"I do, Mister. I swear." His eyelids got heavy, because that touch was warm and solid, sure. "I wouldn't embarrass you for love or money."

"I'm not at all concerned, sweetheart." Sir pressed a kiss to the base of his neck and moved around him again, picking up a pair of pants from the bed. They were a soft, black leather and fashioned like blue jeans. "Pull these on. I considered shorts but decided you weren't really the boy-toy type." Mister laughed and handed him the pants.

"They're soft." They smelled wonderful too—God, there were so many good things about the way leather smelled, so many memories, from tack to Thomas. He guessed that Thomas wanted him to go commando, so he didn't ask. He just pulled the pants on.

Once they were up over his ass, Mister took over, fastening the top button for him and pulling up the fly. Sir took some time to smooth out the areas where they weren't hugging quite right, and the leather warmed anywhere Thomas's hands lingered for more than a few seconds.

They were tight, the leather clinging to him, and he had to admit, he'd worn a lot of leather, but nothing buttery like this.

"Mm. You'll have to let me know if you end up liking these, boy. A tailored pair would look fantastic on you. All right. Your harness."

Mister pulled the contraption off the bed and showed it to him. "Drops right over your head."

He looked at it and said a quick, quiet prayer that he didn't look stupid. Hell, he could look stupid so long as his Mister didn't think so. "Right over my head. I guess I'm lucky I'm not hairy, huh? I bet it would tug."

Mister looked thoughtful as the harness slipped on with more than enough room to avoid touching his head at all. "Hm. I've never considered that. Mine hasn't given me an issue that I recall. Take a natural deep breath, hold it, and keep still."

He held his breath while Mister tugged and shifted the harness, adjusting it. Finally, he felt it tighten flat against his skin. "Good boy. Breathe out and move a little."

Sam rolled his shoulders, shifted side to side, and breathed. It wasn't uncomfortable, just odd, pressing against his skin in weird ways.

Mister stepped back and walked a slow circle around him, admiring. "Not a bad fit for off-the-rack." His Sir tugged him close by the leather straps on his chest and kissed him.

He gasped, arching against the straps and opening up. The kiss was deep enough to make him breathless, make the world swing.

"Mm. Yes, those work nicely." Mister gave him a smile. "Knees, please, boy."

He knelt, one hand on Thomas's hip. He did love that smile, the warmth in those eyes. The sight of his Mister's heavy cock right there where he could admire it.

Thomas ran a hand over his head, starting at his

forehead and sliding slowly back. "At the club tonight, if you're not actively engaged, either under my order or because another Dom has addressed you, I want you to kneel. If we're walking and I stop to talk to someone for example, you should kneel. If you don't have a reason to be standing, you're to be on your knees. Questions?"

Do I get knee pads? He didn't ask because that would hurt Thomas's feelings, and he wasn't all het up. Thomas needed this, and the coldness that bothered him so much wasn't present. "Can I balance on you, if I need to?" He doubted that would be a thing, but he had to know.

"Of course. You understand my expectations, and I trust you to manage. If you need assistance, you should ask. If it's painful or injuring you in some way, don't do it. If you simply can't for *any* reason, don't, and we can discuss it when we have a moment."

Mister's tone was reassuring and not the least bit condescending. "I won't question you. I trust that if you can, you will."

He leaned forward and rested against that warm leg. "Love you."

He was going to hate not having his hat. Hate it.

As if Mister could read his thoughts, his Sir stroked a hand over his head and asked, "Do you want to talk about your hat? I'm listening."

"I don't like not having it." And he couldn't even pretend that he didn't know why or that the reason wasn't selfish. He needed to hide behind it. He felt like everyone in that club understood everything better than he did, like he was bound to get into trouble, like he was going to be exposed, and that rattled him.

Mister snorted. "I know that. But if you'd like me to consider changing my mind, sweetheart, I need a reason."

"You and I both know that the reasons are sort of bullshit, huh? I mean, I still feel what I feel, but when the reasons are that I need to hide in it..."

"You *think* you need to hide in it, but you don't. I want to help you gain that confidence, not force something on you that will make you so anxious you can't function. What do you think?"

"I think we'll do this and, if it doesn't work for me, I'll tell you." He was pretty good at that, these days. Just saying the truth. Even better, Thomas was good at hearing it and knowing that he wasn't being a fuck. He wondered sometimes if James had been one to play games, to push buttons just to push them and see what Thomas did.

Mister's fingers slipped under his chin and tilted his head up. "Good boy. I'm so proud of you."

"Talk to me later when you're about ready to put a bag over my head." He winked up, trying to ease the little bit of intensity that buzzed between them.

"That's no fun. I'll just flog you publicly." Mister laughed and stepped away, opening the closet door and staring into it a second before retrieving a leather ball cap and bringing it to him. "You can keep that in your back pocket."

"That's more than fair. Thank you." And he'd do his best not to use it. Then he looked at it. "Seriously? They make these in leather?"

He'd be damned.

"Mm. Yes." Mister turned and pulled his cuffs off the bed, handing him one. "Wrist."

"Huh. Go figure." He popped the hat in the space in his waistband left by the small of his back real quick before handing Thomas his left arm. "I love those, you know."

"I do know that." Mister chuckled. "See? I'm not entirely an evil ogre."

He snorted, leaned forward and nuzzled his lover's belly. "We'll see about that, Mister Ogre of Evil."

God, he cracked himself up.

"Naughty boy." Mister gently moved him away again. "Other wrist, please. You'll get to wear the chain at the club."

He handed his other wrist over, the heaviness like a...he wasn't sure how to explain it, even to himself. Security blanket was stupid, and comfort wasn't quite right. All he knew was they were there and solid, more than a little like his Mister's hands on him.

"Go and have a look in the dressing mirror."

"You think I look okay?"

"Hm." Mister walked up behind him and reached around to slowly trace the lines of the leather harness, fingers dragging along his skin. One hand slid down over the waistband of his pants and palmed him through the leather. "Works for me."

"That's important." He felt like he was playing dress-up or something, but that didn't stop him from rolling his hips into that warm touch, did it?

"Not to worry, boy. I'm not going to doll you up for every visit to the club." Mister grinned over his shoulder. "All right. Questions?"

Did he have any? He didn't think so. What was he supposed to ask? Sam figured that Thomas needed him to fit in at the club, at least every once in a while, so he'd fake what he had to. Thomas hadn't asked this of him before and, if he hated it, next time he would say no, and they could figure it from there. Simple as that. "I don't think so, Mister."

"Excellent. You may now dress me. I took out the pants I want to wear, black vest is in the closet, you know where my boots are." Mister moved to the center of the room and waited.

He smiled. Why yes, yes he did. In fact, he'd bet he knew where everything in the apartment was, barring the... playroom? Guest room? Whatever. He hadn't been in there but a handful of times. Thomas could keep a dead body in there and he wouldn't know.

Sam looked at the pants, then at Thomas, and the temptation to tell him to lie back on the bed so he could get the pants on was huge. Also, a testament to his nervousness, he'd bet. "Okay, so I've done this a lot with broke-dick cowboys and loose jeans, but never leather. I'm gonna squat down; you hold my shoulders and pick up your foot?"

Mister didn't say a thing, just did exactly as he'd suggested and rested a hand on his shoulder. He discovered that his Sir had excellent balance, as Thomas didn't put hardly any weight on that hand.

He hummed softly, sort of silly with how much in love he was. He took his time, got the pants on up to Thomas's knees. "Okay, we're making progress. Don't let me squish your balls. I ever tell you about when my buddy Rick had broke both elbows and there were three of us trying to get him ready for an appearance? I swear to God, Mister, he was a soprano for a week, and he didn't thank us for it. Of course, I can use my fingers to protect your jewels..."

Rick really wouldn't have thanked him for that.

Thomas didn't seem amused. "I encourage you to do so. I would be a very unhappy Dom and an even more unhappy lover."

"Well, yes. None of us were trying to hurt Rick; we just didn't know what to do. We were teenagers." He'd actually had to help guys get dressed way more than Thomas, he'd bet. He eased the pants up and fastened them from behind. The vest was easy, and he was telling himself "no shit, there I was" stories as he went to get Thomas's boots.

"Well, of course not. This exercise wasn't intended to make you nervous, boy." Mister grinned at him as he came back with the boots. "I'd intended it to be a way for us to connect a little before we left for the club. Is it this, or the evening in general that has you edgy?"

The smile was what allowed him to be honest and say, "I'm not nervous about dressing you. I love touching you. I like the smell of leather. It's all good. I'm just a little... worried. I'm trying not to babble at you."

"Will you tell me why you're worried? You're out of your element, I realize, but that doesn't seem to be cause for worry." Mister let him help with the boots, let him keep his hands busy.

"That's the million-dollar question, isn't it?" He kissed one of Mister's knees. "I guess because I want it to be a good night for us. I feel—" He sighed, then looked up, meeting his Mister's eyes. "I know you don't get it, but I can feel crazy alone in the club, like I'm trapped in my own head."

Please. Please hear me. Please hear what I'm trying to tell you. He was trying so hard, and he wanted to have a good night tonight. He wasn't begging off; he was telling Mister the truth.

Thomas looked at him and frowned, but he knew that look, and it didn't make him as anxious as it used to. He also knew that what usually followed was a long silence, and he'd learned better than to hold his breath.

"Come sit with me." Mister helped him up and led him over to the bed to sit, taking both of his hands once they were comfortable. "Tell me more. You say I don't get it, and I...need to get it."

He held on to those strong hands, trusting in their connection, in *them*. "I don't know how to be quiet at will. In my head, I mean. I'm faking it until I figure it out, and I will. I will figure out what I need to do." He only had to do it once, right? Once he felt it, he could do it again. "It's lonely, because everyone has it reckoned, and then there's me, just trying to pass."

"Sweetheart, you're not supposed to be quiet. Physically still perhaps, often even, but that's not the same thing as being quiet...in your head."

"That's good. I tell myself a lot of stories, sing, you know." It was weirdly freeing, to admit that out loud and believe that he was going to be understood.

"Ah." Mister laughed softly. "Sam, where is your head while you're getting that rope in place on the horse, in those seconds before you give them a nod to open the gate? Where is your head while you're riding? Are you telling yourself stories?"

"No. Time stops." He searched his brain for a way to explain it. "There's no thinking, just...it's not even you and the animal. It's just...the moment. My body knows what to do, and I can trust in that. It's a little like an orgasm, in a really weird way."

"Was it always that way? I can't imagine it was."

"No. No, at first it was sheer terror. Then I had to do it, over and over. I always knew, though, when my mind wasn't in the middle, it was gonna be a bad ride." Sam squeezed Mister's hands. "Question is, how do I keep my mind in the middle for more than a couple minutes at a time, right?" He leaned forward. "I mean, is that a thing, do you think? Can it happen like that?"

Thomas shrugged. "I don't know. The only thing I know for sure is that we've figured everything else out, so we can figure this out too." Mister worked his fingers under a warm thumb, thinking. "Let's start by defining what the middle is for you. You say you tell stories in your head to keep your mind busy, but really you should be focused on me. You should be responsive to my needs. A great deal of submission, put simply, is letting me worry about your needs so that you can focus on mine."

"Don't you think I am?" Sam thought they were touching something tender for both of them. "Paying attention to what you need?"

Mister took a deep breath, watching him. "All right. Let's breathe a little here. Are we only talking about the club now, or are you...asking a bigger question? Because I was focusing on the club."

"Me too. I mean, yes. The club." He knew Thomas was happy at home. He knew it. They had hiccups, but they were solid. "I know we're good. Hell, I know we're good even if I never figure out another single thing about submission."

Mister gave him a smile. "We are. And you're right, but... I think you have it figured out. I just think you're not connecting something. Because at home, your submission is so seamless, I don't even think it's conscious most of the time. That's unusual...or, no, it's remarkable. And rare. But at the club something disconnects. It's like...something happens when it's put under a microscope. What is it you said about feeling alone?"

"I just feel like I'm all by myself. Like..." *I could be anyone and it wouldn't matter to you.* How did that happen, when he knew how his Mister saw him, so well? Thomas even got it —that he was missing some connection, some sense of balance or something. He knew it, all the way to his soul, so why was it different at the club?

"You're fine here with me, but you feel alone there even

though you're still with me. So...the disconnect isn't the club. It's between us." Thomas scratched that sandy hair and stood up. "Can I...? I just need to think." Mister paced away a few steps and back again, thinking out loud. "You feel like everyone has it figured out but you. What do they have a handle on that you don't? What haven't I given you?"

Thomas sat down next to him again and looked at him "Or, is it something I have given you that their Doms haven't? Something it feels like I...take away?"

"I don't know. I don't know what that means." Sam didn't know what to do. "Mister. I swear to God, I didn't intend you to stress. Tonight is supposed to be for you."

Now he felt bad. This was supposed to be Thomas getting what he wanted and now, somehow, Sam'd been a dick and made it all about him and his bullshit. Christ, he never would have thought he was a self-absorbed bastard. Learned something new every day.

Mister took his hand again. "I'm not stressing, I'm thinking. This is for me. It's for us. This is the work that matters, boy. It's just another one of our puzzles. And I think I might have the answer. I *think*..."

"Right. Right, one of our puzzles." He inhaled deep, letting himself fill his lungs and hold his breath for a second before he blew it out, the action helping to stop everything for a heartbeat. "So, what do we need to do, Mister?"

"We, um. Well? Nothing, actually. I don't think. Tonight was supposedly about what I need, right? You're experiencing a disconnect at the club, and I keep thinking that I'm missing something there too. I felt like a little bit more tradition would fill that for me, that I was missing that formality. But I think..." Mister stared at him hard, like there was more to get across than Sir had words for. "I think I've been stuck in one of James's boxes. I think I keep...trying to drag you in there with me."

"I'm pretty bad at boxes, Mister." That wasn't even him being a bitch. It was true. He was who he was. "I want to help you be happy, though. You know that."

"Well, that's just it, Sam. I want out of the box too. We're not missing anything. I think we're just each looking for something that isn't there. Something we don't need." Thomas relaxed a little, tilted his head back and looked at the ceiling. "I just don't know what that means."

"Me either." He leaned in and rested against Thomas's bare arm, fingers trailing along Mister's skin, soothing them both. They would figure it. He had to believe that. "So, we'll go to the club and have a good night? I'm all dressed up and willing..."

"That, or we throw on T-shirts and go have a beer at Mike's." Mister glanced at him, grinning. "Your call."

"Yeah? You want to?" He would love that. To go out with Mister, have a beer, laugh together. Maybe sit on his lover's lap. "I'd love to say hi to everyone, show you off."

Mister reached for the buckles on the harness he was wearing. "Let's do it."

"You could leave it," he offered, carefully. "I have that black T-shirt you like." It was tight enough that Mister would be able to see the outline.

"Oh?" Thomas raised an eyebrow. "Is it growing on you?"

His cheeks heated, but he didn't look away. "The way you grabbed it and kissed me is."

So there.

"Boy." Thomas did look pleased, and he got pulled in again. "Like this, you mean?" This time Sir's kiss was relaxed and curious.

He moaned, his body tightening. Lord have mercy, that casual strength and confidence was hot as hell.

Thomas broke off the kiss, fingers still gripping the harness, and stood, hauling him right to his feet. "Ready?"

"Yes, Sir." He was. More than.

13

Thomas hustled his boy out of the cab and onto the sidewalk outside Mike's, more ready for a beer than he'd been in recent memory. Something cold and hoppy. Bitter.

Every time he and Sam had one of those discussions, he felt a little raw afterward, as if they'd tunneled through something and the resulting clarity was encouraging, but also fragile. Delicate. Sensitive. And as successful as their talks typically were, he knew they both went through the emotional wringer a bit too—each assuming they'd done something wrong, that whatever the issue entailed was their fault, and it was only trusting they'd be forgiven that got them through it.

That was exactly how he was feeling as he followed his boy into the bar. Forgiven. They still had more to think about, but staying in seemed like conceding defeat. Going out to the club didn't feel like the right fit for tonight either. This felt comfortable and safe, like keeping warm and out of the weather on a snowy day. As strange as it seemed, Mike's felt right from the moment he'd suggested it.

The bar was loud and raucous, the crowd greeting them with hoots and hollers, back slaps and rough hugs. He had a beer pushed into his hand even as Sam was whisked away for greetings and hugs.

He looked at the beer and raised it in thanks before taking a sip. It wasn't the nice hoppy ale he was craving; it was something too light and watered-down for his taste, but he wasn't about to complain. It felt like a compliment to have been brought into the fold that way.

Here, have a beer, man. You're one of us.

Sam literally disappeared into the crowd, partly due to the number of people that wanted to say hello, and partly because the boy was half the size of most of these people. He managed to slowly maneuver his way to the bar, with the assumption that when Sam broke free, he'd be easily found.

He set the beer down and watched Darla work, waiting for her to have a minute. She'd get to him; he was in no hurry.

Every so often he'd catch a glimpse of Sam, and his boy's eyes were on him. Every time. He'd smile so Sam knew he was fine; then someone would step between them again.

"Thanks for bringing Little Sammy by. We'd heard he was okay, but it feels better having him here in person where we can see him for ourselves. Is that yours?" Darla pointed to the beer, the look doubtful.

"Technically, but—"

She grinned at him. "IPA?"

"You're a saint."

Darla took the bottle and dumped it, heading for the taps.

Feels better having him here.

He would have brought Sam by sooner, but he thought of Mike's as too rough for someone with a still-healing head injury. Mike or Angel must have passed the word around though, because every time he met Sam's eyes, there was room around the boy. The people that knew Sam, particularly some of the bigger guys, were looking out for his cowboy.

Darla brought his beer back and set it on the bar, and he slid her a card to open a tab.

"You've got time," she said, leaning over the bar to make sure she was heard. Or he assumed as much, he was pretty sure she knew he wasn't interested in the view of her impressive cleavage. "But around midnight or one, it can get a little nuts in here on a Saturday."

"No doubt. I assume Sam knows more than I do, we'll feel it out. It's just...his head you know? He can't—"

"Angel said. We'll look after him. Any more problems at your place?"

God, he hadn't even thought about that since they'd returned from vacation, except to text Mike they were home.

"No, we're still running surveillance. I'm at a loss as to how to find the guy at this point."

"We all are. Maybe he's gone. Maybe he thinks you're gone." She smiled at him, shook her head. "Y'all should come to the back in a bit. There's a more private lounge. You'd appreciate it."

He raised an eyebrow. "Thank you, we will do that." He didn't know there was a private room. Did Sam? He supposed that was why he never saw Mike with a black eye. Then again, he wouldn't want to see what happened to the guy that gave Daddy Mike a black eye.

He sipped his beer and looked around again, not seeing Sam this time. That was all right. There was a game on TV, and his IPA was good company.

A warm hand landed on the small of his back, Sam

grabbing his waistband, holding on tight. "Lord, they won't let me be."

"You want a drink, Little Sammy?" Darla grinned at him.

"Coke, please, ma'am."

"You want to come work a shift?"

"No, ma'am. I'm working with my Mister tonight. He might fuss."

He felt himself relax now that Sam was there—he must have been worrying more than he realized. "You're not really complaining, are you? It must feel good to be missed. Have a beer if you'd like. I felt like I needed one."

Sam smiled at him but shook his head. "Thanks."

He hooked an arm around Sam, wondering if the boy wasn't a little worried himself. "Darla invited us to the private lounge."

"You must be special. I've never been back there." Sam settled against him, relaxing into his touch.

"Never? I'm pretty sure it's you that's special, but I think we'll appreciate the thought. Let me finish my beer, and we'll go see what curiosity gets us." He took another sip. He assumed Sam was looking out for him by not drinking and he didn't say anything about it, but the boy needn't worry. The only reason he had more than one margarita was because Stephanie ordered it for him, and he didn't want to be impolite.

That was his story, anyway.

"Did you see Angel? I'm hoping to run into him and show off my tan." He grinned at his boy. "And yours."

"He texted. He's on his way. He was waiting for us at the club." Sam held up his phone.

Tricky boys! Buzz texted. Be there soon. Do. Not. Let. Tommy. Leave. I want my hugs

He rolled his eyes. He was going to have to answer to

Clint now, wasn't he? "I'm tossing you between us, so he hugs you first."

"Fair enough. He hasn't broken me yet." Sam grinned up at him, winked. "I forgot how crazy it got in here."

"I didn't. I like it as long as it's reasonably safe. This is quite a room full of characters. Friendly. I don't even know the guy that handed me that beer." He laughed and took the last sip of his IPA.

"You're family now." Sam seemed relaxed, leaning into him, chatting with people, but always *with* him, close. "You need another one, Mister?"

"No, sweetheart. One is enough, I just had a craving. Do you want to hang out here a little while longer or find out from Darla what we need to do?"

There was a shout behind them and a bit of a commotion that seemed to get under control fairly quickly.

"I'm not looking for a bar fight, Mister. I want to be with you."

He nodded. "I'm not looking for a misplaced elbow to get you in the head." He gave Darla a wave. "Is there a secret handshake or a nonviolent initiation?" He grinned. "Do I have to kiss Daddy Mike's ring or something?"

"Little Sammy's already done that." She winked and passed him a business card with nothing but numbers printed on it. "Door's at the bottom of the stairs. That works the lock. I'll tell Angel where you are."

Angel must have texted Darla the same orders he texted Sam.

He flipped the card over in his fingers and grinned at Sam. "Come along, sweetheart. It's an adventure. We're good at those." He headed for the stairwell.

"We totally are." The noise faded as they headed downstairs, and Sam chuckled. "So, this is pretty cool."

It really was. A secret door, a hidden area—it was fascinating.

"You've really never been down here? I feel like 007 or Jason Bourne." He found the door and looked at his card, carefully entering the code. He grinned at Sam. "This is a great moment, isn't it? Once we go in, we can't ever be here again."

"I really haven't. I assumed it was Daddy Mike and Darla's apartment, to be honest." Sam pushed up and kissed him.

Maybe it was. God. Maybe he'd just let them wonder and make out with his boy in the stairwell. He loved when Sam initiated things. He wrapped Sam in closer, and Sam moaned for him, bringing them together, fingers pulling him down for a deeper kiss.

He slid his hands up Sam's spine and over the harness, his cock taking notice and his balls growing heavy. He put a hand on the boy's chest and levered him back a step, both of them gasping a little as they separated. "Boy."

" 'M not sorry." Sam blinked at him, the expression more than a little dazed.

That look. It was so lovely, it made his chest ache. Sam had never been that uninhibited at the club. Not without the right kind of...encouragement. He laughed softly, trying to defuse a little of the electricity between them. "No. Not sorry. Never sorry."

Sam's lips quirked in a smile. "Good. I love the way you look in those pants. Have I said?" Sam barely brushed the outline of his cock.

"You may have mentioned it once or twice. I might have to see you in that harness again." He traced a finger down one strap of Sam's harness, then turned and opened the door.

The room was truly a lounge—a few love seats, a couple of heavily padded chairs. The room was comfortable, simple, but obviously well cared for. There were a couple of men down here playing chess, another pair sharing a beer. Two of the men had subs with them, a man and a woman, both at their feet, kept close.

One man—wiry and covered in ink—lifted a hand. "You're Little Sammy's master? Lucky bastard! Come in and have a seat. I was sorry to hear that Sammy got hurt. Mike had a couple of days where we donated to his medical bills. I'm Darren, by the way. Darren St. James."

He felt himself smile as the ease of something familiar settled over him. "Thomas Ward. You know my boy, I see. Thank you so much for the concern. We were comforted by the support he has here. Say hello, Sam."

"It's so good to see you, Sir. It's been a long time." Sam smiled warmly, offering both men a nod.

"It has. There are Cokes and waters in the fridge down here. Mike prefers us to keep the alcohol upstairs."

"Would you like anything, Mister? Y'all?"

"I appreciate Mike's thinking. I'd like a water, sweetheart. Darren?" He took a seat as Darren had suggested, daring to clear a spot next to him for his boy on the floor where Sam could lean on him. He'd see how that went over.

"I'll take two waters as well, Sammy. Thank you." Darren reached down to stroke the head of a well-built, bald man wearing jeans and a T-shirt. "This is my Kynan. He's had a long session under my needles today, so he's floating. Please don't take offense if he's not the most alert boy alive."

He didn't speak to Kynan directly, not wanting to disrupt him. "He's beautiful and blissed-out. The boy looks quite happy."

He thought briefly about the ropes he'd tried to use on

Sam so long ago. His boy wasn't built to sit still for a long session of anything, so it was probably a good thing he wasn't able to get them on. Poor Sam might have needed them off long before he'd finished. Still, Sam was very capable of getting to that point in other ways.

"Thank you. I think so." Darren beamed down at his boy and winked at him.

Sam brought the waters, giving him his first, before offering Darren the other two. Then his boy settled next to him, resting against his leg. No hesitation, no shame, no worry whatsoever. His hand settled on Sam's head, and his boy wrapped one hand around his calf.

"So, how do you know Mike?" Did everyone here just get a random invitation one day to Mike's secret lounge? He wondered what the criteria was. Sam was his chip, clearly.

"We've been friends for a while. I do his ink, Darla's. If you ever want any for you or your boy, holler."

He took a longer look at Kynan's skin, admiring. "I like your work. I have a couple of small tattoos, but Sam has some impressive ink. I'm fairly sure he's always thinking about more." He had no doubt, in fact. He was always considering more himself, something large and intricate.

"You just let me know. I have even worked in a scene environment. It can be intense."

The idea of incorporating that into a scene made his skin tingle. "I can imagine. What do you think of that, boy?"

"It sounds…" Sam cleared his throat. "It sounds hot as hell, Mister."

"Indeed." Exactly what he'd been thinking. He had a look down at his boy and laughed softly at the light tension. He'd bet Sam's toes were curling. "Well, Darren, perhaps you'll be hearing from me."

The door opened slowly drawing his attention, and

Angel stepped into the room and grinned at him. "Here you are."

He gave Sam a pat on the shoulder and stood. "That was the quietest entrance I think I've ever seen you make, Gabriel."

"I know. Look at you, in the basement lounge." Angel laughed and hugged him, then held one hand out to Darren. "Hey, buddy. Ky. Sammy. Someone offer me a seat."

"I know, I'm moving up in the world. Have a seat, won't you?" He laughed. "Boy, offer the man a hug and something to drink."

"My pleasure, Mister." Sam stood up and launched himself into Angel's arms. "I've missed you, old man. We brought you presents from Texas."

Angel laughed happily and held Sam tight for a second. "You're a good kid."

"I am. Coke or water?"

"Coke, Sammy. Please."

"Yessir."

"Texas—" He looked over at Darren. "We just got back from a trip to meet Sam's parents and some sightseeing. So... Texas was a great deal of fun, Angel. I lucked out to begin with because Sam's parents seemed to like me."

They loved him, he thought, as he did them. But he wouldn't overstate things. "Sam is a fantastic trip planner and tour guide."

"That doesn't surprise me. He's a detail-oriented man." Angel sat, sprawling and large. "So, you met the parents. Sam sent me texts of the beach and the rodeo. You look ten years younger."

"Jesus, Angel. You make it sound like I'm ninety." He laughed. Did he look older than his years, or just act it? He shook his head. "It was the most fun I've had on vacation.

And Sam and I just...we discovered some new things and dealt with others, I never dreamed we were capable of an even stronger connection."

He smiled as Sam brought Angel a Coke. "We're talking about vacation, boy."

"We had a ball, Mister. I loved every second." Sam settled right back down at his feet with a happy laugh. "My Mister is adorable, especially after a few margaritas. I took him to his first Walmart."

He snorted. "Tipsy at my first Walmart. Lots of firsts for me. First limeade, first real Tex-Mex, first time in Austin. First time meeting a significant other's parents. Ever." He'd never felt so out of his element.

"It was perfect." Sam rubbed his cheek against Thomas's knee.

Angel beamed at them. "It looks like it, yes."

"How have you been? Keeping busy?"

"Sure. Work's always busy, people never seem to stop being stupid." Angel grinned at him, a big, wide, toothy thing. "And getting legitimately sick, of course."

"Of course." He smiled and caught himself stroking his fingers over Sam's head. "You were at the club tonight?"

"For a few minutes, yes. I was hoping to run into you." Angel grinned at him. "Imagine my surprise when I found out where you were playing."

"Are we playing, boy?" He looked down at Sam and back at Angel. "We're just relaxing, I think." It didn't feel much different than their living room.

"We're having a good evening, Mister. A good Saturday night." Sam looked up at him with a warm, happy smile.

"Sam and I are...we've discovered a road less traveled. We're only just beginning to understand what that means for our time at the club. It bears a discussion with Clint, perhaps. Did you tell him we were here?"

"I didn't. Should I have?" Angel raised one eyebrow. "It never occurred to me, I guess. This isn't his vibe."

"No, no. You're right, it's not his vibe. I don't know how he'll feel about it, that's all. Given our history." Not so much the location but his slow and steady march away from the tradition and formality that Clint preferred. "Are you involved with anything more formal, Darren?"

"Only with my work. I've seen some amazing rituals though, some lovely things. I'm more like Angel, not the most, uh, traditional man, and my boy needs less formality. He finds it distancing, distracting."

He nodded. "Yes. I'm learning that Sam has been experiencing something similar. Distance, a lack of connection. It's actually good to know he's not alone in that." Good for him, better for his boy. Perhaps Sam could meet some kindred spirits here if they got invited back.

"Not at all. I assume that's your experience—something more formalized?" Darren opened the water and handed it to Kynan. "Drink this, boy. All of it." Then he turned to Thomas. "I've enjoyed working with some of those guys. Truly disciplined boys."

"That's my background, yes. Formal training, rules and traditions, discipline and punishment." He glanced at Angel and over to Darren again. "My boy's background is...none of those things." He smiled and reached lower, giving Sam's shoulder a squeeze.

Sam chuckled softly, which surprised him, pleased him. Sam's fingers were wrapped around his calf, petting him in slow, gentle, random touches.

"We have an enormous amount of fun with punishment, don't we, boy?" Darren's laugh was surprisingly wicked and drew an answering laugh from him.

He could hardly imagine a scenario in which he'd punish Sam. The boy was very capable of that without his help. Perhaps if they ever managed to stop finding hurdles to jump, they might get there.

Then again, perhaps not. Sam's integrity didn't allow the boy to offer less than his best. And in truth, Thomas liked the boy a little naughty.

He traced the outline of Sam's ear, the touch featherlight, and he felt Sam's soft, near-hidden moan.

He looked at Angel with a little wicked smile of his own. "You're not the most traditional guy, huh? Whatever could Darren mean by that?" He was joking, and not. They'd been friends for years, but he really didn't know anything about Angel's proclivities, only that the man hadn't had a lover or a sub in some time.

"It means that what I get off on is the fight, Tommy." Angel beamed at him, the expression in those eyes full of mischief.

He grinned back, understanding better now why Sam in particular was such a draw for Gabe. "All this time and I didn't know that about you? I've been looking to set you up with a sweet little thing. Is it the sweet little thing that fights restraint, or someone you can throw a punch at that you're looking for?" This was an important distinction. Sometimes it was both, sometimes it was really the black eye that got a guy going.

"I'm not looking for sweet, Tommy. A beautiful man I can put over my knee and tear his ass up? Sure. Someone I can hold down and drive out of his mind? I'm all over that. Are you sure you don't want to let me have your boy?"

He laughed, positive that Angel's style would never do

more than intrigue Sam for a day or two. "What do you think, boy? You have my permission to speak very freely."

"I think that I'm not available to be 'had,' Mister. I'm yours."

He knew that, but knowing didn't stop the rush he felt at his boy's public declaration, or the deep, delicious ache in his balls. "Sorry, Gabe. You heard the boy, he's *mine*." He reached down and coaxed Sam off the floor and into his lap as a reward.

No question this was a much better atmosphere for Sam, which could only make his own experience fuller in turn. The boy had already shown him more earnest public submission than ever before. Sam wasn't passively telling himself stories; the boy was relaxed and engaged.

He needed to reevaluate their roles at the club. He would have to talk to Clint.

Sam cuddled into him, and Darren beamed at them both. "Oh, how gorgeous is that?" Darren held up his phone. "May I? You have to see."

"Be my guest. If Sam doesn't care for it, we can delete it." He decided not to smile for the camera; that rather defeated the purpose.

Darren took a couple of shots, then showed him. It was gorgeous—from the way Sam's body curled against him, to the look of peace on his boy, to the way his hand looked on Sam's hip.

"Look at that, boy." He took the phone from Darren so Sam could see without moving. "See how lovely you are?" If he didn't know those two people, he still would have thought it was lovely.

Sam smiled, turning his face to drop a kiss on Thomas's chest. "We both look happy. Thank you, Sir. It's a great picture of us."

He gave Darren his cell number and asked the Dom to text him the pictures. He'd make sure Sam got them too. "All right, Gabe." He winked at Angel. "Now I know. I'll keep my eyes out for a naughty boy instead." He wasn't sure he knew a sub that naughty, but he ran across new people in his line of work all the time.

Then again, no one that he knew of was asking Angel the hard questions, and he wouldn't be doing a new sub justice to vouch for someone he was unsure of. "Assuming you want another sub. You do a fairly decent impression of someone that's happy without one."

"I'll find someone that meshes with me. I know it."

Sam reached out, and Angel grabbed hold of Sam's hand. "Have faith, man. I do."

Angel smiled, squeezed Sam's hand. "Thank you, Sammy. You're a good friend."

"Of course you will. When you're ready. There's someone out there for everyone." *Sometimes you have to lose someone to find them.* He gave Sam's thigh a pat, letting the boy know it was okay to go sit with Angel if he'd like.

Sam, though, stayed right where he was. It was lovely to have his boy here, listening and easy, pressed against him.

Mike came through the door, the huge man filling the space. "Well, Tommy! I'm so glad to see you and your boy. Everyone okay down here?"

He should get up and say a proper hello. He should probably instruct Sam to do the same, but honestly, he was enjoying the moment too much.

"Mike! Good evening. We're doing very well indeed. I can't tell you how much I appreciate this invitation. Thank you." He offered a hand to shake. "Forgive us for not getting up, will you? Sam only just got comfortable." His other hand caressed his boy, stroking over Sam's back and shoulders.

"Of course. Your boy looks amazing."

"Thank you, Daddy Mike," Sam said. "I'm doing well."

"He does, doesn't he? We've made a couple of new discoveries today, and I think Sam has benefitted from that more than I could have imagined. How have you been?"

"Good. Good. I'm making money, I have my girl, I have my buddies. Life is good." Mike looked over at Darren. "New ink. He's deep in his space."

"Worked on his spine. That draws some intense shit out. Once it's out, I like to fill it up with something good, right."

"He's sweet, isn't he? We were discussing some similarities between our boys. Darren's been an excellent host."

He wondered about Sam's space. Darren's boy was clearly floating; James once had a similar headspace, the same outward expression. He'd been able to find it for Sam with the flogger, but he hadn't yet tried to keep his boy there. Further, it was possible that Sam was getting more from this experience than the boy would from staying in that place for an extended period. That place for his boy was one strike short of an adrenaline rush. Or sex. And his friends didn't need to be party to either.

"I told Thomas there that I could work on Little Sammy whenever."

Sam grinned against his chest and Thomas wanted to know what was funny, what had amused his boy. He reached down to Sam's leg and stroked down along the muscled thigh.

"On Sam, or possibly on us both. Something new we haven't tried together before." He hooked a finger under his boy's chin and lifted it. "Something on your mind, boy?" He asked softly, smiling back.

"It's just good, knowing I'm not the only one, Mister. I

know how that feels, the slow endorphin release." Sam's eyes were focused on him. "I get it."

"Oh, Darren. We will definitely be in touch." He slid his thumb over Sam's lips and gifted his boy a light kiss.

Sam flushed a deep, sweet rose, and the smile heated him all the way to the bone.

Angel coughed. "How are things on the floor, Mike? Darla okay?"

"Fine. Just fine. Come upstairs, Angel. Have a beer with me?" Mike was a good man—rough as a cob, but good.

Sam pulled away a little, but the questioning look—the "Have I done something wrong?" look—was offered to him and him alone. He gave the boy a reassuring wink and the hint of a smile.

"We'll stop by on our way out, Gabe. Good to see you. Let's have dinner next week. Burgers?"

"Sounds great. You're on." Angel clapped him on the shoulder. "Keep smiling, Little Sammy, it looks damn good on you." They watched Angel head off with Mike. "You got a summer ale yet? Or is it too early?"

The door closed behind them and a quiet settled in the room. "He needs..." *to talk to Clint.* He wondered if Angel had. Clint had a way of breaking through bullshit. "Someone."

"He does." Sam had relaxed back down, resting into him like this was where he belonged. Which it was.

"He's solid as a rock. He needs someone that needs him desperately." Darren shrugged. "Who knows how it'll happen? I found my Ky when I was on a reality show."

That was just it. Angel needed to be needed like air. He squinted at Darren. "A reality show? Real people actually do that?" He always assumed people got paid to look real.

"Yeah. It was for tattoo artists. We had a ball. Ky was the

caterer. Before we parted, I'd inked his sac. He moved here to be with me three months later."

That sounded excruciating. And incredibly hot. "You're both lucky." No one had ever asked him how he met Sam. He wasn't sure how he'd answer that question.

"Yes." Darren stroked Ky's head, murmuring softly to his sub. It was beautiful to see their connection, to see how Ky relaxed even deeper into Darren's leg. "So are the two of you. It's amazing to find the right man."

"It's a gift for sure." His fingers hadn't stopped moving, roaming over Sam's back, tracing the lines of the harness, smoothing over his boy's abs. Sam was right, he liked the shirt. He liked the whole thing.

He took the last sip of his water. And looked at the empty bottle. "Is this just a place to relax, or are there say, poker games or parties down here?"

"Poker on Wednesdays, although I will warn you, that is Doms only, and there is no wager with your sub. Mike had troubles. You're welcome to bring Little Sammy, but he can't play. On Sundays when the bar is closed, we have private parties—dancing, etcetera. Mostly though, this is a place for us to relax—play chess, breathe, visit. It's a place where a sub can show his or her Dom how much they're loved, and vice-versa, hmm?" Darren grinned and rolled his eyes. "And sometimes you don't want a struggle or a fight. Sometimes you want your boy to be affectionate and close."

Often, in fact.

Wager with Sam? Evidently people did that sort of thing; it honestly would never have occurred to him. But poker sounded fun—he hadn't had a regular game since college. Poker with Sam at his feet sounded like a good evening. "I've never been to a club that wasn't all men. The mix sounds nice actually. And it's nice to have a place to celebrate this, in good company, without being in a bar."

He kissed the top of Sam's head. "More water, please, boy. Unless you're tired?"

"I'm happy, Mister. Would y'all like anything else, Sir?" Sam stood and smiled at Darren.

"Two, please. I want him hydrated." Darren tapped Ky's shoulder. "Come up over my legs, boy. You need to stretch out."

"Yes, Sir." That was a dear, sweet little moan.

"Oh, do you mind if I have a look?" He'd love to get a close-up of Darren's work.

"Of course not. Off with the shirt, boy. The air will feel good, hmm?"

"Yes, Master."

Darren helped Ky remove the shirt and get settled over Darren's thighs. The sub's entire back was done—a mass of vines and flowers, a leopard's eye peering from the jungle, a hint of a bright parrot. That was...breathtaking.

"We're celebrating the different environments. His chest is ocean, one arm is desert, one is tundra."

"That is exquisite work, Darren. Ky, you're a work of art." He admired the details especially, the creativity. "Sam, come see." He'd offer to let Darren and Ky see Sam's ink, but Sam would essentially have to undress, and he wasn't going to ask that of the boy. At least not until he knew everyone a bit better.

Sam returned with four waters, offering him one and Darren two, putting the other on the table as he bent forward to look.

"Oh, wow. Oh, y'all. How beautiful! You must be so proud." Sam admired Ky's back, giving it the attention it deserved. "You're doing amazing work."

Thomas took his water. "Thank you, boy. Really, Darren, you're gifted." He looked around the room at the two men playing chess, another one who seemed to be reading, and decided not to bother any of them; he'd introduce himself as the opportunity arose more organically. "Do you need to move around, boy, or are you settled?"

"I'm good, Mister. Where do you want me?"

"Right by my feet again, sweetheart." He took his seat.

Another conversation he hadn't known they needed to have. Another successful outcome despite some struggle. It was difficult to know if they were simply fortunate enough to have been able to work everything out this far, or if it was just so important to each of them that they wouldn't accept the alternative. He assumed more of the latter, but they were certainly under a bright star.

What he appreciated most about this lounge was that they hadn't been here before. It wasn't frustrating for either of them the way the club could be, and unlike nearly everything else in the city, he hadn't gotten there first. It was somewhere they could explore and accept, or not, together. Another adventure.

14

Sam had woken up warm and happy, and he'd spent a lovely half hour sucking Thomas dry. It was the best way to spend a Sunday, especially once they made coffee and shared a couple leftover doughnuts.

Thomas was fighting with the newspaper, and Sam was playing Candy Crush and telling himself it wasn't a time-waster if he didn't have any plans.

"I've got leather for you to clean if you're bored, boy." Thomas's voice floated past the newspaper, sounding equally serious and amused.

"I'm desperately interested in beating this level. Desperately." He fought his laughter, his tease.

"It's good to have goals." Thomas flicked the newspaper and one hand shot out and took the phone from his fingers. "Oops."

"Oops?" He cracked up, climbing into Thomas's lap, straddling his thighs as he reached for his phone.

"No matter how far you reach, my arm will always be longer, tiny cowboy." Thomas laughed, taunting him, the phone out of his reach.

166 | JODI PAYNE & BA TORTUGA

"Tiny cowboy!" Oh, he reached for Thomas's ribs, digging in to tickle. "I'll show you tiny."

"Cheater! Ow. Oh...stop!" Thomas gasped, laughing and squirming from him and his Mister's abs went rock hard under his fingers. *Whoa.* "All right! You cheat, but all right! Here." Thomas grinned at him, panting and holding out the phone.

Sam stood into Thomas's arms, hugging him hard. "I do love you, Mister."

More than anything. Seriously.

"I know. I count on it, my boy." Thomas circled an arm around him. "But may I remind you that tickling isn't love, it's torture."

"You did steal my phone, you know." He leaned into the curve of Thomas's arm. "Mmm. You're warm."

"Mmm. It was chivalry, thank you. I rescued your brain cells from certain death." Thomas kissed his head.

"Are you suggesting you don't love glittery addictive matching games?"

"I've got the only match I need, and he isn't glittery." Mister gave him a toothy grin. "Nice, right? That was a good one."

Sam had to give him that. "Very good."

Sam leaned a little harder, loving the vibe they'd found together over the last few weeks—from Texas to last night. It all felt so good.

"Did you know that lounge at Mike's existed? Wasn't that something?" Thomas bent over him and picked up a mug of coffee, then settled again, tucking him close.

"I knew there was a door down there, but I thought it was their house, that good friends knew where that was. It was amazing—quiet and friendly. Ky's ink was gorgeous too."

"I'm going to talk to Darren and see if he'll design something for us. We'll make a scene of it. I'd like to try a poker night too. I won't make you come with me, but I'd love it if you did."

"I'd like to come, please." He'd felt like he was welcome last night, like he was supposed to be there with Thomas. Like Thomas wanted him there. Him. Not anyone else.

Thomas smiled, looking so damn pleased. "We'll get to know some people, right? Make some friends. See where it leads us."

He nodded. "I'd like that, Mister. I would. They're easy to know." And he was all over a scene with ink, with his Mister right there, sharing it, helping him fly.

"I don't want to give up the club, but...if we do go back, we're going to be ourselves, whatever that means that day. I'll find out if that will work with Clint. It may not, and that's his right. I'd hate to close that chapter completely, but there's nothing we do in the rooms there that we can't do at home, and...you have to feel like you belong. You're a member; it's your club as much as anyone's. If we can't figure out a way to make that happen, it's not a good fit."

"I wouldn't ever ask you to not go to the club. I promise. And...I don't want you to choose someone else to go there with you. That's important to me, Mister. I want to be yours, full-stop."

"What?" Mister sat up, making him sit up too. "What are you talking about?"

"Scotty told me you'd spoken to Clint about..." *Replacing me.* "...finding another sub from the club, giving me to someone else."

He'd made himself clear on that fact last night. He wasn't going to be given away to anyone. He was with Thomas.

"Scotty needs to mind his own goddamn business." Thomas looked like he'd been punched in the gut. "I never said...well. I did I guess, but that's not...Sam, we barely knew each other then. When you flipped out over Blackwell and his Master kissing...you remember that, right? You took off and I thought, there's no way I was going to coax you out of the closet and train you too, it just wasn't right. That wasn't what I wanted."

Thomas sighed. "I may have lost it a little with Clint. We weren't even working together yet when I said that. Scotty wasn't even part of that conversation. What the fuck is wrong with him?"

Mister pinned him with those deep brown eyes. "I have no intention of finding another sub for anything. I have you. I would never just hand you off to someone else. How could you believe that? I love you. You're mine. I don't need anyone else. For anything. Period."

"Breathe, Mister. Seriously." He moved into Thomas's lap, staring right into him. "I'm not hand-offable, one. You're stuck with me. Two, Scotty's a jackass. Three, good. I am yours. All of me. All the way."

Poor worried man. He leaned in and kissed Thomas slowly. "And yeah, I remember that night. Watching them kiss was the biggest thing I could imagine. Then you kissed me, and I knew I was wrong about that."

Thomas sighed and watched him. "We're still pretty good at it." He got another kiss, and Mister stroked a finger over his cheek. "How long have you been worrying about this? About me wanting to take someone else to the club? Seriously."

"He told me right after the new year." Honesty, right? That was their deal. Come to each other first.

"Oh, sweetheart." Thomas reached for him, pulled him

in. "Please don't sit on something like that for so long, hm? I'm so sorry. I could have cleared this up, dealt with Scotty ages ago. I'd have told you the same thing."

"I'm sorry. I just wanted to prove that I could make you happy and, to be honest, Scotty is a bit of a dick. I wasn't sure he was telling me the truth."

"It was true. For five minutes a couple of weeks after James died. It hasn't been true since the day I showed up for lunch with you intending to cut ties, but you'd gotten yourself into a fight and I realized you needed me." Thomas sighed again. "I'm sorry."

"Are you?" He didn't think Thomas was, and he knew he wasn't. "We're making a damn good life, Mister."

"About us? Never. We're solid and happy. About Scotty? More and more by the minute."

"He's a dick, and he's into you hard." Which he could get. He totally understood, in fact.

"Well, he's out of luck, isn't he? I'm into you harder." Thomas winked at him. "A lot harder."

"Mmm...promises, promises." He leaned in, nuzzled Thomas's ear. "Like this morning, for instance."

"Exactly like this morning. And last night. And...oh, in the stairwell. God, you kissed me."

"I did. You tasted so good." He dragged his tongue around his Mister's ear. "You make me ache sometimes."

"Boy." Thomas's tone was playfully stern. "I meant it when I said I had leather for you to clean."

"So mean when I'm loving on you." He bit Thomas's earlobe and tugged.

Thomas laughed, but Mister arched that long neck for him anyway. "Don't make me cuff you to something. Or do. Your choice."

"My choice?" He licked all the way down that still-tanned throat.

"Mmm. Samuel O'Reilly, you are a naughty boy. God."

"Me? I'm crazy good." He chuckled against Thomas's throat.

"You are that. Rather instinctually good. It's insane." He was suddenly moving, Thomas's hands supporting his neck and back as he landed on the couch. "There's a list on the kitchen counter for you."

Mister winked at him and headed for the kitchen.

"Butthead old man," he muttered, chuckling under his breath. He didn't mind cleaning Thomas's boots at all, but he figured there was no reason to let on about that fact. "I thought Sundays were for relaxing."

"Yes, I plan to." Mister poured himself another cup of coffee. "You're still digging out from being on vacation."

"Am I now? You just wait, Mister. One day you'll want me to love on you, and I'll just have things to clean instead."

"Oh ho! But then I can put myself at the top of your to-do list." Thomas turned, grinning, and gave his balls a squeeze right through his sweat pants. "I want you, boy. I just want to make us wait. Remember how you assured me you weren't going to break? I was thinking we could test that theory later. Angel made it sound like so much fun."

A rush of pure need zipped down his spine, and he was totally on board with that plan. "I'm a tough cookie, all right. Let me grab a cup of coffee and my headphones, evil one."

He pushed himself up and took a hard kiss, loving Thomas for all he was worth. "You holler when you're ready to test theories, Mister. I'm all yours."

Thomas snorted. "You won't get a warning." Mister sipped his coffee and pushed the to-do list across the counter to him.

"No? I'll just have to be ready for you." He put the list in his pocket and made for the coffeepot.

Thomas purposefully got in his way, gave him a wicked grin that seemed to settle in his lover's stance and in those brown eyes, and slid past him, leaving the room.

"Butthead." He was laughing as he said it, though. Someone was full of piss and vinegar today. That promised fun and games. Worked for him.

Mister spent the rest of the morning being a playful pain in the ass. He got a kiss, then Thomas pointed at the boot he was polishing and gave him a little shit over a tiny spot he'd supposedly missed. He was remaking the bed, and Mister switched out the sheets he'd chosen for different ones, before saying "I love you." There wasn't a single thing on his list that Sir didn't make a comment about, then confuse him with something sweet.

He saw right through that shit. Mister was trying to set him on edge, rile him up.

Sam considered putting Thomas over his knee and popping his butt. He had himself cracking up, just rolling with merriment at the image.

"What's so funny, boy? Is lunch ready yet?" Thomas sat down on the couch and started texting.

"You wouldn't understand. Trust me. And nope, it's not. What do you want?" And Thomas had better have a decent answer, because he was fixin' to point out that Thomas wasn't broken, not yet.

Before Thomas could reply, there was a loud knock on the door, and Sam went to get it, a frown on his face.

"Hey." Tamara from two doors down was standing there, her pretty face just gray.

"What's wrong, honey. You need to come in?"

"No. No. You need to come out."

He glanced over at Thomas. "Okay."

"Watch your step."

"Oh, motherfucker." He grabbed his flip-flops and shuffled out, his eyes going wide. There were razor blades everywhere.

Literally everywhere.

Stuck in the doorframe like metal, wicked teeth, all over the floor, glued to the door. *Christ.*

"Thomas. Bring me my phone."

"Who is it?" Thomas appeared a second later with his phone. "Good afternoon, Tam—" Mister's eyes went wide. "Tamara, go to your place, all right? One of us will come by later."

Tamara nodded and backed away, then disappeared into her apartment.

"Jesus Christ." Thomas slipped into shoes and joined him in the hall, handing him his phone. "This has to stop."

"You think? Someone's sure pissed off." He started taking pictures. He was going to take these to Blackwell and tell the man to start helping before he started harassing policemen. The bastard had taken James because he had the element of surprise. Him? He was made of sterner stuff than his brother, and he was ready. "This took time. He has to be on our camera. Has to be."

Thomas nodded. "I find it hard to believe he doesn't know we have one by now, but I'll get the recording. And I'll..." His lover sighed. "Call Colletti. For all the good it will do us. I guess we need the cops here before we can clean this up. I swear, Sam, when they find this guy..." Thomas's hands balled into fists, then relaxed. "Fuck."

"I hope I find him first." He'd show the motherfucker what pain was. All the way to the core of every bone. "But I want him found, one way or the other. I'm tired of this."

"We need twenty-four seven surveillance now, not just

Mike's people." Thomas stormed back inside. "They need to keep him out of the building. Period. Where's my phone?"

"Mike's people." Sam blinked, head tilting. Oh. Why wouldn't Thomas have told him? Why wouldn't the guys? They were supposed to have been his friends, and no one said? Hell, Thomas was all about honesty and shit, right? How long had this been going on? Had they been watching when he left the house the day of the attack? Were they supposed to be watching the house or him?

He took pictures of the ground so the police could see, then swept the blades up so no one got hurt.

Sam sort of wanted to go inside, punch Thomas in the nose, and ask if that felt like he needed watching. If that felt like he couldn't handle his own. Of course, he hadn't been able to handle the last one on his own, had he?

God.

He waited for Thomas to get off the phone before he said, "I'm going to get lunch. I swept up the outside floor. I took pictures first."

Then he went to trade flip-flops for boots.

"Colletti's sending someone." Thomas followed him into the bedroom. "I think you should stay here."

"Good deal. I'll grab sandwiches. You want turkey?" Right now he was pissed off—at the killer asshole, at the cops, at Thomas, mostly at himself—and he needed a walk.

"Sam." Thomas stepped closer. "We can make lunch here. There's no need to go out. You're upset, just stay here."

"That's okay, huh? You've got folks watching, right? They'll make sure I get to the corner without hurting myself." He wanted to smile at Thomas, offer a little comfort, but he was giving it all he had already. "I'll be right back."

Thomas stepped between him and the bedroom door.

"Not on Sun...days. Shit." He watched the realization dawn on Thomas's face. Well, that told him what he needed to know. "Look. Don't go out. We don't know where he is right now, when he did this. I want you to stay here."

"Fine. Deal with your own lunch then, man." He was done for right now, and he needed a second to himself. "I'm going to my office. Holler if the cops need me."

Thomas didn't follow him or say another word.

Sam didn't slam the door or anything; he just closed it and opened up his laptop. He logged on, but he didn't actually do anything.

Then he grabbed his phone and texted Angel.

How many guys were watching me from Mikes?

Angel didn't answer right away, and when the text finally came in, it wasn't an answer. *You're trying to get me in trouble*

Answer the goddamn question

He wasn't playing some bullshit game here.

8, covering two shifts a day on weekdays, don't swear at me

Yeah, well, he'd fucking swear at whoever he wanted to. He was...well, if he was honest with himself, he felt like a fool. Worse than that, everyone knew he was a fool, one that couldn't be trusted to be outside on his own. Thomas, Angel, Mike, the guys at the bar. He'd thought he could have friends here, but...

His phone started ringing, Angel's name popping up, and he silenced it.

Hell, he'd thought, of all these men, Angel was his friend. Had really been his friend. *Shit.*

Sam did some math. Eleven thirty p.m. in Afghanistan. He texted Bowie.

u up?

Yeah. What's wrong

Lots.

15

Thomas hadn't seen that O'Reilly temper in a long time. But he'd known, hadn't he? He'd known Sam would be upset that he'd arranged surveillance, or he would have told his lover a long time ago.

He'd wanted to. He'd thought about it a few times, but every time he felt like he should level with Sam, something else happened and he...just hadn't.

This asshole was after Sam. It wasn't him the guy wanted to hurt, it was Sam. Whoever it was hadn't darkened his door until Sam moved in. And it was James before Sam. He had a hard time believing that the issue was O'Reillys in general, so somehow all of it was his fault. He'd known that for a long while. He couldn't help James, but goddamn it, no one was taking Sam from him.

He tried to decide if he was sorry. He felt like he should be—he'd essentially been lying, after all. He'd had a lot of support from a lot of people because obviously no one else said anything either, but ultimately it was his responsibility. He understood that, accepted it.

He hadn't done it to be mean, to make Sam think less of

176 | JODI PAYNE & BA TORTUGA

him, hadn't hidden it to hurt anyone's feelings. He did it because…being honest? He was terrified.

And in love. He'd told himself all along it was because he loved Sam.

And he promised Bowie he'd keep Sam safe.

He'd wanted Sam whole more than…more than he cared about his own integrity.

Jesus Christ.

He had no idea what to do now. He should be proactive, get up and go talk to Sam instead of sitting on the couch and letting the darkness fall around him, but he didn't know what the hell to say. He bent over and looked at his phone, finding a string of missed calls from Angel. He must have had it on mute.

One of them had to say something. He tapped Sam's name and texted, *Hungry?* It was the closest thing to an olive branch he had right now.

Ordered you a pizza about half an hour ago. It's paid for.

He dropped the phone on the couch next to him and sighed, then hauled himself up and headed for the office, feet and heart equally heavy. When he got to the door he knocked, not having any expectation that Sam would let him in, but at least he could say he tried.

Sam opened the door, the look on his face completely neutral. "What's up?"

What's up. How was he supposed to answer that? "The sky" came to mind, his old standby from when he was eight, but it wasn't funny then, and it certainly wasn't going to amuse anyone now.

"Would you like a glass of wine?"

"No, thank you. I want you to leave me alone. Go eat your pizza." Sam's lips tightened, his boy's cheeks going a dark, painful red.

Come on Thomas, you must have something to say. You always have something to say. His fingers itched to reach out and comfort his boy while he searched for the words...for their words. The ones that Sam would hear. But there just weren't any.

And he couldn't leave Sam alone. Not like this, not in this much pain, not when it was his fault. He wished that he was someone with answers like Clint, that didn't have to think so damn hard about everything. He couldn't think, he didn't have time to think, his boy was hurting right *now*.

"Sam." Right. *Fuck it.* He just wasn't going to. He reached for Sam and pulled him in, tightening his arms around the boy.

Sam stayed stiff for a long time. Then he sighed and shook his head. "You fucked up bad this time."

This time. He let out a heavy breath. All right. No one shattered, and the boy was talking, he'd listen.

"I did."

"I'm real pissed at you. All that shit about trusting each other and coming to each other first, and you were having me watched the whole time? Like I was a kid or something."

"I don't know how to explain my thinking to you without it sounding like I'm making excuses for bad behavior. I should have told you a long time ago. I wanted to. I didn't ask you when I set it up because I knew you'd say no, and I didn't want to hear that. I wanted you safe. And every time I thought I should tell you, razor blades showed up, or you got beaten and mugged. It just felt relentless."

"And no one—not one person—thought to tell you this was a shitty idea?"

In fact, it was Mike's offer, but he had no intention of throwing anyone under the bus. "I should have known. I did know, I guess. It wasn't...I didn't do it because I thought any less of you, I did it because I was...worried about *him*."

Terrified, Thomas. Just tell him.

"That's not what I asked you. Pay attention to me. These people were supposed to be my friends, at least some of them, and they were all good with this? With months of lying to me?"

Pay attention. *What's the boy really asking you?*

"I can't say whether they were good with it, but to answer you directly, no. No one told me it was a bad idea. Everyone seemed to think keeping you alive and catching this asshole was a pretty high priority. But they were following my lead, Sam. I told them I didn't want you to know, and I'm your Dom. They weren't going to question me."

Sam closed his eyes for a second, a look of hurt obvious, but only for a second. "You get what you ask for, I guess. Call them off. Now. I don't need a babysitter. This is not negotiable for me."

"This is not about a babysitter, sweetheart. It's about your safety. It's about keeping that asshole out of our building, away from you. You've been cut, drugged, mugged, harassed, beaten...and there's no question in my mind he's the same man that killed James. How far do you think, in good conscience, I can let this go? Please. Think about what you're asking me to do."

Sam stared at him for a long minute before the doorbell rang. "That's the pizza. It's been paid for online."

Thomas nodded and let him go and went to get the pizza. He'd forgotten the state of their doorway completely until he saw it in the delivery guy's face. "Just a prank," he told the guy, took the pizza and closed the door.

"Would you like some of this?" He took it into the

kitchen and put it on the counter. He wasn't hungry, he felt sick.

Not negotiable. Everything with them was a negotiation. Sam's well-being and his safety were not about Sam in a box anymore. Sam had him, the boy was surrounded by people that cared. However they dealt with the sins of the past, if Sam was staying, if Sam still wanted him, then he had a say in this going forward.

"No, thank you. I might later, but right now I can't." Sam headed for the coffeemaker and the whiskey, taking one shot out of his old coffee cup before pouring a second to go with his coffee.

Sam's phone rang again, but his boy looked at it, turned it off, and put it in his pocket.

"Look. What do you want from me? I lied to you because I wanted you safe and I love you. Should I have lied? No. I accept that. But it's not Mike's fault, or Angel's, it's mine. You could do a lot worse than having a half a dozen or more friends that love you enough to want to take care of you. And while I'm sorry I lied, I'm not sorry I had you looked after. I'm not. Your brother was murdered, and you're being harassed because of me. I don't know why, but I'll be damned if I'm going to sit by and not do everything I can to keep you safe. So you want to paint us all with a broad brush as liars, that's on you. I love you. That bastard isn't taking you from me."

That was it. That was as truthful as he could be. He didn't much care if it was what Sam wanted to hear, it was all he had.

Sam looked at him for a minute, before he turned around and washed out his coffee cup. "Fine. Whatever gets us through the night, huh? I'm fixin' to get the razors out of the door before someone hurts themselves. I'm not going anywhere, just right outside." Sam grabbed a pair of pliers from the junk drawer and a glass.

What the fuck did that mean? He blinked at Sam. "Fine." It wasn't fine, he wasn't just trying to get by.

He watched Sam step through the front door and watched the boy yanking one of the razor blades free as the door closed. Then he went for the wine.

16

S am hated weekends. Hated the motherfucking things.

Monday morning, as soon as Thomas left, he gathered his laptop and headed to the coffee shop first, then the library, then the park. He applied for a half dozen professional positions, found out what he needed to do to get back into school, and answered his emails.

He needed to get his shit together.

Bowie had listened to his raft of bullshit last night, and said, "If you lay down with dogs, baby boy..."

And he'd gotten it. If he wanted to be with Thomas, if he wanted this life, he had to put up with the fact that no one in Thomas's life was going to question the man.

Okay, fine, but he needed a life of his own. He needed something he could trust.

Or something to just get his happy ass out of the house.

What the fuck did he know?

The part that sucked so hard was that he'd thought that he had a place, he thought he was figuring it out. Hell, he thought he was doing good, and he was reduced to a sleepless Sunday night and Monday morning crashing down like he was a drunk.

But he'd dealt today—he'd stayed out of the house, he'd done things, and now it was five o'clock and he was heading home. His bodyguards could check in with Thomas.

By the time he got home, Thomas was already there, sipping a glass of wine and flipping through a magazine in the living room. Thomas looked over at him, brown eyes meeting his for just a moment, then going back to reading.

Oh goodie. It was his favorite game, Ignore the Redneck. "Hey, you. I'm home."

He plugged in his laptop and his phone and went to take off his boots. Maybe Thomas wouldn't notice if he just stayed in here. He was mad, and he had a right to be, dammit. Hell, at this point he'd gotten a half-assed sorry buried in between a bunch of reasons why Thomas wasn't really sorry and how, if he felt betrayed, well, that was his fault for thinking those good people didn't know what was best for him.

Okay, so, he was pretty pissed off.

After a little while, he heard Thomas moving around the apartment, but the steps never came near the office. Finally, he heard the shower turn on and the bathroom door close.

He sighed softly, stripped down, and just went to bed. Maybe he'd hate on Mondays too. At least this one.

17

S anity day. That was what they called it when life got so out of control that you just needed to take a day off and step out of it for a few hours, right?

Thomas took a walk in Central Park in the morning, wandering and sipping a latte. He'd had a nice lunch completely solo, and while he was there, he'd called Bryan and booked a massage at the club.

He hadn't said a word to Sam since Sunday. He had nothing to say. He was sure eventually something would come to him, but he wasn't interested in talking to a wall of pissed-off cowboy anymore. "Whatever gets you through the night" wasn't the response he'd been after when he said I love you, but it was what it was.

He'd made a mistake and taken responsibility, but somehow one breach of trust had outweighed absolutely everything else they had going for them. One lie of omission balanced against months of truths. He'd accept that if he'd cheated, or done something cruel, or told Sam's secrets. But how was keeping Sam safe the crime of the century?

Not to mention that his intention, and his own mental

state, had absolutely no impact. It was all about how wronged Sam was. As far as he could tell, why he lied was of no consequence at all, only that he had.

He was going to wait for Sam to come to him.

He went into the club, squinting as his eyes adjusted to the low light.

"Master Thomas! Welcome home!" Scotty was behind the bar, grinning at him.

He'd been expecting that, and he rather felt like as long as he was in a foul mood, he might as well get the rest of it off his chest. "Boy." He stepped up to the bar but didn't sit. "What room will Bryan and I be in?"

"Four, Master." Scotty blinked at him, obviously confused.

His phone rang, Sam's name popping up.

He snorted. That was one way to get him to talk. He gave Scotty a "one minute" finger and answered the phone, dreading whatever Sam had to say. "Hello?"

"Hey. I'm sorry to bother you. I was wondering if I could meet you somewhere to talk for a couple minutes."

A couple of minutes? "I took a sanity day. I've just arrived at the club for a massage with Bryan. You're welcome to join me here, or I can meet you somewhere after we're done."

"Oh." There was a long silence, then a gentle, sad sound that might have been a chuckle. "I'll just meet you after when you have a second. Enjoy your massage. Good-bye, Mister."

Jesus, that sounded final.

He looked at his phone and quickly texted, *where am I meeting you? Home? Coffee?*

Coffee shop is fine. Just tell me when & I'll be there

don't read more into this than is there, it's just a day to myself and a massage. I'll text you in an hour or so

Though he wasn't sure he was going to be able to relax now.

"Scotty." He moved to the bar. "My boy tells me you shared details of a private conversation that I had with Master Clint with him. Details that were out of context and also out of date."

"I'm sure I don't know what you're talking about, Master Thomas. I would never."

That was the kind of lie all of them should be worried about.

"Good. Because if I hear of it again from my boy, or from anyone, Master Clint will not be kind. And neither will I." He gave Scotty a look. To the boy's credit, those eyes fell quickly, but that didn't stop him from keeping Scotty pinned there for a long, silent moment.

"The key to room four, boy." He held out his hand. "Send Bryan in the moment he arrives."

Scotty quickly and silently handed over the key. On the way to the room, Thomas texted Clint. *We need to talk about Scotty. Call me tonight?*

Everything all right? The text came back gratifyingly fast.

Not in the least. But the Scotty situation is probably salvageable. That was vague and worrying wasn't it? He followed that quickly with, *I'll explain later.*

Fair enough. I'll call.

———

SAM LOOKED around the apartment after he'd put a couple of shirts and a pair of jeans in his backpack, his laptop in his briefcase.

It had been, not the longest week of his life, nor the worst, but enough to know that he needed to spend the weekend somewhere else. He had a cheap hotel with Wi-Fi, somewhere no one would look for him.

Now he just had to tell Thomas.

He hadn't known that he was making the right decision, but he knew now. He hadn't found Thomas at work, but at the club, which was cool. Thomas needed a place to be, but he couldn't face two days in that apartment without anyone answering him when he talked.

He'd be less alone in a hotel room.

Sam couldn't just go, though. He wouldn't scare Thomas like that. He wasn't threatening to move out, he wasn't being a bitch. He was lonely and tired, and he was going to go somewhere he could watch silly TV, get really drunk, and... well, talk to himself about what happened next, he guessed.

Maybe call his momma and admit defeat.

on my way to our usual spot

The text came in almost exactly when Thomas said it would, an hour later.

I'll be there

He grabbed his two bags and a gimme cap, heading downstairs to order their coffees—a fancy-assed caramel one for Thomas and a black coffee for him.

Thomas came through the door looking anxious and not very relaxed the way one should after a massage at all. He stuck a hand up and Thomas spotted him, hurrying over, but stopping before sitting down, eyes falling in his backpack. "What's going on?"

"Sit down, please. I wanted to talk to you. I won't bother you long." He didn't ask about the massage because he didn't want to make small talk. He didn't know how to do this, but then he didn't imagine anyone did. This was a stupid situation. How did you tell the person that you loved more than anyone who wasn't talking to you, that you weren't leaving him but if you had to live in that apartment in silence for two more days, you might lose your mind?

"Bother me." Thomas sat, looked at the coffee but didn't pick it up.

"I'm going to spend the weekend at a hotel. I can't...I'm not leaving you, but I can't sit in there a whole weekend without you even answering me. I'm sorry. I just wanted you to know so you wouldn't worry." Okay, that was good, right?

Thomas nodded slowly, lips pursed and forehead pinched. "I don't know what to say to you, Sam. You throw platitudes at me, you don't accept my apology, you don't tell me to fuck off, where do we stand? It's your show. I'm sitting smack in the middle of I can't do anything right. If you think sitting in a hotel room all weekend is what you need to do, you've made it clear you know best. But don't expect me not to worry, because I will. And don't expect me to sleep either, because I won't. I don't want you to go, but you have your bags packed, so I assume that doesn't matter to you."

"I want to go home, and I don't have one right now, so yeah, I'm going to a fucking hotel. And I tell you what, you stop assuming shit about me because no matter how many O'Reillys you've been with, you don't seem to know dick about me. You know you fucked up, and you don't like it, and I am trying to figure shit out. I'm trying my ass off." He closed his eyes and breathed, calming himself down. "You don't want me to feel shitty because people that call themselves my friends lied to me. Fine. All the people I know here assume that I'm not capable of facing the truth. That's a deal I took up when I took up with you. I'm sorry if I didn't come to that fact fast enough."

"Those are good people. The best. You want to write them off, it's your loss. But I'm not concerned with other people right now, I'm concerned about you and me."

Thomas shifted in his chair, leaning closer. "The only thing you share with James is a last name. I know everything about you. Everything. I knew you would think that hiring surveillance meant that I thought you were somehow incapable of taking care of yourself. I know that when you get to that hotel you're going to turn on Boomerang, pull the whiskey out of your backpack and wake up on the bathroom floor. I know you love me. And I know that you and I have never solved anything—*anything*—without working through it together. So I know you're going to come *home*—" Thomas drew the word out meaningfully. "You're going to come home on Sunday with a hangover and very little else in the way of answers."

Thomas leaned back in his chair. "I did fuck up and you're right, I don't like it. But you know, there was nothing malicious about it at all. Not from anyone, but especially not from me. It was a bad call. Somehow weighed against everything else we have, it seems like you might find some forgiveness. If you think you might find it in your whiskey bottle, great. Otherwise it's a waste of time. Come home."

His cheeks felt like they were on fire, but he wasn't going to let that go unanswered, for fuck's sake. "Jesus, you're a drama queen. You don't speak to me for damn near a week, then bitch about how I'm not forgiving you? I've talked to you every motherfucking day. It was a bad call. It was a bad call made worse because y'all didn't say so. I'm mad at you, asshole. Trying to work shit out, but I'm not going to let you sit there and accuse me of being unfair to you." He stuck his tongue out at Thomas. "I swear, I'm going to kick you."

"You know, you're right. You have talked to me every day. I just didn't know 'You want an omelet, honey' meant 'Fuck off, asshole, I'm mad at you.' "

Oh, Sam did not think so. He held up one hand, cutting

Thomas off. "No, you giant ass. 'You want an omelet, honey' means 'I may be mad at you, but I still love you and want to take care of you.' Just like 'I ordered your supper' and 'I pressed your work pants' and 'Here's your coffee.' "

Thomas laughed. "Because you couldn't just say, 'I still love you'? And by the way, I did manage to figure out that 'I paid for your pizza' meant 'You're in serious trouble, asshole,' so I deserve a little credit."

"Right, just like you couldn't just say 'I'm sorry' without a thousand reasons why I shouldn't be pissed."

Thomas just grinned, bit tight lips together, and gave him a shrug.

"Don't you grin at me. Butthead." God, he wanted to come home. He really wanted to just come home and let Thomas hold him a second.

"There was nothing I could say to you that that wasn't going to get me in trouble." Thomas picked up his coffee finally and took a sip. "Still warm. Can I carry your backpack?"

"Yeah, you can." He needed a hug in the worst way. "You want to take the coffee upstairs?"

"Yes." Thomas stood right up and shouldered his backpack, making a face. "Did you pack anything other than the whiskey?"

"Two shirts and two pairs of briefs."

"Momma would be so proud."

"I will beat you to death, Mister. I have a terrible headache and no patience left."

"Bryan beat you to it. My massage was more like a wrestling match. Wait until you see the bruises." Thomas hooked an arm behind him and led him out of the coffee shop. "You can still watch Boomerang."

"Hush, you. I might still get drunk off my ass too."

Thomas laughed softly and kissed his head as they got on the elevator. "Well, at least you know the bathroom floor is clean. Oh! This will make you feel better. I saw Scotty."

"Goodie. Did you give him my regards?" *Fucker.*

"I did. I told him to mind his own fucking business and keep his mouth shut. Then I texted Clint."

Well, that was something. He headed down the hall, his head pounding. Maybe he'd just stroke out. Somehow he doubted Thomas would appreciate that much.

"Looks okay," Thomas said casually. Door check. Welcome to their new reality. The door swung open. "After you. Bedroom."

"You don't mind?" He nodded even before Thomas answered.

"That's a rhetorical question, right?" Thomas took all his bags and his cap and everything and made them disappear.

"Yes, Sir."

Thomas led him into the bedroom, hands smoothing over him, getting him bare. With his head pounding he just followed Mister's lead, and in a second he was wrapped up in cool sheets and warm arms.

"Just sleep for now. I've got you."

18

Thomas was already awake when his phone started ringing and he fumbled around, yanking it off the nightstand to silence it before it woke Sam. It was Clint, though, and he wanted to take that call, so once he got the phone quiet, he texted quickly.

Sam is sleeping. Call you right back.

I'm here.

He carefully worked his arm out from under his boy, relieved in a way because his fingers had fallen asleep, and managed to get out of bed and tuck Sam in again without waking the boy.

He looked at Sam, cuddled safely into bed and snoring lightly, and realized that he'd nearly lost everything today. Again. There was no doubt in his mind that one weekend away would have started that ball rolling. Once you needed space, all you did was crave more.

After finding sweats to pull on, he wandered out into the kitchen, poured himself a cup of cold coffee, and stuck the cup in the microwave.

Sam hadn't liked his policy of silence at all, but it had worked. Sam had finally asked to talk to him. Granted, it was to say good-bye, so the plan had been a near failure, but as much as their joking about pizzas and omelets was fun, code wasn't really a conversation, and food wasn't really the same as saying I love you. Sam had finally asked to sit down with him and had opened that door.

He looked at his phone and dialed Clint.

"Good evening."

"Good evening. Thank you for calling."

"I wasn't sure whether to be worried, intrigued, or both."

He took his coffee out and added a little milk. "I'm not sure either. Scotty's been stirring the pot, and I just wanted you to know about it, if you didn't already."

"What happened?"

"He passed on details of one of our private conversations to Sam. He told Sam I was thinking about finding him another Dom, that I was looking to take on someone else. I remember having that conversation with you ages ago before Sam and I were...anything. I'm not even sure how he overheard us. But he apparently brought it up as if our conversation were more recent, and Sam feels it was done deliberately. He thinks Scotty is jealous."

He pulled his coffee out of the microwave and sank down onto the couch.

"It wouldn't be the first time boys didn't get along, or squabbled over Masters. But it certainly shouldn't happen with someone I employ. I'll have a talk with him."

"I don't think you need to, I said something today, and that might be enough. He denied it, but he looked properly contrite."

"So that's it, then? An important phone call about a situation you've already handled?"

Dammit.

"I was having a bad day. It got better."

"Oh? I saw you booked a massage. Did that help?" Clint was such a shit.

"If by help you mean that Bryan isn't as sweet as he looks, yes. For future reference, he doesn't take 'Maybe this was a bad idea' as a legitimate reason to get out of a massage. My shoulders are covered in bruises." Bryan had found knots inside knots. It did help, but he was going to need to find the arnica.

"Poor Tommy." Clint laughed at him, the sound husky and soft. "Are you ever coming home again? I miss you."

"I hope so. Yes. But Sam needs—" That wasn't fair. It wasn't just Sam. "*We* need to play by different rules. Sam's submission isn't like other subs'. It's every bit as complete, it just looks very different. He has a different...show. I need to find a way to make sure he feels included. Confident. Respected, not judged."

"All right. How can we make that happen for you?" The words were immediate, nonjudgmental, and welcome.

"I'm not sure. He feels alone...left out. It'll be better now that I understand, but I think some validation would go a long way. I wonder—it's your club, perhaps you could speak with him? Let him know you have his back? You're the highest authority there, if he knows you accept him, accept us, that might be enough."

"Of course. Perhaps we could have lunch together here, just the three of us. Or somewhere out."

Clint's calm, capable air made this so easy. "That would be perfect. Let me see what his schedule looks like, and I'll get back to you." This wasn't something he'd commit his boy to without buy-in, but he felt like it might work.

He was starting to wonder if he'd ever know what it was

like to not be working something out with Sam. But then again, growth was important, so maybe that wasn't something to wish for. Sam loved him more completely than he could ask for. That sort of thing took work. Right?

"Just let me know when. I'll make time for you two." Clint cleared his throat. "Have you spoken to Gabe?"

He sighed. Obviously Clint had.

"No. Why?" He could be a shit too.

"He's worried about you, I think. He keeps coming in and looking for you."

He'd missed a dozen calls, and he couldn't imagine how many Sam had ignored.

"I'll call him. Thank you." Angel was worried, he knew. Sam must have gotten information from him. But he knew his friend—their friend—wasn't looking for gossip about the surveillance; it was genuine concern for both of them. It wasn't fair to keep the man in the dark. "Sam and I had a misunderstanding, but I think we're going to work it out."

"Good. I appreciate that. I'm sorry. I can imagine you and Mister O'Reilly have more than your fair share of those."

"They're not unusual, for sure. But we're learning." First stop, Sam. It felt strange not to just put it out there to get Clint's feedback, but he'd made that promise for a good reason. "You know I'll ask if we need help."

"I'm here for you, however you both need me."

He heard Sam begin to move, then watched his boy stumble toward the kitchen, and blindly make a fresh pot of coffee.

"Thanks, Clint. My boy's up. I'll call you about lunch."

"Talk soon." Clint hung up; so he felt like he could. He'd been well trained years ago not to hang up on Clint first.

"Hey, sunshine. Did I wake you?" He wandered into the kitchen and put his arms around his boy. "You're more ambitious than I am. I just warmed up a cup of whatever had been sitting in the pot."

Sam turned in his arms, abandoning his coffee-making endeavors, and held on, hiding in his throat.

God, so sweet it made him ache. "Are you all right, sweetheart? I'm sorry I left you, I'd asked Clint to call me about Scotty, and when the phone rang I didn't want to wake you."

" 'm...I just needed a hug." Sam stayed right there. Poor boy. They hadn't been connecting at all, and Sam needed this, craved it on a cellular level.

He was starting to feel the same way. After spending a couple of days with Sam's parents, he'd come to understand that this too was an important part of how they communicated. That sometimes words weren't anywhere near as necessary as this. He held his boy close, already resolved to spend the day refilling Sam's reservoir. "My pleasure. I'm yours, love."

He wasn't sure if the sound Sam made was a sob, but it was desperate, and his boy stayed right there, arms around him.

"I'm right here. Let's sit, hm?" He scooped Sam right up and carried the boy to the couch where he settled them both, Sam in his lap and cradled against his shoulder. "I've got all the time you need to hold you, boy. This is our weekend."

"Love you, Mister." Sam relaxed against him, and he started petting, stroking slowly. He'd needed this too, he thought, because he could feel his own tension melting away.

"How is your headache? Any better?" He kissed Sam's forehead, resting a hand on his boy's hip.

"It is. Thank you. It's been a hard week. I've been working hard."

"You must have been—I came home to an empty apartment most days. What were you up to?" He didn't know what his boy had been doing all week. God, he was never letting this happen again. Never.

"I was at the library. I started looking at more PhD programs, or a job. Somewhere I could find new friends, people that are willing to talk to me." Sam sighed. "I feel like a fool. I wouldn't have let my guard down with some of those people, if I'd known. Worse, now I do know, so it's like all the safe places are gone, even the ones I worked hard for."

"If you'd known...known what, sweetheart?" This was a big deal. Sam's trust in their mutual friends was important.

"That they were comfortable lying to me. Eight guys from the bar, Mike, Darla, Angel? Not one said to you, look, you might want to talk to Sam? Hell, I took Buzz for coffee. You were there. I understand why you did it—I don't agree with lying to me about it, but I understand why you're scared. I don't understand why people that are supposed to be friends were all okay with lying to me." Sam shook his head. "It sucks, but it is what it is, I guess. I'll just have to try again."

"Why is it understandable that I was scared, but not that they were? Why do I get the pass and they don't?" Sam's take on this made no sense. He didn't understand it at all.

"Those people love you too, sweetheart. Is that so hard to believe? The day you ended up in the hospital, there were four men in this apartment. Me, Clint, Mike, and Angel. Clint was here to support me. Mike and Angel were looking for you. Angel was especially worried about you. He has connections and was helpful, but I think that was the only reason he wasn't a wreck. You're going to write those people off without even discussing this with them?"

"You lost James, and like Bowie told me, this is part of the deal. I want to be with you, I love you, and I get the parts that make me stupid happy, so I get the parts that are crazy-making. It's what gets us through the night, like I said Sunday. The lying? That's off the table. I'm willing to accept having someone watching the building because it's so important to you. Clint isn't my friend, and I know that. Daddy Mike, either. But some of the guys? Darla? I thought they were. I'm happy to be friendly with them, but right now, I don't trust them."

It didn't escape his attention that Angel wasn't mentioned at all.

"Ah. I see you and your brother have something in common after all." He shifted so he could look at Sam. "No one gets second chances. Is that an O'Reilly thing? Is Bowie like that too?"

"That's not fair. There were a lot of chances. I had to catch y'all out. If I hadn't, the lies would still be going on. You keep going on like I don't have a reason to be hurt, and that's not right, Thomas." Sam lifted his head. "And, FYI, Bowie demands perfection. He doesn't even give first chances."

"I never meant to imply you didn't have a reason to be hurt. Of course you do. But if you turn your back on every friend that makes a mistake without giving them a chance to step up and apologize, you're going to run out of people to be friends with. Everyone fucks up, Sam. Some of them might deserve to be forgiven."

"I'm not stupid, you know." Sam shook his head, sighed.

"I mean, give me a little credit. I'm the easiest motherfucker I know. I forgive and I let live and I let it go. God forbid I need a few days to lick my wounds, and I don't get with the timeline you've set or then I'm getting a 'how to forgive' lecture. I'm not an asshole. If I was, I wouldn't fucking care that I was easy to lie to."

"I'm not lecturing, I don't have a timeline and...Christ. I guess I *am* stupid because I don't understand. Why are we arguing? I don't want to argue."

"I don't know. I'm sorry." Sam settled back down, going quiet against him, still.

"I'm sorry too. We don't need to be talking about those guys anyway, we need to be talking about us. I need to promise you I won't do this again." No amount of righteous justification was worth all of this heartache. Nothing was. He'd let go of every friend he had for Sam.

"Just be honest with me? I'm not unreasonable. I try hard for you."

He hugged Sam closer. "I know." The issue was that he hadn't seen it as lying. He wasn't sure what it did fall under, though. So he was going to have to do some soul searching. Was it lying not to tell Sam that? He saw a lot of second-guessing in his future. He could only be as honest as he knew how to be.

"Thank you. I love you, huh? I think that was the worst part. It had been such a good weekend. We were having so much fun together."

"That asshole set us off. And the surveillance I lied about? That's because of him too. We have to find him. We have to stop this. He's throwing things into a tailspin for us over and over again. His bullshit is complicating everything."

God, that pissed him off. And he hadn't heard from Colletti all week, either. *Dammit.*

"Yes. Please God, yes. It's time for us to have a little peace."

"Past time. We complicate our own lives just fine without his help, thank you very much." He laughed, trying to lighten things up a little. His poor boy needed to breathe.

"Yes." Sam kissed his shoulder. "Are you hungry for supper? Did you eat already? I haven't been good about it and I'm starving."

"I haven't eaten. Would you like to take a walk? Maybe get some air and a slice or something? Or if that's too daunting, we can make eggs or grilled cheese." He could be convinced to go out. He could be equally convinced to stay in.

"It's beautiful out there. I'd love to go out with you, wander."

"Great. All we need is clothes." And arnica. And some Advil. God, his shoulders were sore. He stood up, lifting his boy upright and heading for the bedroom.

"You want a bottle of water, Mister?"

"Yes, please. Do you know where the arnica is? I'm positive you were the last one to use it." He gave Sam an evil grin and pulled out a pair of jeans.

They had been having fun that day, hadn't they? And he didn't get a chance to follow through on his nefarious plans. It wasn't ever too late for that kind of thing was it? They did have all weekend.

Which reminded him... "Shit. I have to call Angel. He even asked Clint if we were okay."

Sam brought him the tube of salve and the water, putting on his jeans from earlier before going to grab his boots and button-down. "Holler if you need me to put the arnica on, Mister."

"That would be nice, boy. Thank you." He pulled out his phone, sat it on the dresser and called Angel on speaker.

Sam didn't say a word, just carefully smoothed the arnica over his shoulders.

"Jesus. Tommy! What the fuck? I was going to show up on your doorstep next."

"Sorry, Gabe. I know you've been calling. Sam and I have been busy." Busy not communicating. Their Achilles' heel.

"I assume I'm on Sammy's shit list and I'm not welcome for dinner anytime soon, but...can you and I have coffee, man?"

Good for you, Gabe. He hadn't prompted that or anything. He looked over his shoulder at Sam. "Sam's right here Angel. You're on speaker."

"Hey, Sammy. I'm sorry about this. I did what I thought was best for you, huh?"

Sam sighed softly and shook his head. "Thank you, Sir. Have a good evening."

Well, now what was he supposed to do? If he accepted Angel's invitation was he betraying Sam? Was he allowed to have friends that Sammy didn't like? Didn't trust? Did Sam expect him to give up on Angel too? "Angel, just give us some time. I made a big mistake, and it seems as though I've dragged everyone down with me. I'm sorry. I'll call you again soon, all right?"

"Of course. Sure. I'll—good night." The line went dead, and Thomas rubbed his forehead, sighing softly.

"Why don't I just run out and pick something up? I can tell you're hurting, and you can call him back, make plans to see him next week. He loves you dearly." Sam kissed his temple, the touch gentle as hell. "I'll be back in a jiff."

"No. No, don't. Don't do that. You do that a lot, you know. Say you need to go out, you need to get air, you need to clear your head, get coffee, get lunch. No. No fresh air for you. This time you stay right here in this horribly uncomfortable moment, and you breathe it with me."

"I'm good at being busy, and I was polite, you know. I accepted his apology."

"You did. And you broke his heart."

Sam stilled behind him, then handed him his shirt without a word.

"Thanks for the arnica." He pulled on the button-down Sam had grabbed for him. "Boots, please, boy." He wasn't going to lecture; he wasn't getting in the middle. He'd stood up for Sam on the phone, and he was standing up for his friend now, and the rest was between them. He'd call Gabe from work on Monday. This was their weekend. He didn't know what they needed, but they damn well needed something. He'd figure it out.

Sam got Thomas his boots before heading to the bathroom to smooth his hair and brush his teeth.

"Did you want pizza? Or do you want to sit down someplace?" He pulled on his boots and stood up, hoping they'd give him confidence.

"I could be convinced to go either way." Sam looked him over, nodding to him. "You look fine. Just fine."

"Thank you, sweetheart." He sighed and reached for Sam, tugging the boy in tight. "I love you. We'll feel better after we eat something and get some air."

"I love you. Come on. We'll wander, see what we can see. Maybe, if you're very good, I'll even buy you a cookie." Sam winked at him and kissed him, obviously willing to find good in their day.

"Maybe a tequila-flavored cookie?" He grinned back, letting Sam lead him out of the building.

It was late for dinner, but it was a warm Friday night and there were plenty of people out. He hooked an arm around his boy's shoulders and told himself that once they figured this out, once they got each other through this, they'd be able to get through anything.

19

Sam headed home, whistling to himself.

He had spent three days working at home, but everything was starting to get to him, thoughts buzzing at him. He didn't like it, so today he'd gone to work at the coffee shop, then taken a long, long walk.

He was doing good with Thomas. He was. They had spent two weekends hiding from the world, had spent evenings together. Had been okay.

So why was he so frigging restless, and why was...

The sound of a motorcycle cut in front of him, and Angel was there, great big and scowling. "You want a ride?"

"I live right there."

"I know. Come have a cup of coffee with me. We need to talk."

The temptation to ask why was huge, but he knew why, and maybe it was time. "Okay. I'll need to holler at Thomas. I don't want to scare him."

Angel gave a wave across the street and Buzz nodded and waved back, turned, and headed toward the subway. "You do that. And then hop on."

Sam gave Angel a look. "You want me to salute?"

"No. I want you to hop on, so I can take you for coffee."

He chuckled softly. "It's been a few weeks since you took me for a ride."

"Just a few. Did you finish that text yet? I'm ready to tear up Fifth Avenue. I mean, go to Starbucks." Angel gave the throttle a twist and the engine roared.

He texted Thomas and crawled into the bitch seat. "Tear it up."

Angel took off along the park, headed uptown, away from busy Midtown to where the park and the street got quieter. Well, quieter except for Angel's bike, which roared for long stretches and sputtered when they idled at red lights. Finally Angel pulled over and shut the engine off, but there wasn't a single Starbucks in sight.

He sighed and shook his head. "What's up, Angel?"

Was the bike acting up? Lord knew he had about no experience working on one of those.

Angel grinned at him. "You and I can't afford coffee on the Upper East Side. Thought we could sit by the reservoir. Come on."

"Dork. Why didn't you just say so?" Sam would have come to sit and talk. Probably.

"Honestly? I had no plan beyond seeing if you'd actually take a ride with me. I wasn't counting on it. That was a nice ride, and this is just where we ended up." Angel laughed and led him into the park. It was quiet and green up here, and the sun was strong as they approached the water.

He shook his head but smiled. "So, are we going to fight or make up, do you think?"

He knew that he was still hurt, and he knew Thomas didn't understand why. He also knew he was going to have to figure it out on his own, if he was going to do this—live with Thomas, give them both what they needed.

"Well, we're not going to fight." Angel pointed to a bench and led him over that way. "And you didn't call me 'Sir,' so maybe there's hope for me."

"Maybe. I don't like being on the outs with a friend."

Angel sat, feet kicked out, and leaned back on the bench. "So. I don't have a lot to say." The big man looked out over the water. "I was in the room when Mike made the offer and the decision was made. I should have spoken up then, and I didn't. Everything after that was just a lie." Angel looked over at him and shrugged. "I screwed up. I'm sorry, man."

Sam nodded. Fair enough. It sucked to have to admit you were wrong.

"Thanks. I appreciate that." He bumped shoulders with Angel. "How've you been?"

"Keeping busy. Thinking a lot." Angel squinted at him. "Trying to figure out how the hell you and Tommy work."

"Are we that different from other people?" God, that was a question he'd wanted to ask Thomas and couldn't figure out how.

"Yeah. And you're that different from each other." Angel winked at him. "When Tommy and James got together, I got it right away. It took me a while to figure out what you two had in common other than, you know, your grief and all. And now? Anyone who knows you can see you're solid, but the two of you together in the scene? It doesn't look like anyone else I know."

"I don't even know what that means, Angel. I do everything I'm supposed to." Christ, he was tired. Bone-deep. He was doing his best to take care of everything, and it didn't seem to matter in the least.

Angel's head tilted at him. "What's the matter, Sammy? Tommy said you two were okay."

"We're fine. We're good." He wasn't sure how they were supposed to look in a scene. "So what am I doing that's different?"

Because Thomas knew what he was doing.

"Well, you two were way better at Mike's a couple of weeks ago. But at the club...I mean, seeing you hiding in your hat...it's just odd. I don't know. Tommy is so proud of you, you should totally own that room, right? He's yours."

"So this is about my hat?" Seriously? He hated the idea of just having to be all exposed. He wasn't even sure he was going to Mike's again, and the club? He didn't even want to think about all the bullshit and pressure from having to worry about every single fucking thing and about the fallout on Sunday after.

"What? No. I meant...no. It's not about your hat, Sammy." Angel laughed, that big, booming happy laugh that could make him jump, except outdoors it didn't hit him quite so hard. "Your clueless thing is really convincing, that's all. The way you let Tommy look after you is sweet. He needs that."

"I don't have a clueless thing. I'm just trying to not embarrass him in public. I don't have a 'thing' at all." He wasn't sure there was a thing to have. Did James have a thing? Did Thomas have a thing?

"You're joking, right?" Angel squinted at him. "Wait. You're serious? You're Master Thomas's boy. Tommy was hand-picked by Clint. You can't embarrass him. You're basically the top of the sub food chain over there."

"Right. I'm the idiot that can't figure dick-all about... anything. I'm just trying to make it through a single weekend without a disaster, man." He looked over at Angel, chuckling softly, although it wasn't funny. "I got to tell you, I dread weekends a little bit. I'm...I'm not very good at this."

"What are you talking about? Dread weekends? When you took the job at Mike's, Tommy missed you like crazy on Saturdays."

Shit, marthy. Just shut up. Angel is Thomas's friend. Just shut your stupid trap. "I'm talking out my ass, man. It's no big. I hated never seeing Thomas."

That was what he needed to think about. He needed to focus on taking care of Thomas, just going to the club and following the rules and making it to Monday. Someday it would stop feeling like he was an imposter.

"Listen. Doms aren't that complicated, Sammy. Let us take care of you, feed our egos often, and we're good." Angel laughed again.

"Y'all sure as shit feel fucking complicated." He winked over at Angel. "I'm just tired. Been a long week."

"Does Thomas know?"

"Know what?"

"That it's been a long week, Sammy." Angel asked it like he was insane.

"I doubt it. He's been working and..." What? He was supposed to be all, "Hey, I'm a dipshit and half a titty baby and I need a hug and..."? Right.

"And? Sammy, if you're stressed, if you need him, you have to let him know." Angel looked at him. Hell, stared at him. "It's part of the deal, kiddo. Don't you know that? He needs it, maybe more than you need to give it. Shit, no wonder you're so fucking stressed out. I swear, I thought you were pulling some shit, but you're not, are you?"

"If people don't stop acting like I'm either a liar or stupid, I'm going to lose my motherfucking mind!"

Angel stared at him for a second, then grabbed him and

208 | JODI PAYNE & BA TORTUGA

held him tight. "Okay. I hear you. I get it. Not a liar. Not crazy. Not stupid."

"Thank you."

"Okay. You know what Tommy told me on the phone the morning after your initiation at Mike's? When you were all beat to hell? He said, 'The boy needs me.' Tommy needs to be needed. He needs to know he can be what you need. Does that make sense?"

"I'm trying not to stress him out."

"Shit, do me a favor, Sammy. Stress him out. Fucking dump everything in his lap until he squeaks. After you do that? Come on to the son of a bitch. Drive him out of his tiny little mind."

"Angel!" He cracked up, just tickled as all get out.

"Seriously. Do this. Drop all your mental shit into his lap and see what happens. If I'm giving you bad advice, I swear to God, I will buy your coffees for a year."

One of his eyebrows went up. Okay, that was a serious offer.

Angel echoed the look. "The good stuff."

"I-I got nothing."

"Just say you'll try it. Trust me."

"I'll try it. If he gets really pissed, I'm calling you."

"Deal. And when it works, you can give me the credit." Angel snorted a laugh. "No. No, don't do that. What happens at the reservoir stays at the reservoir."

He shook his head, smiled. "Yeah, yeah. I just want to be what he needs."

"You are. You just have to make sure he knows your needs too." Angel stood up, eyes on the sidewalk. All right, Sammy. I'm going to take you home. Thanks for hearing me out."

"Thanks for the ride." He gave Angel another hard hug. "Even if there wasn't coffee involved."

Angel hugged him back, holding on tight for a second. "We're good? Because I missed you."

"We're good. I missed you too." Stupidly. Angel was his best friend, for fuck's sake.

"Right on, man." Angel cleared his throat and let him go. "TGIF." He grinned and started off toward Fifth and that loud bike.

20

Sam and Angel had a good talk. That was what Sam told him last night, and Angel confirmed it when he texted to check in.

We're good. You guys want to come out to Mike's tonight?

Thomas looked at Angel's invitation and sighed. *Not sure. Might stay in again.*

Again.

This would be the third weekend in a row that he and Sam would be spending enjoying each other's company and no one else's. Going out had become complicated. The club was still out—he hadn't had gotten Sam's buy-in on lunch with Clint yet, and it was just too stressful for the boy. And Sam still felt like he'd been betrayed by too many people at Mike's, including Mike himself, so it was possible they'd never go back there either.

The consequences of not being truthful with his boy were high. He just wished the universe would figure out he'd learned that lesson and be done with it.

He didn't even have it in him to pick up a flogger today. He'd decided he would just let Sam find them a movie, and they could snuggle on the couch. There was really nothing else he could do for his boy right now, not until he found his own bearings again and stopped second-guessing himself. He wasn't at all confident that he wouldn't add insult to injury.

He headed for the kitchen and the coffeepot, thinking maybe he'd take Sam to the Guggenheim tomorrow, get them out of their living room. They couldn't go wrong with a museum, right?

He found Sam there with two mugs, carefully making his coffee, a deep frown etched on his face.

Shit. What was that about? What had he done now? And when was he going to be able to see that look on his boy's face and not assume he'd put it there? He stepped up behind Sam and wrapped his arms around his boy. That, at least, he knew was something he could do to help. "Hey."

"Hey." Sam leaned back, inhaling deep. "I made us coffee. I was...I was hoping you had a couple three minutes for me, Mister."

Jesus, it was Saturday. Did the boy really feel like he needed to ask? "I have all day for you."

Throw me a bone, sweetheart. Anything.

Sam nodded, cheeks turning a bright pink. "Yeah, I know that, but 'I want to talk to you' sounds like I'm mad at you, and I'm not. Come sit? Please?"

The coffee was perfect—just the way he liked it, and when Sam turned to give it to him, his boy looked a little nervous, a lot determined.

"Sure." He would ask what was wrong, but Sam was obviously about to tell him, so instead he just leaned in a took a kiss, hoping that would offer some reassurance.

They ended up on the sofa, Sam shocking the hell out of him by settling on a pillow on the floor and leaning against his legs, one cheek on his thigh. "Lord, Mister. It's been a weird, rough week. I mean, I swear to God, everything's felt like sandpaper, even the good stuff. And there's been that. Good. But there's all the other."

Sam began to talk to him, a steady stream of worries and random things that had happened to him, the meeting with Angel, a fight with a client, how he worried about his hair growing in funny, the fact that their coffee shop had stopped carrying his favorite muffin.

He was glad that his boy wasn't looking right at him, because he wasn't sure he could hide the stunned look on his face. It was replaced fairly quickly by a smile, though. Not because Sam's week had been rough, of course, but because he suddenly recognized the boy sitting at his feet again.

He stroked his hand over Sam's head and shoulders, listening to the tangled mind that somehow attributed an equal amount of anxiety to everything, whether it was career-oriented or simply interfered with the boy's breakfast, and began to feel like he could breathe a little. None of that insanity had his name attached to it.

"I didn't know any of that was weighing on you this week. I wish you'd told me sooner so that I could help you. We have a rule for this, remember? Speak up."

"I was worried about stressing you out, but...I need you, you know?" Sam held his ankle, fingers tracing patterns on his skin.

I know, I need you too. He breathed in deep, as if Sam had offered him oxygen, but he treaded lightly, not wanting to make assumptions. "I'm right here boy. Tell me what you need."

"I need you. I-it's hard to ask, you know? I don't know

how. I don't want to do it wrong, but...I want you. I want you to help me let it all go. I need to let you, too."

He nodded slowly, aware of the way his own posture changed as Sam spoke to him and understanding better what it was he needed as well. "I hear you, boy. We'll talk about how to ask another time. Let's move, shall we?"

Sam glanced up at him, a tentative, warm smile on his face. "Thank you, Mister."

"My boy. I hope you understand the gift you've given me. If you don't now, you will." He stood and pulled his boy up and into his arms, already feeling like they were healing one another.

Sam pressed close, the soft moan a mixture of emotions, all offered to him openly, and they began to move to the bedroom. Thomas had a determination to his movements now, and Sam did too, his boy totally focused on him.

"Find your cuffs, make sure the chain is attached, and bring them to me." He released Sam as they entered the bedroom and moved to the closet to find his pants. He knew just the pair he wanted, the supple leather calling to him. He moved with purpose but not in a rush, letting every step he took straighten his spine and square his shoulders.

Sam retrieved the cuffs from the heavy chest at the bottom of the bed, kneeling down to fasten the chain before standing up and coming to him. Those pretty eyes dragged over him, admiring him, loving him.

He left his boy to stand there, holding them while he changed, welcoming the attention and the confidence Sam's appreciation brought with it. When he was ready, he took the cuffs and smiled. "Strip, please, boy."

"Yes, Mister. I love how those pants look on you. They make me a little goofy." Sam stripped for him—baring himself, folding the T-shirt and jeans.

"I'll take goofy." He pulled Sam in by the chin and kissed him lightly before putting on the cuffs. The ritual of strapping his boy into them held meaning for them both, so he took his time, making sure they didn't pinch the boy, and the heavy chain that hung between them didn't twist. "Bring me your flogger. Then you may go to the wall."

Sam nodded to him, whispering, "Yes, Mister." His boy's cock was already heavy, proving his interest, but it was the set of Sam's shoulders that proved his need. Sam brought him the flogger, stealing a quick, hard kiss before moving to the wall.

"Hands wherever you are most comfortable. Just breathe, sweetheart." He took in the sight of his boy, the offer, the willingness just as he remembered. He retrieved the chair and set it in the middle of the room in case Sam needed it, then picked up the boy's blindfold and moved in close, hips and chest pressing into his boy. "I have missed you. You look beautiful."

"I need you, Mister." Sam leaned into him, and he smiled as he covered Sam's eyes. He swallowed the rush that came with his boy's words and stepped away, rolling his shoulders and letting his arm swing the flogger in front of him, the weight and feel of it familiar and exhilarating. He didn't go far, intending a few lighter falls at first, just to give his boy something to feel, and something for them both to focus on.

"Give me your words, boy." Another ritual that was important for their focus.

Sam answered him easily. "Yellow and revolver, Sir."

"Yellow and revolver. Good boy. We'll begin. Just light for now."

He brought the flogger down on Sam's shoulders, going for the rhythmic thud, relentless but light, watching Sam's skin blush just slightly. He was very aware of the moment things started to let go in him; his breathing grew even and his weight settled into his hips, anticipating the stronger blows to come.

Sam danced for him, the motions slow and undulating, the soft sighs and moans like music on the air. Thomas was soaring with the knowledge his boy had come to him, freely and openly.

"Good boy." The praise was real, and it was gratifying to be able to say it, to know it was deserved. "Tell me how it feels."

"Necessary." There wasn't a moment of hesitation, of second-guessing.

"Yes. For us both, my own. Imperative, in fact. Harder now." He took a measured step back, knowing the distance he would need to use the full length of his arm. "Count, please."

He took a deep breath, focusing as he let it out. He gave his boy two strikes, paused, and added two more, smiling at the way it felt, at the knowledge that his boy needed this, needed his arm and his attention, his validation. Him.

Sam groaned between counts, the sound making him smile with its freedom. He watched as Sam stretched under the blows, the tension dissolving.

With that sound, any lingering thought he'd had about holding back dissipated and he let his arm fly, leveling one solid blow after another at a steady pace, listening to the strength in his boy's voice as Sam counted for him.

His arm felt good, strong and loose. He watched, transfixed, as the skin on the boy's shoulders slowly progressed from a light pink to a heavier red, stripes rising on Sam's skin.

"Mister..." Sam moaned for him, forehead resting on his

hands. Thomas could read the lines of need, the deep burn that his boy craved.

Eventually, Sam stopped counting, distracted perhaps by endorphins or simply floating, and he slowed his blows, then stopped them entirely and stepped closer. It would be easy to push too far, to step over the line unintentionally, given how desperate they'd both been for a scene, and he knew he needed to check in with his boy before either of them allowed that to happen.

"Boy," he said softly, resting a hand on Sam's lower back, a spot that he never touched with his flogger. "Are you with me?"

Sam moaned for him. "Mister. With you. Love."

"You're stunning, boy. Your color, your sounds." God, just the mention made him ache, and he pulled the boy's hips against him and rubbed his erection against Sam's ass, making them both moan, his need stretching the leather.

"Yes." Sam spread for him, hips rocking in a clear offer, a desperate offer. The action was honest, wanton, and made his mouth dry.

"Soon." He pushed away from his boy with every bit of restraint he had in him. But it wasn't about making them wait or teasing his boy. He could feel that Sam hadn't had enough yet. The boy wasn't quite there. He considered whether he ought to get out the heavier flogger and decided against it, opting to add effort rather than let the tool do the work. It would tire his arm and be more satisfying.

"Breathe and count, boy. A few more."

"Yes, Sir. Breathe and count. I love you. Thank you."

"I love you." His boy's expression of thanks was surprising and unexpected, but it was appreciated, and he knew in that instant that Sam truly understood him now. "Mine."

He raised his arm again and brought the flogger down in solid, forceful blows with his full weight behind them, listening for a safe word but not letting up until the first sign that his aim was off. He tossed the flogger to the ground, panting, and approached Sam again, walking tall and feeling strong. "My boy."

"Yours." Sam's voice was raw, husky, the boy breathing like a bellows. "Burn for you."

He took a quick, critical look at the boy's back to make sure there was no worrisome injury and reached up to remove his boy's blindfold, leaning close enough to feel the heat coming off Sam's skin and to grind against the boy's ass again. "Fuck, you feel good."

"Yes, Mister. Please. *Please*. All yours."

Thomas craved that—how Sam never shied away from begging for him, for his touch, his cock, his love. Now that he understood Sam hadn't known how to beg for his flogger, for a scene—they were going to fly.

He made it to the nightstand and back with the lube in just a few long strides, then pressed slippery fingers inside his boy and blew cool air across Sam's shoulders.

Sam barked out a short, sharp scream, his ass gripping Thomas's fingers like a fist.

He couldn't stop the wicked grin, but he sobered quickly as the leather pinched and tried to strangle his aching cock. He tore his fly open with his other hand and pushed the fabric away enough to free his balls too, dropping his head down with a sigh. "Christ, boy. I want you."

"I'm all yours. Please." Sam moved on his finger, riding him like a wild man. He grabbed Sam's hip, stilling Sam's frenetic movements.

"Breathe, boy." The order was gruff, and his voice was

deep and heated. He pressed close and took his boy without grace or subtlety, grunting as he hauled on Sam's hips.

"Yes!"

That wild cry suited him to the bone, vibrated in his balls. Sam took him, every inch, again and again, that sweet hole gripping his shaft, trying to keep him in deep.

He closed his eyes for a bit and just listened to their breathing, his boy's moans, and when he opened them again his view was almost entirely Sam's reddened, striped skin. Beautiful and raw, his marks were a reflection of his boy's need and his own.

He leaned over Sam's back, letting his chest touch that sensitive skin and curled his fingers around his boy's cock. "This is us, boy. This is what we have to believe in."

"Us. Oh, Mister..." Sam spread his fingers out on the wall, the chain jingling. "So good. Need this. You. Us, huh?"

"Nothing matters more." He groaned in Sam's ear and tightened his fingers, stroking Sam root to tip. "Fuck, yes."

Each stroke made Sam work him, milk his cock with that tight, tiny hole, the burning heat that fluttered around him. He gasped as his balls drew up, and he knew the sound he made as he fought for control was more desperate than determined.

"Yours." Sam moaned and arched, fucking Thomas's hand with a strong, steady motion, pressing back on his cock.

"Mine." Sam felt so good, the boy making it impossible for him not to give in and take what he wanted. He shifted and took his boy by the hips again, his thrusts erratic and searching for just the right resistance. Finding it was pure heaven. He closed his eyes and took his boy, grinding in and out, his balls going tight and hard. "Gonna...Sam!" He grunted and his orgasm rocked him, flowing through him in long, breathless waves, hips jerking and fingers digging into Sam's skin.

Sam moaned low, shaking around him, panting like he'd run a marathon. "Feel you. Fuck. Feel you everywhere."

He heard that, but could only nod in answer at first, his cock still tender and spasming inside his boy. He braced a hand near Sam's chained hands on the wall and steadied himself, finding air as his boy rocked against him. He reached around and snorted softly at the boy's stiff prick, grinning into one shoulder. "Stud."

"Yours. Yours." Sam squeezed him tight, making him grunt.

Naughty, naughty.

He could play along; his head was starting to clear. A little. "Mine. Mine to fuck. Mine to...deny? If I want to."

To his surprise, Sam nodded, even as he groaned, ass fluttering like mad around him. "Yours. All the way."

Denial was an entertaining tool, but his boy's words were so touching and sweet, he couldn't actually bring himself to do it. Today, anyway. He took Sam in his fist and braced himself, giving his boy something to work against, then whispered in the boy's ear. "I can smell you."

"Oh." Sam's eyes flew open, and it didn't take four or five hard strokes before his boy came for him, shooting hot and wet over his fingers.

He groaned with his boy as Sam tightened around him again. "Oh, my love. You're a wonder." He continued to fondle and stroke his boy, making Sam shiver.

"I'm all yours. God, I needed. I needed this. Thank you."

"Thank you, Sam." There was more to say, about need, about gifts, things he wanted to help Sam understand. Later. Right now, the boy's fingers were probably tingling, and he needed to see to Sam's back. He reached up and loosened the buckle of one cuff, sliding it over Sam's hand, then the other.

"Mmm. It makes them feel like they're floating."

"Because they're so light now?" Carefully, he got Sam moving toward the bed.

"Yes, Sir." Sam settled on his belly with a soft little moan.

He reached for his kit, and the muscles in his shoulder pulled a little, making him grin. Oh, that little bit of soreness felt good. It felt so right. He went to work, checking for and dealing with raw spots and broken skin on his boy's back.

"I want you to rest. I don't want you to give a single thought to anything other than staying here with me. We need to savor this together, boy, we deserve it."

"Yes, Mister. That sounds magical."

Maybe it was magic. Maybe it was magic named Angel. Maybe Sam had come to it accidentally. He wasn't questioning anything. Something had clicked for his boy, and everything felt balanced right now.

By the time he'd finished with the ointment, Sam was so relaxed, the boy seemed boneless. He climbed in beside his boy and Sam molded against him, both of them sighing and closing their eyes.

21

Sam woke up around suppertime, went to the bathroom, grabbed some water, then cuddled right into his Mister's side.

His world was quiet, easy. Thomas's heart beat steadily in his ear, and he felt like he could breathe, like the world was solid under his feet. It seemed like Mister was solid too. Sir was perfectly still, face relaxed, not at all restless or uncomfortable. Sleeping like Thomas hadn't in a while.

He rolled his shoulders and stretched, the deep burn in his back joining with the ache in his ass to pull a long, low sigh from him.

Thomas hummed softly. "Mmm. That is a marvelous sound." Mister was smiling, but those sleepy eyes were still closed.

He kissed Thomas's chest, the curve of his jaw. *Love*.

Thomas reached one arm up, and pressed it against the headboard, stretching out long. "I'm going to open my eyes, and this all going to stay real, right?" Mister chuckled, chest vibrating under him.

"Yes, Sir." He let his leg slide up along his Mister's, loving the way their bodies made friction.

"Good. I was afraid it might be too good to be true. Oh, but look at your back. That's very real, isn't it? How does it feel?"

"Burns so good. It's like...I know you're right here, under my skin, inside me." Keeping that blessed clarity close.

Thomas's smile lit up the darkening room. "I like that. I hope it steadies you some. I know sending you out in the world wearing my marks, whether anyone sees them or not, makes me proud."

"It makes it easier, quiet. Like I...like the load is lighter." *Please say that's okay. Please, Mister.*

"I'm glad that you let me do that for you. We should help lift each other's burdens, shouldn't we? Isn't that one of the responsibilities of our commitment to each other? I want...I *need* to know that I can do that for you. I could explain but... well, truthfully, I haven't ever with a sub before. I don't know how it will sound to you."

"I don't either, but I want to know. Angel told me that I could just let you have all the stuff filling me up, that it wouldn't break your back." Sometimes he felt like it was fixin' to break his.

"Yes. Yes, please. I want all of it. Even if it could break my back, I want it. I need that from you...because I—" Mister stopped abruptly and took a deep breath. He could feel Sir tense and start to relax again. "Sorry. I've never told a soul any of this except for Clint, I'm not sure I know how. And Clint would tell me not to, not because you shouldn't know as my lover, but because you shouldn't know as my sub." Thomas snorted. "But we're not very good at following the rules, are we?"

"No, Sir. That's not really our way." He stroked Thomas's

belly, nice and easy. "Besides, how can we give each other all we need if we don't say so? I'll tell you a secret I learned a long time ago, and that is that ain't none of us perfect. We're just men."

"Shhh. Wrong. I'm a Dom. I am supposed to look perfect even if I'm not. And that's exactly why I'm not supposed to share these things with you. But I agree with you. This isn't about the lifestyle anymore, it's about us." Thomas kissed his head, ghosted a hand over his back, and let it settle on his spine.

"I need you to give me all of that because I have to understand what you need. I have to know that you need me." Sir spoke slowly, not just finding words but as if to make sure he was following. "I have to know, I have to really believe or I can't...it feels so strange to say this out loud, but...I have to believe that you need me without any doubt, or I can't pick up that flogger. And...I have to be able to do that."

"I hear you, Mister." It sort of suited him, down to the bone. "I've been trying to save you from all my shit, but, I got to say...I need you. You..." Thank God the sun was going down. It made it easier to confess. "You make things so clear inside me, and I need you to take me there. I didn't want to bother you, and I want you to know I'll always take care of you, but...I need this from you, bad."

"I understand. I've known that to some extent since before I decided to leave that journal where you'd see it. Where you'd know I left it for a reason. Your needs were obvious to me then, you couldn't hide them even though I know you wanted to. But when things are more day to day, more subtle, or there are issues I can't anticipate, I need you to tell me. I'd decided we wouldn't do a scene today because I didn't...I've used a flogger before on subs that just wanted to hurt. I felt like an asshole. I can't do it unless it means something."

"The hurting isn't the thing. I mean, it makes me hot..." And wasn't that a little hard to say. Hard, but good. "...but it's the part where there's no more counting. Where I don't have to hold it together because you are."

"The part where you can't be anything but honest. Where your trust is so complete that I'm your whole world." Thomas nodded, his words soft and reverent. "That's precious to me. It's a gift that I need to treat with care."

He dropped a quiet kiss on his Mister's chest. "Thank God we found each other."

"I love you, sweetheart. I know conversations like this are difficult for you, and I appreciate that you try. This hasn't been an easy road for either of us. I sometimes wonder what made us each believe we had to stick it out. I'm pretty good with words, but those I don't have. I just...knew."

"When I took the beating at the bar, I knew. I knew I'd do anything to stay here, with you. I knew you were mine." He'd known that there was something about Thomas that he needed more than anything.

"I am." He waited for Thomas to say more but his lover just left it at that. Simple and unqualified. He nodded his head and smiled. There they were.

They snuggled in silence for a while; then his belly informed both of them that he was empty as a worm.

"Oh, thank God. I really want enchiladas." Thomas laughed. "Surely we can find decent Tex-Mex in this city."

22

Thomas stood up, put his fingers on the handle, and flushed the toilet, watching the water in the bowl disappear and the tank fill up with water. A grin spread across his face. *So there, James. I can be handy after all!* He'd have stuck out his tongue too, but that seemed a bit much given that James wasn't actually there to see it.

He laughed at himself, put the cover on the tank, grabbed up the tools, and dumped them in the toolbox. "I did it!" He shouted down the hall and ducked back into the bathroom to wash his hands.

"Oh, rock on!" Sam leaned against the doorframe, applauding, a huge grin on his face. "Nicely done, o handy-dandy one!"

"Your brother is rolling over in his grave. He never even let me try. I'm sure that had nothing to do with the time I fixed his dishwasher and it flooded the kitchen." He dried his hands off and picked up the toolbox to put it away.

"He just needed to have faith in you. I knew you had this."

He smiled and hooked his free arm around Sam's waist. "You're lying, but I love you."

"Never." Sam lifted his face, begging a kiss.

He chose to believe because he wasn't saying no to that face. He kissed his boy, tugging Sam in tight to his chest. He loved how open they'd been in the last week. It felt a lot like their vacation had, and he was glad to get back to that.

"Mmm..." Sam smiled at him. "I got all my ends and odds done too. I think we're going to have to think about taking your boots to get resoled, Mister. You have some wear and tear."

"Is it strange that I love that you just said that?" Something about knowing his boy was taking such good care of his boots kind of turned him on. He'd admit it.

Sam laughed for him. "I have to make sure my Mister has what he needs."

Sam cupped his jaw, fingers stroking for a second. Oh, wasn't that a satisfied look?

"Thank you, boy." He gave Sam another quick kiss. "Now I need to put this toolbox away before I drop it on my foot."

"Here, hand it over, and I'll put it away." Sam took the toolbox and went to store it under the sink in the kitchen.

He followed, partly to be polite and partly to admire the way Sam's sweats rode low on the boy's hips and showed off that tight ass. He leaned in the doorway as Sam tucked the toolbox away. "So...have you given any thought to whether you'd like to go out tonight?"

"A little, yeah." Sam stood and faced him. "You?"

Of course he had. He wanted to go to the club. Despite being sensitive to his boy's needs, he was still having a hard time accepting that they couldn't go back. "A little. Yes. I'd like to."

Sam nodded, just once, expression going from carefully

neutral to...Thomas wasn't sure—peaceful? Determined? "You want to sit, have a cup of coffee together?"

He smiled at his boy. Coffee meant they were going to have a talk. Determined meant Sam wanted him to understand something, and peaceful meant that his boy knew he'd try. All of it suited him fine. "I'd love that."

"Me too." Sam went through the process of making their coffees. Sam took great care with his, and Thomas liked to think it soothed them both, readied them for a talk.

There was a time even very recently when being asked if he had time to talk made him anxious, made him worry about what Sam could possibly want, what was wrong. But standing here now, leaning in the doorjamb and waiting for his coffee, he was completely relaxed. Curious, sure. But not worried in the least. Whatever it was, they'd figure it out. He had confidence.

What he needed to do was hear Sam. He knew his boy needed to be listened to, understood, even when Sam didn't understand himself.

They moved to the couch, Sam settling down near his leg. That position allowed them both to speak freely, not have to control their expressions, and still touch constantly. And it didn't hurt that he liked having his boy at his feet.

He took a sip of his coffee as they got settled, and waited to see if Sam wanted to start, or if he needed a springboard. He finally decided a prompt couldn't hurt. "This is about tonight, is it?"

"Yes, Mister. I'm...I'm worried. I worry that we'll have a terrible time. I worry that I'll mess up. I have loved this—what we have. I feel like you hear me, like I hear you, like we work—good work. I worry so much that worrying will just make it a self-fulfilling process. I don't want this—Mike's or the club—to be something to dread, and I don't want to have to give up going out, knowing people. I like making friends. I always thought I was good at it."

Once his boy opened up, it was like a faucet, everything offered in a rush.

"Thank you. Breathe, boy." That was good advice of course, but really he needed to buy himself a quiet couple of minutes to think about the actual words in between all the worry. He rested a hand on Sam's head, a little extra contact to steady them both. "First of all, I won't take you anywhere you dread going. I simply won't do it. That's not constructive. Nerves are one thing, dread is another. And if we can't manage to make the club or Mike's work for us, this is a big city. We'll find our place in it. Does that reassure you a little?"

Sam nodded, cheek rubbing against his knee. "I know how important the club is to you. I want to fit in, so much. I want to be able to be comfortable there—like it was at Mike's that night. Angel said something to me about my 'clueless thing' and how it was working for me. I'm not playing games, you know, and if I was, it sure doesn't seem like I'm doing myself—or you—any favors."

Clueless thing? What the hell was Angel talking about? "I don't know what that means, but I assure you I never thought you were playing games." He took another sip of his coffee. Sam seemed to understand now that taking a pause only meant he was thinking, not avoiding something.

"All right. I'd like to get back to the club, and I take you at your word when you say you'd like to try. So let's talk about the club like one of our puzzles, then. The goal is that we're both comfortable, right? What do you need, just generally speaking, to feel comfortable?"

"Oh. Okay, right. Good idea. I...can you touch me?"

Sam's cheeks were lit up, but his boy was with him, trying so hard. "I need that a lot. Your hand."

"Oh." His sensual boy. He set his coffee down and combed his fingers through Sam's hair again. "Of course. Come up here if you like. Whatever you need."

Sam climbed up next to him, melting into him, drawing comfort. "This is heaven. It may be unusual, but I need this. You...you settle me."

It was perfectly normal for them. That was what mattered. "I'm glad. So. Can you answer my question? What do you need to feel comfortable? Never mind whether you think it's possible or not, just tell me what it would be."

"I felt comfortable at Mike's, like I belonged, like I was doing the right thing. You act so different at the club. I don't know how to be who you need. I know that's important to you. Can you help me?"

He thought about that. He'd already been considering his role at the club, his expectations, what was expected of him. "Well, yes. But perhaps not in the way you're asking. The only way the club will work for us I think, is if I am more of who you need too. I acted the way I did at the club for two reasons. First, it's what I was accustomed to. Habit, nothing more. And second, because I was trying to fit in myself. Whether I like it or not, people watch me at the club. I sit with Clint, and Clint has a very strict set of rules for himself and any sub he may choose. I naturally assumed that he expected the same behavior of me."

He stroked a hand over Sam's shoulder and down one arm, making sure to keep active contact with his boy.

"Right. I understand that. It happens at the rodeo—you have to act a certain way, especially around the sponsors." Sam inhaled deeply, let the breath out. "I sort of sucked at that part. I know, you're stunned."

He laughed. Oh, he could only imagine. "Shocked. Just as I am sure that you are taken aback that I am very, very good at following rules when I have to." And that was the important distinction, wasn't it? When he had to. Clint told him they didn't. "I'm ready to break out of the box, and Clint has given us his blessing. So we can decide who we want to be and try it out. If you're up for that, it will bring along a different set of challenges I'm sure, but at least we'd be navigating those together."

"I like that idea. The together part. We're good at together. So, what do we do, Mister? I think we need a little bit of a plan. I mean, can I stay close to you? I'll leave the hat here if we don't have to pretend we don't like each other."

"Oh, Sam." He laughed again. "Regardless of what we decide, I'm going to explain all of it to you a little better. Service is about showing love, though I can understand your impression." He rested a hand on his boy's knee and kissed Sam's forehead. "We do need a plan. So I was thinking about the things I would miss most about the club. The things that mattered to me. And as it turns out, they're actually very simple, I think. I'd miss my leather. I love how attentive you are. And, honestly, I'd miss showing you off."

"Showing me off?" Sam cupped his jaw. "Like anyone would see me with you there."

"Are you kidding? Everyone sees you there with me. They see my sub. Outside the club, and places like it, they see my lover. It's different."

"How? How is it different? I mean, I understand that you don't kneel at a restaurant. Is that it?"

"Would you?" Object lesson. It was the only way he knew to explain it.

"For you, yes. You wouldn't ask me if it wasn't important." Sam winked at him. "Or clean."

He snorted. *So much for that.*

"You've already destroyed my object lesson, my boy." He smiled and gave Sam a squeeze. "I ought to have known. All right. How about this. If we walk into a pub holding hands and take a seat at the bar, everyone will assume we're a couple. If we walk into the club holding hands, everyone will quickly assess which one of us is the Dom and which is the sub. It's about mindset. Context. At the club I want people to see my sub. I want them to see your service. How we care for each other in that context. Does that make more sense?"

Sam's head tilted like he heard a whistle. "Yes. I think so. I was trying not to be seen."

Wait. He leaned a little, catching those hazel eyes. "You were? Well. That would be a rather serious oversight on my part."

Sam shrugged, looking a little uncomfortable but not hiding away from him, not masking his discomfort with fury. "I thought that was what you wanted, Mister. Out of sight, out of mind. I thought that was what I was supposed to do."

He sighed. "It wasn't at all. But that's not your fault, boy. It's mine. I wasn't clear, obviously, about the purpose of the rules I'd asked you to follow. Keeping your eyes low and being respectful doesn't mean you should disappear. I'm so, so sorry." His stomach twisted, and he felt sick with the realization that he'd done this to Sam. That he'd made the boy feel so insignificant. He tried to console himself with the notion that Sam knew better now, but it was cold comfort in light of all the pain it had caused the boy. "Entirely my fault."

Sam crawled into his lap, holding on to him. "It was a misunderstanding. We have a lot of those. Now we figured it out, right? Or we are figuring it out."

"It was a big one." The best he could say for himself was that it was an honest mistake. But honesty carried a lot of weight with his boy. He'd be soul searching for a little while yet, but Sam's instant forgiveness mattered. He tightened his arms around his boy and decided if Sam was more interested in moving forward, he could be too. "And we will figure it out, yes."

He took a breath and loosened his grip on his boy. "So." Where were they? He'd taken one hell of an emotional detour.

"So, no invisibility. Got it." Sam kissed him. "Can I lean on your leg at the club? Is that too much? To be affectionate?"

"Not at all. Certainly, you may." Frankly, he dared anyone to tell him affection was inappropriate. He'd seen plenty of blissed-out subs crawling all over their Masters. "What else do you need?"

"You."

Well, that was clear enough.

"Done." He tipped Sam's face up and kissed the boy gently. "So, the rest we play by ear. You need a way to speak up in the moment so I can pay attention to what's happening. I suggest your soft limit safe word." That would offer him both a clear understanding that Sam was uneasy and a convenient excuse to step away.

"I can do that, Mister. I will do that." Sam met his eyes. "And it's okay, right? It won't get you in trouble with your people?"

That was a reasonable question. "It will be fine. There are advantages to using it, in fact. Because we can step away and talk, and when we come back, no one will ask us about it. They'll regard it as personal and it shouldn't even come up."

But the way Sam had phrased that question brought up a question of his own. "What can I do to help you make the club your place as well? Are you interested in making friends there? What do you want to get out of going?"

"Those are two different questions. One's easy. I want to make friends, but Mister, how on earth can that happen when you can't talk or smile or look? I mean, I'm good at friendly, but no one's that good."

"Telepathy isn't a common trait among subs, no." He laughed. "There's a sub's lounge, sweetheart. I've just never sent you because you haven't seemed ready to leave my side. I'll make sure you get some time. And there are parties." Well, not the New Year's party, but holidays and such were far less formal.

"That's fair, and you're right. I wasn't ready. This is a whole new land. I want...I loved that night at Mike's. I felt like I was where I was supposed to be—not at Mike's, I mean. I mean with you. I felt right. I know that...I know that part of it is about pushing too, right? Like the collar thing, the bad one, not mine." Sam stroked his collar with a single finger, smiled softly. "I think that now I could tell you better that I was stressed, and I didn't know why and you could help."

Thomas had to wonder how his boy had managed not to just stroke out, with all these things trapped in his brain. But the way that Sam looked touching his collar was worth every second he'd spend listening to the boy tell him all about it.

"I hope so, love." The irony being, of course, that he'd had no idea he was pushing so hard by putting his boy in that collar. Sam's boundaries, even still, seemed unstable and mercurial. At some point he'd find one that stuck. "We have to push each other some, right? Or we can't grow. Growth is important." For example, the very fact that Sam called it a bad collar meant they'd be revisiting it at some point.

"We could talk this to death, you and I." He grinned and eased Sam off his lap to the couch. "Or we could get dressed and go."

He needed to know if all the talk meant Sam was ready to try going out tonight.

"Okay. Let's do this, you and me." Sam smiled at him, nodding once, so determined.

The nod was everything. He knew when he got it that Sam meant business. He'd pull Sam into the shower, make a big deal of getting dressed, fuss over his boy a little, and give Sam every advantage he could to start their evening off right.

23

L eather pants made Sam feel...he wasn't sure. Different, absolutely. Sexual, yes. Not comfortable. He was comfy in jeans, but the leather pants were...new.

And they didn't look as good on him as they did on Thomas.

The harness deal under his shirt, now? That he didn't mind at all. Add that to his black Luccheses and his felt hat, and he was okay.

He had to admit, he liked how his Mister looked at him in this getup, like there was no one else Thomas wanted to see.

Thomas had on the usual uniform, with the pants and the vest, a tight black T-shirt, and stompy boots. Maybe if this worked out for them, he'd go online and find his Sir a couple of new options.

"If you're comfortable wearing them, bring your cuffs to me and I'll put them on. No chain unless you want one—the lighter ones are in the bottom left there. You'll see."

"I like the cuffs, Mister." He liked the weight on his

wrists, the way it made him feel like his lover was touching him.

"Well, let's get them on you, then." Thomas smiled at him, obviously pleased with his answer. Mister seemed pretty pleased all around, in fact. Energized. In a good mood.

They spent a minute putting the cuffs on, Mister taking his time with them like always, making sure they fit right. "I think we're ready." Thomas smoothed knowing hands over his chest, tracing the lines of his harness. The touch made his nipples draw up, hard and tight, and he groaned softly, his eyelids going heavy. *Damn.*

"That's my boy." Mister kissed him, grinning against his lips. "Let's go."

Thomas sprung for an Uber and tucked him close on the ride, even though he'd said he was perfectly happy to walk, and they climbed out of the car into a lovely night. Summer was coming; he could feel the humidity in the air.

Mister stopped them just outside the front door. "Any questions before we go in?"

"No, Sir. No invisibility, yellow if I need you, and tomorrow is going to be a good day, regardless." *Dammit.*

He was nervous, sure, but he was determined to do his best here. To let Thomas help make it okay.

"It is. And I'll start tomorrow off early for you when we get home tonight." Mister winked and kissed him quickly; then they headed inside.

He was still buzzing from that kiss when they headed into the big main room. It was a busy night; the dance floor filled with men, and there was even a little line at the bar.

Mister actually tugged on his hand, scooting him around in front as they made their way through the crowd, hands resting on his shoulders. "Don't want to get separated."

Thomas seemed to know where they were headed though, steering him along the bar toward the back. It was slow-going because, as usual, everyone knew Thomas and had to say hello.

"Thomas!" Oh, that guy looked familiar, and the guy's sub too. Thomas stepped around him and gave the man a hug.

"Adam. How've you been?"

"Me? I've been fine, but where the hell have you been?"

"Sam and I took a vacation."

And it had been amazing. He couldn't have stopped his smile if he wanted to.

"Oh, lucky! Where did you go?"

"We went down to Texas so I could meet Sam's parents, and Sam arranged the most amazing tour of...where did we start, boy? Before Austin?"

"Fort Worth, Mister. We went to the Stockyards, to Billy Bob's. I think you liked the steak supper at the Cattlemen's the best." Watching his Mister eat steak was in the top twenty glorious things in life.

"Oh, that steak." Thomas grinned at Adam. "And Austin and the beach at Corpus...such a good time."

"Sounds like it. You both look fantastic. I'm a fan of your boy in leather."

Mister grinned, gave him a hot once-over. "Me too."

"There's room at Clint's table; have your boy grab you a drink."

"Thanks, Adam. We'll see you over there."

Maybe he could talk Mister into a steak tomorrow. Something decadent and juicy. He chuckled softly, and Thomas looked at him, eyebrow lifting. "Just remembering watching you eat steak, Mister. It's a happy-making thing."

Thomas nodded. "I love a good steak. That was a damn

good steak." Mister slowly steered him over to the bar. "Water?"

"Yes please, Sir." Sam didn't know whether he was supposed to go get it, but surely Mister would let him know. He had to trust that.

Scotty was busy, but Thomas got his attention and the bartender came right over. "Welcome back, Sir. Good to see you. What can I get for you and your boy?" He didn't hear one hint of sarcasm, and Scotty's eyes were low, pinned to the bar.

"Two waters, boy."

"Yes, Sir."

Oh, that was kind as hell. He hadn't realized how worried he was about this part, and Mister just fixed it. *Boom.*

Scotty placed the waters on the bar, never once meeting his eyes or Thomas's. "Have a good evening, Sir."

"Thank you, boy. We will." Scotty may have been watching his manners, but Mister had a little bite in his bark. "Clint's table, Sam."

"Yes, Sir." He took the waters and headed to the table on the wee little dais. He smiled at the folks at the table and nodded. "Good evenin', y'all."

Then he pulled out the empty chair for his Mister.

"Gentlemen." Thomas started shaking hands and a look passed between his Mister and Clint that he had a hard time reading.

"It's a pleasure to see you again, Tommy. And your Mister O'Reilly, of course. Welcome home."

"Thank you, boy." Mister took a seat.

"You're welcome, Sir." He got Mister settled with a smile. "Let me hang up my hat, Mister?"

He got a tilted head, a nod, a smile. "Good idea, boy."

Sam found a hook for his hat close by, one his Mister could keep his eye on, then he found his place next to Thomas's chair. He loved the way that there were soft places to settle. He could touch, he could relax, and he could breathe a little.

"Tommy, your boy's stool…" Clint inclined his head.

"Thank you. He'll let me know if he needs it."

"Very good. So this is a nice surprise; I wasn't aware you had plans to be here."

"We've been playing the last few weekends by ear." Mister rested a hand on his shoulder.

He leaned his head down, rubbing the strong hand with his cheek. They'd been figuring things out, together.

"It's good to see you. Seriously. I want to hear all about your vacation sometime. I've never been to Texas." Adam's laughter was friendly, low. "Tell me it's full of stunning cowboy butts, man."

Mister chuckled. "I ought to have known that would be your first thought, Adam. Wranglers do have a certain appeal, yes. But I think I was more impressed by the boys in chaps at the rodeo in Austin."

Sam grinned. Lord have mercy. He had offered more than once to ride, but he guessed he was well and truly retired. Mister worried about his head.

Of course, there was nothing that said he couldn't wear his chaps for a certain man's gratification.

Adam laughed. "I don't know, I have a hard time picturing you in Texas."

"I can't imagine why." Thomas gave that leather vest a tug. "You ask Sam, I fit right in. Didn't I, boy?"

He looked up into those gorgeous dark eyes. "Yes, Sir. My folks adored you, and you cowboyed up, all the way."

"There. You see?"

"Your Mister O'Reilly is very loyal."

The whole table cracked up, and eventually even Mister rolled his eyes. "Fine. Fine." Mister stroked a hand over his head.

"He seems well, I hope he's fully recovered?"

"Sam, you can answer Master Clint."

"Yes, Sir. I'm doing real well, thank you. Even the headaches are gone." And thank God for that. The low-grade ache had been irritating as hell. "Thank you for all your help when I was hurt. I appreciate it, more than I can say."

"You're welcome, boy. Anyone that is important to Tommy is important to me. You have a great deal of support here, you'll come to learn."

Mister's hand that had been absently stroking his hair stilled, then dropped to squeeze his shoulder.

"Thank you, Sir. I appreciate it." He wrapped one hand around Mister's ankle.

The conversation wove around after that from summer plans, to work, and he was able to just settle, listening but mostly focusing on his Mister, and the comfortable warmth between them. It wasn't quite the same as Mike's had been —he still felt eyes on him—but at least it was without the worry he'd had before.

"Are you interested in visiting the lounge, Sam? Adam's boy is taking a break if you'd like to go with him."

"I think I will, for a second." He was curious—both about this lounge and meeting folks. Hell, he was a little curious about the club. He stood up and smiled at Thomas. "I'll be right back."

Rick smiled at him and led him down into a comfortable, good-sized room, filled with soft furniture and low lights.

"Isn't this nice?"

"It is. Haven't you been back here before? It's nice to have a place to kind of turn your brain off for a minute, you know? Because...God." Rick flopped on one of the couches.

"I haven't, no. I'm new at everything, but I'm learning." He sat too, spreading out a little bit. "I swear, these pants get warm."

"So take them off." Rick sounded completely serious.

He smiled, but he thought that might be a little far for him.

Another man—an older guy with a warm smile and twinkling gray eyes with the best laugh lines—shook his head. "I always use an ice pack."

Rick snorted. "That's because your master has always got you caged up, Ty."

Okay, Sam didn't even want to know what that meant.

"I won't argue that. I'm Ty Little, Markus's boy."

"Sam O'Reilly. Pleased."

"Sam is with—"

"Master Thomas, I know. It's not you, it's warm out there tonight. What do you do, Sam?" Not hey, I knew your brother, or how are things with Thomas. Ty was asking about him.

"I'm a specialist in Old West art and costuming. I do research, consulting, and I'm working on a book." He grinned over and winked. "In other words, I work from home and try not to spend all day playing Candy Crush."

Ty and Rick both laughed, and Rick's head tilted at him. "That's crazy. Who do you consult for? Like, TV or something?"

"Sometimes. Mostly I work with set designers and authors, but I've done a bit of television." He shrugged but let himself be proud of what he'd done. "It's a strange job, but I'm making it work for me."

"Sounds like fun." Ty sighed. "Rick, how's the yoga working for you?"

"Oh." Rick sat up. "It's going okay. I think I like it? I don't really know if it's helping with the whole concentration issue yet, but it's not as out there as I thought it would be."

"I told you."

"I used to love yoga. I spent a lot of time training myself to stand on my head."

"See, Rick? It's good for the soul." Ty stood and got himself a water from a small fridge. "Sam, are you one of those people that likes to hang out in a headstand for a while?"

"Lord, yes. It's sort of comforting. All that blood rushing to your head." He chuckled at himself.

"Can't you just smoke up and get the same effect?" Rick cracked himself up.

"I've been trying to convince Rick that yoga would be good for his—"

"Restless thing. I get restless. I have the worst subspace ever. Makes Adam crazy." Rick flopped onto the couch again.

"I get that. The restless thing. A lot." He liked the way his Mister helped with that. It made him feel strong and quiet and solid.

"Yeah. I'm okay most of the time, I just don't do the whole kneeling and being still stuff very well. Ty thinks the yoga will help. Sir's been good about it. He's patient. And he's into the whole over his knee thing when I don't quite meet his expectations."

Ty laughed. "That's why it works. He looks forward to you not quite managing it."

Rick blushed. "Maybe."

Okay, that was...a little shivery, a little odd, a lot understandable. Mister promised to tell him how to ask for what he needed, though. He wasn't exactly clear on that part. Not yet.

Ty drank down the water in four huge gulps. "Okay, boys. I better get out there, I'm at my ten." Ty bumped fists with Rick, then smiled at Sam, easy and open. "Great to meet you. See you out there."

"You know it." Sam smiled right back. "It was a pleasure."

"You must get a long way on those manners, Sam." Rick shook his head. "They're charming."

"I was raised with them."

"I like it, it suits you. I'm not sure I knew how to say please and thank you. I'm totally an expert now, though, right? Is it weird for you, living up here?"

"Sometimes, yeah. Everything is different, but so interesting, so new. I'm just beginning to feel like I'm not a babe in the woods."

"You did seem pretty nervous when you started here with Master Thomas, I have to say. You've totally got it now, though, huh? Adam was right, you look great."

"Thanks. I'm trying to figure everything out, you know?" He was trying, and he was starting to get it, he thought. He was starting to understand how to talk to Thomas.

"Aren't we all?" Rick looked at him, the expression more serious. "Sometimes it feels like I just figure things out and then we'll do a scene together, or Sir will say something and things kind of tilt a little, they're not the same."

"God, yes. There's so many things I don't get."

"That's a part of it, huh? They keep us off-balance a little on purpose."

Huh. He didn't think Thomas did that with him, but there was a voice inside him that said it was because they hadn't gotten to the point where they could be off-balance on purpose quite yet.

"It's all good. We have the real power, right? They know it." Rick grinned, conspiring. "Master Thomas is wrapped around your little finger. Anyone can see that he loves you. I bet you could get anything you wanted out of him."

"He is a good man. The best." And the rest wasn't anyone's business. Sam felt like it was holy and precious, their love, their connection, not up for discussion with a stranger. He let himself smile, though, and show how happy he was, how truly loved he was.

He popped the whole "real power" thing in his pocket to chat about with his Mister. Sam suspected this was one of those things he understood but didn't *know*.

Sam just flat-out ignored the suggestion that he was trying to get something from Thomas. That was uncomfortable, because wasn't that just life? Everyone had needs...everyone. You needed things from your friends, from your folks, from your lover. You needed to give things to them, take things. That was just life.

"We should probably get back, don't want to be gone too long, you know? Adam might need me." Rick stood up and stretched, reaching up high, then bending over his toes.

"I'm ready." He stood up and made sure all his everythings were in order. Bags of ice? Really?

"Thanks for keeping me company. You're...real. I like that." Rick adjusted the tiny leather shorts that looked like they were still pinching anyway and rolled studded cuffs around thick wrists.

"You're more than welcome. It was nice to visit. You ready?" He sent up a prayer of thanks that Thomas was not in the least interested in looking at his legs beyond the ink that covered his scars. He'd look like an idiot in that getup.

"After you." Rick followed him out. When they got back to the table, everyone had a new round of drinks, and Thomas was sipping a glass of wine.

"Definitely *Jaws*."

"*Jaws*?"

Thomas nodded sagely. "It's got the best one-liners."

One of the other Doms set a glass of what looked like iced tea down on the table. "He has a good point, Clint. That was a good movie."

Master Clint sighed. "It certainly beats *Die Hard*."

"That was your pick, wasn't it Master?" Rick smiled and knelt beside Master Adam.

"It certainly was, boy." Adam tangled fingers in Rick's hair and tugged on it, making Rick's eyes cross.

He chuckled as he settled. Lord have mercy. *Jaws*. He hadn't seen that in a month of Sundays. He'd probably have to go with *Tombstone*.

Mister reached for him instantly, fingers running along his shoulder and resting behind his neck. "Did you like the lounge, boy?"

"Yes, Mister. It was quiet, real nice." He loved how he could feel each and every one of Thomas's fingertips.

"Would you like a sip of my wine?" Thomas held the glass down for him. "It's a very nice Malbec."

He steadied the glass, inhaling deeply. Oh, that was lovely. He took a sip, letting himself taste it. "Thank you, Mister. That one's lovely."

"Isn't it? I knew you'd like it." Thomas sat up again, took another sip and set the glass down.

"Tonight's demonstration is underway if any of you gentlemen are interested. Master Garett and Paul."

"Garett?" Thomas sounded interested.

"I thought that might intrigue you, especially, Tommy." Master Clint's tone was suggestive.

Oh, now what was that about? Who was Garett and what was he fixin' to do that was interesting?

Thomas cleared his throat. "Well, I might like to go watch for a bit."

Clint laughed, and Sam was very sure he was missing something. "Shall we?"

There was agreement all around, and the entire table stood.

He followed Thomas's lead, whispering as low as he could. "Mister, is my hat safe where it is?"

Thomas met his eyes, stroked a thumb over his cheek. "It is. No one will touch it."

"Thank you." He let himself lean into the touch, let it rev him up a little.

Thomas leaned close, kissed his temple and whispered, "You're doing so well. We'll only stay a little longer."

"Mmm. Thank you, Mister." He smiled, unaccountably pleased. The praise felt like magic, though, and he loved it.

The group grew quiet and entered one of the public rooms together. Thomas took him by the hand and led him in, moving to a chair and taking a seat next to Master Clint. "Be comfortable," Mister told him quietly.

He took a quick look at the room, then followed suit and settled at Thomas's side, leaning hard against one leg, cheek against one knee.

There were two men in the center of the room, one completely naked and stretched out prone on a raised platform, and the other in black jeans, boots, and a T-shirt, working at a small table beside the platform. He assumed Garett was the one standing.

Lord, he couldn't imagine being all exposed like Paul was. Well, he could imagine, but he couldn't see doing it without dying of embarrassment. Still, obviously the guy up there wasn't dying of anything. He looked fairly happy.

Garett turned and looked around the room, nodding to Clint and Thomas and others, but only spoke to his boy, leaning over the table to whisper to Paul. Then the Dom picked up what looked like a cup and poured liquid out of it from a good height onto the inside of his own bare forearm.

Garett's eyes narrowed, and Sam realized as Garett peeled the now-solid substance off that it was wax.

Oh. Whoa.

He blinked a couple of times, fascinated, and when Garett picked up the cup again, he found himself tensing.

"Hot. High right shoulder." Paul didn't get much warning. Garett held an arm about a foot and a half above Paul's shoulder and poured out a long thin line of dark wax in a spiral pattern on one of Paul's shoulders.

Sam reached up instinctively, fingers touching his own shoulder as Paul groaned, the sound filling the air.

Mister touched his shoulder at the same time, encountering his fingers and tangled them together.

"High left." Garett had a different color now, a light blue, and drew another line, this one snaking in an overlapping S pattern down Paul's shoulder and over one side.

Paul hissed as the wax ran onto more sensitive skin. "Sir."

"Good boy."

Jesus. That made his belly tight, made him shivery and uncomfortable, and he'd be damned if he could look away. This was hot as fuck.

His Mister's fingers kept moving on him, touching him

—on his jaw, on his neck, on his shoulder, and that threatened to drive him out of his mind.

Garett started switching out colors and changing up patterns until Paul's entire back, ass, and both thighs were decorated, and Paul was moaning softly and almost constantly. Garett behaved as if the room had disappeared and was speaking to and praising his boy loud enough for everyone to hear.

He looked up to his Mister, needing to make contact. He didn't know what he was feeling, but he knew, one way or the other, Thomas would understand.

He managed to catch Thomas's eyes, and they widened a little; then Mister's lips curved into a smile. "Garett's going to roll him over next. Why don't we call it a night?"

Sam nodded, that smile telling him everything he needed to know. His body ached and he needed to move, something not sitting here, but that was just fine with his Mister. "Yes, Sir."

Thomas leaned over and whispered something to Clint, who nodded and said good night. They left the room hand in hand stepping out into the empty hallway.

Sam vibrated as they moved, his cock heavy and full in his pants. He swore he could smell Thomas, too, and it was heady.

Thomas turned suddenly, wordlessly pushed him against a wall and kissed him hard, fingers threading under his harness through his shirt. He pushed up into the kiss, arching deep. His nipples ached and he was burning up. God, he needed.

He felt hands on his ass, and Thomas pulled their hips together, but it didn't last long. Mister released him with a frustrated groan, hands going flat on the wall on either side of him instead. Still, it was long enough for that hard cock to rub up against his own, and he knew Mister needed as bad as he did.

"Want you," Thomas growled low in his ear.

"Yes." God, yes. He tangled his fingers in Thomas's hair and pulled him back far enough that he could take a kiss. On fire. He was on fire.

Thomas flattened a hand on his chest, breaking off the kiss and pinning him to the wall. "Stay." The air around him went cold as Thomas left him there, but his lover wasn't gone long, returning with a purposeful stride and brandishing a key. "Room nine."

Oh, thank God. He licked his lips and followed that perfect, leather-clad ass. He would have given himself to Thomas right there in the hall, but he loved that his Mister knew him. Knew he'd stress it after.

He watched as Thomas got the key into the lock with shaking fingers and it seemed an age before the door finally opened, but they made it inside, and Mister locked the door behind them.

"Need you." Sam went right to his lover, one palm pressed hard against Thomas's cock. He felt like he'd had too much caffeine, like he was fixin' to tear his lover up. Thomas was harder than Chinese algebra, and he went to rubbing through the leather, teasing them both, wanting them both to be shaking for it.

"Yes. Fuck." Thomas kissed him, only breaking off long enough to get his shirt off over his head, fingers a little clumsy. His lover was so eager, wanting that friction, wanting a kiss, wanting everything at once. He tore at Thomas's belt, tugging at it so he could get to skin. He wasn't careful—neither one of them were fixin' to break.

He dared to fasten his lips over his Mister's collarbone as

he worked to get that sweet cock free, and began to pull up a mark. After all, Thomas was his, balls to bones.

His lover accepted the advance, head falling back and letting out a lusty sigh. Thomas reached out and found the wall, taking a step to steady them.

"Swear to God, I could climb you and ride you like a prize pony." He looked around the room, finding one of those massage table deals and a big old chair. That would work for him. A little sucking to get Mister wet, a good hard ride, and they'd both be better people for it. "Come sit, Mister?"

"Mm. I like that kind of talk." Thomas went with him, cock pointing the way, hands and mouth busy the whole time. "Want that mouth on me."

"Yes, Sir. I need you." He got Thomas settled the way he wanted, one leg up over the arm of the chair. He groaned at the sight; the only thing keeping him from creaming his jeans was the promise of his ride. "Jesus. What I'd do for you."

Then he hit his knees, latching on to Thomas's cock and sucking like a starving man.

"Fuck!" Thomas gasped and tensed, one hand reaching out and gripping the nape of his neck. A couple of breaths later, Mister relaxed into the chair, fingers sliding into his hair. "Jesus Christ, boy."

He slid his hands under Thomas's ass and tugged, totally surrounded by his Mister. He slapped the heavy shaft with his tongue, his hips rocking like he was already filled up with what he needed.

"God, your mouth. So good." Fingers kneaded his scalp and pulled his hair, and the rich, deep sounds Thomas was making weren't helping him keep it together at all. "Saving it for your ride, boy. I want to see you, fill you up."

He sobbed around Thomas, making sure that fat cock was slick and ready. He started working his pants open, desperate to get what they both needed.

Sam pulled off, rocked back on his heels, and stood. *Fuck.* Boots. *Motherfucker.* He kicked off his boots like they were filled with fire ants and those offending pants went flying as he moved to straddle Thomas and yanked his T-shirt off, leaving him in the leather harness. "Need. Now, Mister. Now."

"Look at you. So fucking beautiful." Thomas sat up, pulling him in, helping him get his knees and feet settled, making room. "Come on, stud."

Sam reached behind him and rubbed the tip of Thomas's cock over his hole, slicking it a little before he bore down and took what he needed. The head popped in, scraping, the burn and sting fierce and sharp and wonderful, all at once. "Fuck!"

Thomas's fingers dug into his hips, and he knew his lover was trying to slow him down a little, make it go easier. Not that it was easy for Thomas either—his lover's chest heaved, and the groan he got in answer was dark and heavy.

"Mister." He curved forward and took the kiss he needed, beginning to fuck Thomas's lips with the same rhythm of his body. The world went away, the places they connected lit up and raw but so necessary.

Thomas's fingers moved to his harness and tugged hard, his lover using the leverage to roll up under him.

The pressure and pull cracked something loose inside him and he let himself go, let Thomas give him everything and let himself take what he needed.

"Sam. Love." They moved together, Thomas looking up at him, watching him the way his lover always did.

"Yes. Love you. All the way to the bone." He rocked, his eyes crossing as lightning shot up his spine.

"More, Sam. More!" Thomas growled at him. "Not... gonna break...right?" His lover gripped him by the hips again and bucked.

He couldn't answer. All he could do was ride Thomas and hang on, make the buzzer and get them in the short go.

"Yes!" Thomas's eyes slammed shut, mouth open and soundless. His lover arched, fingers bruising his skin and hips rolling under him. He felt Thomas's cock pulse, heat spilling inside him, making everything that much more slick.

He grabbed his cock, pumping once or twice, hard enough to feel it in his spine; then he shot, milking Thomas's prick as he came.

"Fuck." Thomas reached for him, pulling him down for a hard kiss, sweeping a tongue through his mouth.

He melted, his heart slamming, rattling his rib cage. The kiss went sloppy, damn near lazy, and he held on, so he wouldn't just shake apart.

"Need to breathe you like air, Sam." Thomas whispered to him, holding him, keeping him steady.

He nodded, nuzzling into Thomas's throat. God, yes. His love.

They stayed there so long, he felt like maybe they'd dozed off for a bit. The next thing he was really aware of was Thomas chuckling, his lover's chest vibrating against his cheek. "I think we found that pit bull your mother was talking about. I like him off his leash."

"I got no idea what you're talking about." He was all grins. "None."

"That's a shame, because I'd love to do that again." Thomas smoothed a hand over his thigh.

"Mmm…" He lifted his face and took another kiss. "That was…yeah. I was burning for you."

"Your eyes. You looked up at me and I just…God, you made me ache. I'm surprised I could walk. I wanted you right there in that hallway."

"I would have let you. I was…riled up." And that, ladies and gentlemen, was the understatement of the century.

Thomas laughed again. "Clint would not. It's against the rules. But that is very, very good to know."

They looked at each other; then they began to cackle together, both of them just rolling.

Thomas lifted him and set him on his feet, standing and still giggling. "Towels in the cabinet, bottom shelf. I think there might be baby wipes too. Yes, I really said that."

He cracked up, heading for the cabinet. Baby wipes. Good Lord and butter, they had a life and a half.

24

Eggs and bacon, coffee, toast...Thomas was just about done making breakfast and no sign of Sam yet. He felt rather smug about that, his boy, all worn out. Breakfast would keep warm.

He was high over the whole evening, as a matter of fact. Sam had done so well. The changes they'd talked about making seemed so big when they discussed them, but in context they didn't feel out of place, or even all that different from everyone else. Not really.

Clint had been a gracious host; Sam had taken time to explore the lounge and maybe meet some people. Even he hadn't felt so relaxed there since perhaps Thanksgiving.

He was smug, he was proud, and damn it, he was sore. He grinned again, as he had been on and off since he woke up. Sore in all the right places and in all the best ways.

"Mmm...bacon. Love. Morning. Coffee." His boy was a bit like a caveman, grunting and nuzzling into his shoulder.

Oh, that was going to keep a smile on his face. He turned and tucked Sam against his chest. "Good morning, stud.

Coffee is ready." He reached up with one hand and pulled out a mug. "You just woke up, hm?"

"Mmhmm. I did." Sam stayed close, fingers teasing over his ribs, his belly. "Smells good, Mister."

"Don't tempt me to climb right back into bed with you." It wouldn't take much. Sam was so warm and pliable. He picked up the coffeepot and poured Sam a cup. "Fork. Eggs. Sit."

"Mmhmm." Sam pinched his nipple, playing with him.

Oh, damn. He hissed and took Sam's chin in his fingers, giving him a kiss. "Naughty."

Sam grinned at him. "Maybe a little. The eggs look amazing. Thank you."

He handed Sam the mug of coffee. "Well, I was making myself some, and I thought I might as well make enough for you, too." He grinned. It was actually the other way around. "There's a plate for you there, help yourself." He stepped out of the way to let his boy get breakfast first.

Sam hummed and fixed their plates, then handed him his before grabbing the coffee cup and heading to the table.

He should have known better. "Thank you, boy." He followed Sam, stomach growling and still smiling, dammit. It was unnatural. And wonderful. "How are you feeling this morning?" He was looking forward to his boy's answer to that one.

"Like a million bucks. Last night was...mind-blowing, Mister."

"You were mind-blowing, boy. From the moment we arrived. I was...I *am* so proud of you." He picked up a piece of bacon and took a bite, knowing his Monday workout would be payback and not caring.

"I felt like...like we were there together. Really together." Sam dug into the eggs like they were the best thing ever.

He understood what Sam was telling him, and he was relieved for both of them. He couldn't imagine losing the club for good, but he wouldn't have stayed if it wasn't good for both of them. "It's interesting, because I felt more relaxed as well. I suppose a part of me was worrying about you in the past, and last night I didn't feel that way."

"No. You didn't seem tense at all." Sam's pretty eyes twinkled. "A little stiff maybe..."

"Mm. A little. I'm a little stiff in other places this morning." He winked over the top of his coffee cup.

"Tell me about it. I like it, though." Sam blushed but met his eyes.

"I like it too." He didn't blush at all. "You know what else you're going to like?" He put his fingers in the collar of his T-shirt and pulled it down, showing Sam the purple mark his boy had left on him.

Oh, wasn't that a perfectly smug, satisfied look on his boy's face. "My Mister."

"Just so, boy. Yours. All the way, as you say." Strangely, he liked his boy's mark. He was proud of it. In his head it seemed to symbolize so perfectly how far they had come together and the ownership Sam was finally taking over those accomplishments. So much more than a bruise.

"I wanted you like crazy. We tore each other up, didn't we?"

"We did. I couldn't get enough of you. I just...wanted you all over me." They hadn't had a lot of opportunity to be spontaneous, and now that he knew what that felt like, he was going to make room for it to happen more often. "We'll have to thank Garett and Paul for their incredibly hot display, hm?"

Oh, that blush became a blaze. "That was...something else."

He put his fork down and looked Sam over. "You enjoyed it."

"I don't know how I felt, exactly. I felt a lot."

That was interesting, because obviously it had been a turn-on. Something about it had made Sam pretty damn hot. "All right. I suppose I can understand that, there are a lot of layers. The feel and look of the wax, Garett's artistry, Paul's reactions, and of course their dynamic, which is always breathtaking."

"You could tell they were connected. It was something else." Sam sipped his coffee. "I couldn't look away, I'll admit that."

"I think Garett and Paul's practice with wax is a lot like ours with the flogger. They've just found that single thing they both need. It's transcendent, when you're both getting your needs met by each other at the same time." They'd been there, he and Sam, whether Sam had figured that out yet or not.

"Yes. And it was hot too. I felt a little bad for getting all het up, but..."

"Don't. I...enjoyed the display as well." Now would be a good time to blush if he were someone that did that sort of thing. "Nothing wrong with an honest reaction."

"No. No, I guess they wouldn't show it if they didn't want us to look." Sam met his eyes this time, and that flash of heat was there between them again.

He let it vibrate, trying to figure out what it meant, why they were meeting so strongly in that space. "Is it something you'd like to try?"

"Yeah." The word was barely breathed out. "Would you?"

He swallowed, goose bumps rising on his arms and a delicious ache settling into his groin. "I would."

He wondered whether Sam understood his full intention—that he wasn't thinking about it in terms of a scene, but as something to share with his lover. He wasn't even sure how to ask that question; he'd never been in this position. "So...we will."

"Okay. You and me." Sam licked his lips, eyes focused on him.

He never felt the need to shy away from Sam's eyes, even when he was feeling less sure of himself. They didn't judge, they were only looking for honesty, and he always seemed to find whatever assurance he was looking for in them, however subtle. A grin gently tugged at his lips and grew into a smile for his lover, those eyes assuring him that Sam understood him just fine. His cowboy even understood his difficulty in asking, ironic as it was that they now had that in common.

He winked at Sam and picked up his fork again, banking that fire for later, letting it smolder. "You seem to have a better understanding of what you were feeling now, hm? We should discuss it, I suppose, but...I don't seem to know what to say."

"Maybe we can just be excited together about planning something new. We have a couple things—talking about ink, last night, hell, our cooking class idea even." Sam finished his eggs before continuing. "We could even talk about your playroom, maybe. Like, do you think we ought to dust it?"

He glanced back up at Sam. He wanted to cover all those things as well, and he'd been thinking about that room lately, too. "I think we should dismantle it."

"Really? Why?" Sam didn't seem upset, more curious than anything.

"Well, I have several reasons. We don't use it for one

thing, and I haven't had any inclination to, nor have you seemed particularly curious. The rest of the reasons aren't tangible, but I know you'll understand." He was certainly very clear on them in his own mind.

"Thinking about taking you into that room makes me feel different, more like I used to be at the club. The playroom belongs to that Dom; it's set up to his specifications, not ours. That room belongs to James's Master. My mindset is constantly evolving as I work with you. I'm not the same man I was; I'm not the same Dom either."

If Sam decided he wanted a playroom, they could rebuild it together. But as it was, it would never belong to them. Their playroom was their bedroom. Sam's needs bent toward the sensual and nearly always involved intimacy, and they hadn't yet had an intimate encounter as Dom and sub that didn't blur the line into their needs as lovers.

"Fair enough. What should we do with the space?"

God, Sam made him smile. That easy understanding, that acceptance of what he'd used to be versus who he was now. The belief that this was their home now, that they would build something new together.

"I thought we could rent it out to Angel." He took his last bite of eggs and managed to keep a straight face.

Sam didn't bother to try. His boy cracked up, the sound filling the air. "Oh, good Lord and butter. Can you imagine? He'd be making you crazy in about two seconds." Sam wrinkled his face up. "Tommy! Tommy, what do you mean you don't have the NFL package? Tommy! Are you sure I can't borrow Little Sammy for a couple hours? I'm bored."

Okay, that was a pretty good imitation...

"Possibly the worst roommate I could imagine." He laughed along and finished his coffee. "All right, so, the easiest answer is a guest room, but I'm not sure you'd want your family staying with us." No. Just...no. "We could make it...a library? A gym? Knock the wall down and expand the study?" The fact was, they didn't need another room that he could think of, so it was more a matter of either comfort or convenience.

"Well, we could put in a media thing, but we spend a lot of time reading." Sam's smile was blissful, easy. "We've got all the time to ponder and plan."

"You mean like a big screen? That's an idea, too. Why don't we think about it while we pack up what's in there. You could comb through things, see if anything intrigues you, and we'll keep it." He could send his boy on a hunt for the wax and see what he dug up while he was looking. That might be amusing.

"Sure, if you don't mind. I mean, it's got to be a little weird, huh?"

He nodded. "The room does hold some ghosts, it's true. It was worse before we went to the graveyard. I was able to put a lot of that in perspective when I was there. The few things I knew I couldn't use again are put away and there are a couple of things I've used with you without mentioning, but only if I didn't have an equally good option."

Sam reached out for him, took his hand. "I love you. I'm sorry we lost him, but I'm glad we found each other."

That was the bittersweet truth, wasn't it? If not for losing James, he wouldn't have found Sam. "I treasure everything I had with James. But we were meant to be together. I know that." Someone out there didn't think so, but he and Sam would find him. He smiled. "I would be happy to give new life to anything you discover that intrigues you."

"We can talk as I clean things out. Do you want to get out

of the house today? Go for a wander before our week starts?"

"Yes. I'd love that. We can walk, get some coffee, and discuss our ink." He stood up and took his dishes to the kitchen.

"Oh, that will be fun. Do you have any ideas, Mister?" Sam's chatter filled the air as they cleaned and got ready for the day. Sam touched him constantly, sharing kisses and little strokes. Joy. There was this easy, lazy, wonderful joy.

It made him smile, the way that joy called to him. He wanted to be around it, nurture it, for Sam of course but also for himself. He had a tendency to see everything as complicated, but this wasn't. Sam made this simple. All he had to do was watch his boy, touch him, keep him close.

So that was the plan.

"How about queso and a movie later?" He went looking for a sweat shirt and found a black hoodie he could zip on.

"Sounds perfect, Mister. One hundred percent."

He grabbed Sam up and took a kiss, hard and happy.

Hell, yes. One hundred percent.

25

"Two hundred and ninety. Two hundred and ninety-one. Two hundred and ninety-two."

Sam did his afternoon crunches, moving fast and easy, belly tight. He loved this part of his day—after working on cleaning out the spare room and doing his research before he got to work on his book.

It was pure peace.

Today he'd cleaned out the awful black dresser of doom. The whole top drawer had been filled with nipple clamps. The whole drawer.

He wasn't sure what anyone would do with a whole drawer of them. Hell, he wasn't a hundred percent sure what they'd do with any of them. He'd tried one on for a second and...*whoa.*

Just whoa.

Intense whoa.

He'd put most of them away and put two in the very back of his underwear drawer. The very back.

Lord have mercy.

His phone rang and he grabbed it, the club's number

coming up. "Hello?"

"Sam? It's Scott from the club. Master Thomas left his wallet at lunch. I can't get ahold of him."

"He's in meetings all afternoon. I'll come by and grab it. No problem." *Dammit.* Thomas would need it, too. He could just drop it on Thomas's desk and leave a message on his phone.

"Thank you." The phone call wasn't friendly, but he didn't expect friendly from Scotty. He was happy enough with general toleration, to be honest.

Sam grabbed his boots and put them on, then texted Thomas. *Fixin to get your wallet & bring it to you. Love you. Greek 4 supper?*

Then he headed to the club.

God, it was a glorious afternoon—warm and sunny, a perfect day for a long walk. Summer was well on her way, and Sam was loving it.

He wanted olives and feta, spanakopita and some gyro. More than that, he wanted to feed Thomas baklava. That would be messy and hilarious and would bring Thomas some laughter and relaxation after the day of meetings. He'd never had Greek before Thomas, and now he was an addict.

He went into the club, blinking a little at the darkness. *Lord, come on eyeballs, adjust.*

"Over here, Sam." Scotty, still a bit of a dark form, waved at him from behind the bar. "Bright out?"

"You know it. It's a gorgeous day out there. Thank you for calling, man. My Mister will appreciate it a lot."

"I figured he'd need it." Scotty poured him a Coke, set it on the bar, and slid it toward him. "Dr Pepper, right? Warm out, I bet. Did you walk?"

"Thanks, man. I did. It's too pretty not to." He drank

deep, the bubbles perfect. "Oh, that hits the spot."

"Listen, I just wanted to tell you, Master Thomas kind of laid into me the other day." Scotty leaned toward him, sighing. "I didn't take you for a snitch."

"We don't have to be in each other's business. I got no beef with you."

"Oh, I think you do. I think you have a few."

"What?" What the hell did that mean?

"I get that you're cute, but I really thought Thomas would figure out that a club like this is no place for a shy, dusty little redneck cowboy. I honestly thought you were smarter than that, too. You were supposed to give up and go back to Texas where you belong." Scotty pressed in close. "You just wouldn't take the hint. A pipe against your head and you wouldn't take the hint. Your brother was just as dumb."

"Motherfucker." He stepped forward, but his knees buckled, his chest hitting the bar.

Scotty slowly moved out from behind the bar. "Gosh, are you okay? You look a little woozy."

He reached for his phone. *Thomas. Thomas. Come on. Please.*

"Oh, I don't think so." Scotty took it from his fingers. "Come on, now. Let's get you upstairs to rest."

"Fuck you." He couldn't make his fingers work. He couldn't remember how.

Scotty got hold of his shoulders and spun him around, lifting him off his feet and over one shoulder. "Damn, you are tiny. My Thomas will never make me lower my eyes in front of your scrawny little ass again."

He felt himself moving, felt the world going dark. He turned and bit, as hard as he could. He heard the short, pained scream before the world went black.

26

Thomas trudged back to his office after his final meeting of the day. He needed to remind Ally that three in a row without a real break was too many. But then again, they'd been productive, especially the last one where he'd secured a legacy gift from a longtime donor's family. Such kind people helped to remind him why he'd chosen this line of work.

He pulled out his phone to see what Sam was thinking for dinner. Oh, Greek was great. But he'd lost his wallet? Where had he left it? Did he drop it somewhere? The last time he had it was...oh. The club. They'd been joking around and Scotty asked to see his driver's license picture. He must have left it on the bar.

He texted Sam back.

Sorry for the delay. Was in meetings. Greek sounds great. Did I leave my wallet at the club?

He ducked into his office and checked his email, giving Sam a chance to reply.

He didn't understand how any human being could get sixty emails in a single afternoon. He opened one from a coworker and half an hour went by before he realized he'd gone down the rabbit hole. But at least he'd managed to clean out most of his inbox.

He picked up his cell, ready to apologize for not hearing Sam's reply, but there wasn't one. He grinned. His boy must have gone home and gotten lost in writing that book. He knew Sam had been making some good progress on it. He packed up his briefcase and texted again.

I'm on my way home.

But he didn't get a reply to that text either, and when he arrived home, their apartment was quiet, and Sam wasn't there.

Hey, where are you?

He waited a few more minutes, telling himself not to get worried, that Sam's phone was probably just dead, and the boy was likely down at the club making friends.

Right?

Except his hands started to shake, and his stomach twisted and he just...knew.

His boy would never give him time to get worried. Not after...no. Sam would call from wherever he was, have someone else text. Something.

He picked up the phone and called the club.

"Good evening, this is Scotty. How can I help you?"

"Scotty." He took a breath, trying to keep the anxiety out of his voice. "It's Master Thomas. Is Sam there? I think he might have come down there to pick up my wallet."

"He said he was going to stop by, yes. I haven't seen him yet, though."

His mind started racing. Where else would Sam go? "You...you've been there since I left earlier?" He put Scotty on speaker and started texting Mike.

Hey Mike. Where is your tail on Sam right now? Can you find out?

"I have. I called him. I'm sure he just got busy."

Sure. 2 seconds

"He said he was on his way there...listen, I think maybe his phone is dead. If he comes in, please have him call me right away?"

"Yes, Sir. Will do. Hope everything is okay."

"Me too. Thanks, Scotty." He hung up his phone and waited for Mike to get back to him. It didn't take long, but he stared at the text when it came in.

Buzz says he's at your club

That didn't make any sense. He wrote a quick note asking Sam to call if he got home, left it on the kitchen counter, and headed down to the club himself.

Tell Buzz to stay put and keep his eyes open, I'm on my way

Will do

Something was up. His boy would no more fuck with him, worry him, than he would be caught in a lie. Something was fucking wrong.

He hailed a cab to the club, texting Sam again on the way just in case, but again, hearing nothing back. When he got out of the car the first thing he did was look for Buzz.

Buzz was sitting right there, a confused look on his face. "Man, what's up? Is everything okay?"

"No. What time did you get here?" He squinted down over at the club entrance. "Did you see Sam go inside?"

"I did. Hell, he knew I was here. He got here...three-ish? He was all smiles." Buzz shrugged. "I just figured he was hanging out, having a beer."

He looked at Buzz. "The bartender says he hasn't seen Sam."

"There's no way, man. He hasn't come out. I've been right here. It there another way out?"

There was, but Sam would have set an alarm off. Scotty would have seen him on the security camera and would have known Sam was there. Plus, Sam knew Buzz was here —there'd be no reason for him to evade the man.

Thomas stared hard at the entrance to the club, his pulse starting to pound in his ears. Buzz saw Sam go in hours ago. But Scotty said he hadn't seen Sam at all?

He stalked over to the front doors and stormed inside.

Clint was sitting at his table, looking at his phone, and there were a few people scattered around, but he didn't see his boy. He did see Scotty, though.

He took a breath and made his way over to Scotty, leaning across the bar. "Seen him yet?"

"No, Master, I haven't. I do have your wallet. I'll grab it." Scotty smiled at him, reaching under the bar.

He reached across the bar and grabbed Scotty by the front of the shirt. "Surveillance saw him come in here hours ago, asshole. Where is he?"

"Thomas?" Clint's voice rang out.

"Master!" Scotty's eyes went wide. "What's the matter? What are you talking about?"

He didn't have time to explain to Clint or worry about making a scene. He kept hold of Scotty and dragged the sub down the bar, then yanked the fucker out from behind it. "Where the fuck is Sam? Tell me."

His boy had to be somewhere on site, right? Locked in a room or some storage room somewhere?

"You've lost your mind. How dare you accuse me of hurting James!" Scotty pulled at his wrist, the strength surprising him. "Like I would bother."

He was shocked enough at the mention of James that he

almost let go, but the little silver ring hanging from a strip of leather around Scotty's wrist caught his attention.

Sam's collar.

Adrenaline shot through him like he'd never experienced before and he surged forward, slamming Scotty into the wall. "You little fucker! He's in the building, right? Where?" He hauled on Scotty and slammed him back again. "I'm going to find him whether you're still standing, or you're in pieces on this goddamn floor. Tell me. Now!"

Clint was suddenly right there, hand on his shoulder. "Tommy? What's going on?"

"Sam's collar! He's got Sam!" His boy. This son of a bitch had his boy. He flattened his forearm over Scotty's neck and leaned in, choking the bastard. Scotty might have been strong, but Thomas had never been so angry. "I can't explain now. No time. Look at his wrist!"

"What the hell? Dan, call the police. Now." Clint came up, grabbed Scotty's wrist, shook it. "What is this?"

Thomas didn't even have time to understand what the glimpse of metal was before it flashed out, slashing Clint's forearm.

"Clint!" He glanced at Clint, but he knew he had to get that blade under control. "Motherfucker."

Thomas shoved Scotty and hooked a fist into his jaw, the punch hard enough to make the bastard's head snap to the side and slam into the wall.

Scotty went down, and Thomas landed a foot in his ribs before flipping the sub onto his stomach, wrenching an arm up and taking the blade from his fingers.

"The cops are on their...Jesus fuck, Clint." Dan grabbed a bar towel and rushed past him.

He looked over at Clint, where Dan was putting pressure on his mentor's forearm. He kept one knee in between

Scotty's shoulders as he took Sam's collar off the bastard's wrist. "Are you all right? I need to find my boy."

"Go. Go, find him. Jesus Christ. Go." Clint handed him the key ring. "Opens every fucking door."

"He's out, Dan. Don't you let him get up."

"No, Sir."

He looked at the key ring in his shaking fingers and the master key hanging on it and nodded to Clint.

He checked all the locked playrooms down the big hall first, heart pounding harder as he found each one empty. The hall that went down to the fire door was deserted as well.

That was as much of the club as he'd ever been in, apart from Clint's office, and he took a second to catch his breath and think where to try next. He jogged past everyone again, and into the storage areas behind the bar, forcing himself not to panic when he found no sign of Sam there either.

He almost missed the door at the far end of the room because it was dark down there, and he ran toward it, getting out the key again.

Thomas heard it then, a steady, sharp banging. Over and over. One, two, three, four, then a break, then one, two, three, four.

Sam.

He unlocked the door finding a dark stairwell and bolted up the steps. He reached for the doorknob, but suddenly thought better of it and yanked his hand away just before he gripped it. *Fuck,* that was a good call. The blades on the doorknob could have been laced with anything.

"Sam! I'm here. Are you all right?" He called through the door. "Blades on the doorknob, hang on, sweetheart."

The banging sped up, got harder, rocking the wall.

Fuck. Sam wasn't all right. He needed to get in there quick.

"Moving as fast as I can, Sam." As fast as he dared. He didn't want to cut himself. "Breathe," he told Sam out of habit.

He carefully removed the blades, tossing them into a corner of the stairwell. Then he covered his hand with his shirt hem and opened the door.

Sam was duct-taped to a pipe—arms and mouth and ankles. He'd managed to break the tape holding his arms and legs together and was making as much noise as he could.

"Sam!" He rushed to his boy and knelt close, taking the tape off Sam's mouth first. "I'm here, You're safe. I found you."

"Thomas! Thomas, it's Scotty. He killed James. It's him. He killed James!" Sam's eyes rolled, the whites bloodshot. "He drugged me. Again. This is him. You have to be careful."

He put an arm around Sam's shoulders for a second and gave a squeeze, then kissed his boy's forehead. "I know, sweetheart. We have him." He let go and started working on the tape on Sam's wrists. "Breathe. Tell me how you feel."

"Pissed off. So glad you're okay. Glad I'm not dead." Sam took one deep breath after another, sucking in lungfuls of air. "I'm feeling about ready to not be in this little room anymore too."

"Yes. Not dead is a good thing." He got Sam's hands free and started in on the boy's feet. He was still so angry, so shocked it was Scotty, and trying to get his head around everything. "We need to get downstairs. Scotty cut Clint, and the cops weren't here yet. They'll be worried."

"Go on. Help. I got this. I'm okay." Sam tried to find him a smile, a nod.

"No, sweetheart. You're more important than any of it."
He got the last of the tape off Sam's feet and pulled his boy
into his arms. He didn't know what to say, didn't know how
to tell Sam everything he felt right now, but he knew that
his boy would understand, would feel it in his touch.
Words would come, but right now this was what they
needed.

Sam held him tight, shudders rocking the tight muscles,
fingers fisted in his shirt, almost tearing it. "Fuck. Fuck,
Mister."

"I know, love. I know. I've got you." Fuck, did he know,
but he made himself be what Sam needed right now,
holding tight, stroking a hand over his boy's back, soothing
away the trembling. "You're safe. We're safe now. This is
over."

"Not until they've got the motherfucker locked away."
Sam stood tall—as tall as his boy could. "He has my phone
and wallet, my hat, my collar. I want them. Now."

He has James's coat too.

"Oh!" He pulled Sam's collar out of his pocket. "He
doesn't have your collar." He reached out and fastened the
leather around his boy's neck where it belonged.

"Motherfucker. I'm going to beat him to death. You gave
that to me." Sam closed his eyes and swayed, his boy about
as pale as milk. "Get me out of here. Let's make sure he goes
away."

He would make sure that happened. He kissed Sam's
temple, holding on to steady the boy. "Let me help you on
the stairs."

They made their way down and through the storage
room, running into a couple of cops on the way who'd just
been trying to find them. Back at the bar, Clint was sitting
on a stool, being looked after by an EMT. Scotty was in cuffs,

but standing now, though his jaw was swollen and purple and Thomas wondered if he'd broken it.

He hoped he had.

Not bad for a first punch.

Sam stared at Scotty, stared the man down with an icy gaze. Scotty began to shake, face going bright red. "I'll kill you, just like I killed your asshole brother! You hear me! I'll fucking kill you!"

Sam's lip curled, and for a second, Thomas was sure his boy was going to attack. Sam though, he simply smiled. "Bring it on, motherfucker. You need your ass fucked? I bet you get to bottom in jail whenever the fuck you want." Then Sam turned his back on Scotty, heading toward Clint. "Man, you got to hire better people."

Thomas didn't say anything at all, just glared at Scotty until the boy lowered his eyes and the cops dragged the man that murdered James—that tried to kill Sam, that had tortured their lives for months—away.

He saw his mentor breathe in deep. "Mister O'Reilly." Clint's voice was low. "Sam. I'm...glad to see you're all right."

Somewhere in those words was a sincere apology that Sam would never hear any clearer than that. He hoped Sam understood it.

"Oh, Mister Clint. I'm glad you're okay, too. Seriously. Your poor arm." Sam reached out and grabbed Clint's hand. "We got your back. You're okay."

He made his way over and rested a hand on Sam's hip, catching Clint's look as the man caught Sam's eye. "Thank you, boy."

"We got to take care of our own, don't we." Sam wasn't asking a question. "Do you need to go to the hospital?"

Clint cleared his throat and sat up straighter, and Thomas would have laughed at him in a different context.

"No, boy. This lovely young man is going to stitch me right up. I'm fine. How's the hand, Tommy?"

"My hand?" Thomas lifted it to look at it, only then noticing how purple his knuckles were. "Oh."

Sam took his hand. "Well, I'll be goddamned. You left that bruise on the little fucker's face. Good job. Feels almost as good as if I'd done it."

Then Sam kissed his hand, the touch painfully gentle.

"First time for everything." He winked knowingly at his boy.

Colletti appeared, looking concerned. "Gentlemen."

"Detective."

"Mister O'Reilly, we're all relieved you're okay. As you can imagine, we have questions. We'll need a statement from each of you. If you'd prefer, I could meet with you in the morning."

"Let's get this shit done. I want to go home after and eat Greek food." Sam's voice was hard, firm. "I have to call my momma and tell her the motherfucker that killed my brother is in custody."

Food didn't really seem in the cards tonight, but he understood where the boy was coming from. He wanted to be done with it too. He'd had it with the games, with taking two steps forward and one step back. With surveillance and looking over his shoulder and wondering where the razor blades would show up next.

Clint nodded. "Use my office."

He handed over the key, and Sam and Detective Colletti disappeared behind closed doors.

27

"I love you too, Momma....Yeah. Yeah, I'll call tomorrow." Sam sighed softly and pulled off his boots. "Bye."

He plugged his phone in and went to find Thomas. He needed. He needed to touch. He needed a hug. He needed to know he wasn't alone.

"Mister?"

"In here, boy." He found Thomas in the living room, looking out the window at the streetlights.

"Hey. You...you need anything?" *Coffee? A hug? Me?*

"Yes. You." Thomas reached for him, wrapping strong, sure arms around him.

"Oh." He held on, trying to remember how to breathe.

James. God, the bastard had killed James, and everyone knew now. Had killed James, hurt him, over and over, and now...*God*.

Thomas kept him close, longer than seemed necessary, longer than should be comfortable, longer than seemed to make sense. But it felt right anyway. "I...feel terrible for Clint."

What? Clint?

"Yeah?" *Come on, Sam. Think. Thomas said it because he needs you to hear it.* "He's known that asshole a long time."

Sam was never going to say the motherfucker's name ever again.

"We all have. He was a good bartender. I just...you know how it is. All the personal baggage you end up telling a bartender? You trust them. They're in your corner." Thomas sighed. "You want some wine?"

"No, but I'll get you a glass." Sam thought it would be a while before he felt like having a drink. He wasn't sure he'd ever want anyone to pour him a drink ever again.

He headed to the kitchen and fixed Thomas a glass and grabbed himself a Coke.

"Thank you." Thomas took the glass and sat on the couch, holding a hand out to him. "I suppose it doesn't do us any good to try to make sense of something that makes no sense. But a lot of us trusted him for years. I have no idea when all of this started. I'm...just glad it's finished."

He didn't know what to say, so he just listened. He hadn't trusted Scotty, but that was James's touch on his soul. His brother's hand guiding him. He knew it.

He also knew that he never ever wanted to be drugged again. Ever.

No drugging. No hitting him with a pipe. No cutting him with razors. Nothing.

"I think it's just going to take some time to process it all. I'm just relieved for..." Mister looked at him. "Relieved isn't even the word, Sam. I'm so glad I found you. I'm so glad you're not hurt. I needed you to be whole, I needed us to be able to walk away from it. From him. I couldn't do it again."

"No. No, neither of us needs more shit. You found me." He touched his wrists, the crap from the tape gone, but he could still feel it.

Thomas reached over and touched his wrist too, purple knuckles less swollen after some ice. "I did. He made a mistake, and I figured him out."

"Thank God." He looked down at their hands, shocked to see his fingers trembling violently. *Stop it. Stop it, Sam. Thomas needs you. Stop it.*

Thomas put the wine down and gripped his hands tight, his lover's composure slipping along with his own. "Fuck, Sam. I was desperate to find you, I was terrified for you. Talk to me."

"I'm tired of that asshole drugging me." Suddenly Sam couldn't breathe, the whole world going swimming and unfamiliar. Thomas, though, Thomas he knew.

"He's weak and he's a coward. He couldn't get to you any other way; you're too strong for him, and he knew it. We'll make sure he gets what he deserves and make him miserable while we're at it." Thomas cupped his cheek and caught his eyes. "He will never touch you again."

"Jesus, Mister. Tell me it's real. Tell me we can just be... us. Just us now." They'd done it. They'd found James's killer.

"Breathe, boy. It's real. Your parents can rest easy, we can move past this. You can get Mike on the phone and call off your surveillance yourself." Thomas winked at him, leaned in, and took a kiss.

Sam hung there a second, almost perfectly numb; then he grabbed ahold of Thomas and clung, kissing his Mister right back.

"There you are," Thomas whispered on a breath between kisses and pulled him closer. Thomas's words had been strong and reassuring, but other things that weren't said were in his Mister's kiss. A depth that was hard to put into words. "We're all right, boy. Just us now."

"I can't hardly breathe. I thought...I thought he had me

this time, but you came." He rested his forehead against Thomas's. "Nothing ever sounded so good as you calling my name."

"I wanted to kill him, Sam. I swear, I've never felt that urge in my life, not like that. I worry that I might have had he told me where you were, but he wouldn't answer me. He was saying crazy things, hateful things, but he wouldn't answer me." Thomas rested a hand on his neck, staying right where they were. Close enough to breathe each other's secrets.

"I couldn't move. He said you deserved better than a piece of shit cowboy." Sam chuckled, the sound raw, rough. "Fuck that. We totally deserve each other."

"I got better than a piece of shit cowboy anyway, I got a rodeo cowboy. In chaps." Thomas gave him a half smile and kissed him again, stroking fingers over his cheek. "Breathe. I'll try too. We can just make that the plan for the next day or two. Just breathe."

"Sounds perfect. You. Me. Together. Breathing. I'll watch you sleep. Hold you." He didn't know if he'd ever sleep again.

Thomas's head tilted, the look in those dark eyes curious, concerned. "Ah. So neither of us wants to sleep. We didn't talk about how to ask for what you need, did we?"

"No." He didn't even know what to need right now, much less know how to ask.

Thomas stood, pulling him to his feet. "It's simple, sweetheart. Come with me."

He let Thomas lead him down the hall to their bedroom and through the door. After stripping his shirt off, Mister leaned him up against the wall, left him standing there, and crossed the room to pull his cuffs from the trunk. "If you can't find words, all you have to do is kneel. Anytime, and I can help from there."

Thomas moved back to him, cuffs in hand.

He searched Thomas's eyes, his heart fluttering like a million butterflies were caught in his chest. Then he slid down the wall and held his hands up. "Mister."

"That's right, sweetheart." Thomas took one of his offered wrists gently in one hand. "No one will ever bind you again but me. You're mine."

"Yours." It wasn't the same. It wasn't. It couldn't be. They were safe here. The door was locked. Thomas had him.

Mister spoke to him softly and strapped on the first cuff, the second hanging from it by its heavy chain. "I do this with respect and love, boy. Remember. I promise to keep you safe. You always have a way out if you want one. Give me your words."

"Respect and love. I remember." That had been the first thing that had clicked. Something that he understood, believed in. "Yellow and revolver, Mister."

"Yellow. And revolver." Thomas smiled down at him, strapping the second cuff in place before guiding him to his feet. "Tell me how you feel right now, boy."

"Like I'm fixin' to shake apart. Like there's a...a hole or something. I wasn't trying to be stupid. I was trying to get your wallet. It was a beautiful day."

Mister took him by the shoulders, strong, steady hands keeping him in place. "You were doing something kind for me. You were thinking about your Master—your *Mister*." Thomas gave him a fond smile. "Just as you should. Just as I would have wanted you to. Let the weight of that chain reassure you, boy, you were doing the right thing."

"I was." He did as his Mister said, focusing on the

heaviness on his wrists. That feeling belonged to Thomas. All the way. "I love you."

He needed Thomas to believe that.

"I know. How could I doubt it? You wear my collar, which is given and worn in love. I'm as much yours as you are mine." Mister touched the ring on his collar, pressing it slightly against his throat, and took a hungry kiss, tongue forcing its way in as Thomas pressed him into the wall. He opened up, gasping as he accepted Thomas's passion, and answered it with his own. He let his hands rest on Thomas's chest, the chain heavy between them.

Thomas pushed away finally, breathing heavy, eyes heated and focused on him. "Do you need my flogger, boy?"

All the questions he would ask—Was it okay? Was it normal? Did Thomas need this too?—he let them be. "Please, Mister. Help me."

Mister reached for him, turned him carefully to face the wall, hands moving over his skin. There was the strangest pause; then he got the answer to all those questions as Thomas's forehead came to rest on one shoulder. "Thank you, my boy."

He took a long, shuddering breath, allowing himself to believe Thomas would give him what he needed.

He heard the trunk open and close and the sound of the flogger in the air behind him. "Count, boy. Use your words if you need them. We'll start light until our heads are right and build from there."

The flogger came down light but steady, the falls showering his back again and again making his skin warm. It was harder this time, to begin to relax, and for a minute Sam worried that it wouldn't work. It did, though. The breath and the connection and the burn coalesced into something familiar and necessary.

The blows stopped and Sir approached him, stepping close and trapping the heat from his skin between them. "Are you with me, boy? How do you feel?"

"With you, Mister. Right here. Real. Clear."

"Good boy. Do you need your blindfold?" Thomas reached around and rubbed him through his jeans.

"No, Mister. Please. I need to be able to see." He didn't know if he could bear the darkness right now.

"That's fine, sweetheart. I don't need you to have it." Mister stepped away again. "Harder, boy. Count, please." This time he heard the flogger before he felt it.

He counted, his voice going husky almost immediately. His fingers curled against the wall, his hips beginning to move, to fuck the air. Home. He was home. *Thank God.*

He heard Mister huff out a breath behind him. "My God, boy. You're beautiful. Full arm now, remember your words. Breathe. Count."

There was a short pause; then the loud swoosh before the falls of the flogger made contact with his shoulders. The connection was a line of numbness, then fire, and he gasped out, his focus shattered. He bit out a "One, Mister" because he simply didn't know where they'd been, only where he was.

He heard Thomas praising him, reminding him to breathe, the rough voice weaving in and around his own sounds, and all the while the burn and sting, the power of his Mister's arm, made it hard to concentrate. He sucked in air, moaning deep in his chest as he flew, his whole world the rhythm of his lover's will.

Then suddenly he was in Thomas's arms and realized he'd lost count. His skin was on fire, every breath a kiss, and soon after, cool sheets and hot hands touched him everywhere.

"Mister," he moaned. He was lit up, desperate for those maddening, wonderful touches.

"Gorgeous, boy. So perfect. Right here." Fingers breached him, swirling and stretching.

He arched, his legs spreading wider as he begged for more.

"Boy." Thomas sounded impatient, hungry. It wasn't long before the fingers slipped away, and Mister's cock pressed against him. He felt Thomas's heavy breath across his back. "Want you."

"Yours." He arched, but just barely. Mister would give him what he needed. "Please, Mister. I'm yours."

Thomas sank deep, filling him, that low, needy groan for his ears only. This was something only they shared, that no one could know or understand. He stared at the headboard, not seeing a thing, his world distilled down to their need.

"Fuck, Sam." Mister's thrusts were smooth and strong, rocking them both, the pressure grinding his hips into the mattress. A finger dragged across his spine in a long, burning line, and the world snapped to rights. Suddenly he could see every grain of the wood, the heavy leather weighing his wrists.

"Mister!"

Thomas grunted, laying into him and panting through every stroke. "Sweetheart!"

Thomas slammed into him, pegging him hard enough that lightning shot up his spine. "Fuck! Right there!"

His Mister panted through a dark laugh and kept it up, working that spot over and over, hard enough Thomas's arms started to tremble with the effort. "Good...boy."

Sam shook, so close, right on the edge, and when Thomas bit at his shoulder, the burn, inside and out, pushed him over.

Thomas went a little wild, thrusts quick and shallow, fingers digging into his hips until his Mister howled and shot, hips stuttering through it.

He slumped down, letting the world swing. No thoughts. No worries. No stress. Just Thomas.

Thomas hung over him, kissing his neck and breathing in his ear. "Love you." Finally, Mister collapsed beside him with a sigh. "Sweetheart."

"Love." That was all he had. Love.

28

A t some point while he tended to Sam's back, the boy did seem to doze off. He'd spent a long while with the ointment because he'd laid in a little hard in a couple of spots. Sam had stubbornly continued counting and hadn't tired as quickly either, emotion and adrenaline driving them both to push more than they might have otherwise. Going over it—what he could clearly remember of it anyway—he was confident he hadn't gone too far, but it had been their longest session yet.

They'd both be feeling it for a while; his shoulder was stiff and his arm was weak even this many hours later as he watched the dark sky turn blueish with dawn coming on.

He'd slept for sure, not long, but longer than he thought he would. He was sure Sam had as well, but if they had been awake at the same time at any point, he couldn't be sure. It had been a long, silent night. That was fine, though, there wasn't anything either of them needed to say that the other didn't already know, and they both had plenty to process.

The only thing he had on his mind now was moving forward. Whatever was left of the damage that monster had caused Sam, they would fix together. He didn't think it would take long at all.

Every now and again Sam would reach for him, hold his hand, murmur something nonsensical, then relax again. Thomas had absolutely zero doubt his boy was comforting him, loving on him. He accepted that gratefully, knew he needed care, needed perspective as much as his boy.

That session hadn't just been about reminding Sam where he belonged but also *to whom* he belonged. Putting those cuffs on, sharing the intensity of that flogger was about the two of them together, taking back what someone had tried to steal away.

Sam was *his*.

His boy. His lover. His friend. His partner. His sweetheart.

"Mister." The soft word made him smile. His sensitive boy.

He kissed Sam's forehead. "Right here, sweetheart." Where else would he be? That was what mattered to Sam, that he was within reach.

"Thank you." Sam smiled for him, still mostly asleep.

He was glad Sam had gotten a little rest. Everything was easier after some sleep, especially emotional things. It wasn't a Sunday, it was...what? Wednesday or something? But he was going to treat it like one. He'd roll over and text work in a bit to let them know to reach him at home.

"Sun's coming up." He reached over and gingerly checked his boy's back over, thinking it was time to reapply in some spots. When he wanted to leave a mark, he'd do it on purpose; he didn't want these to scar.

"It's tender. You took me somewhere else last night."

He smiled. "That's a compliment I'll remember. My shoulder will too. That was quite a session." He rolled up on his side and found Sam's lips, dropping a light kiss on them. "You were stunning, flying. You made me feel powerful. I needed that." He sat up, reaching for the ointment.

"I needed you. I thought there was no way I'd ever rest. I was wrong. Thank you."

It was something to know they'd found answers together. To be with someone you knew could get you through anything. "My pleasure, boy. This is going to feel cold." He'd rolled the tube in his hands, but it never really got warm enough. He started on the least angry areas first, easing into it. If he could get the boy on a little endorphin rush, the rest wouldn't be as bad.

"Mmm..." Sam stretched, moving slow and careful. "With you, Mister."

"Good boy." He grinned. Some things about Sam were hard to get his head around sometimes. This was easy. "Today is going to be a good day."

"I'm in. I never have understood people who...uhn, aches there...who go out of their way to have a shit day."

"Right here?" He touched that spot again, just to hear that wonderful sound. It made him smile, and he moved on to more sensitive areas that might be...a little less fun. He'd save the small spot he'd had to cover with gauze for last. Sam had been somewhere in a space between sleep and the moon when he'd treated it last night.

Sam's breath deepened, his boy sinking into both the pain and the sensation.

"I'll find some chores to keep you busy for some of the day, but what else would you like to do? I'll have to be home in case work needs me, but we could...I don't know. Binge-watch something. Try to cook?"

He knew Sam was finding a good space, so he just offered his voice for his boy to listen to.

"Mmm...I bet we could find something to stare at. No murder mysteries, though." Sam tried to make a joke. It was weak, but it was a try. "We need to call Angel today. Mike too."

He laughed softly. "I'm surprised Angel hasn't shown up —" His phone lit up on the nightstand and he leaned over Sam to read it. "Watch that be...oh." He swiped it to answer. "You're on speaker, Bowie."

"You okay, baby boy?"

"I am."

"Tommy?"

"We're both fine. We were even awake." He chuckled. "We got the bastard, Bowie. He's done."

There was a long, long silence, then an, "Okay. Have they set bail or anything?"

"It's been less than twelve hours. I don't imagine they've done much but lock him up. I'll fight for no bail. I'm not sure who would put it up anyway." He knew, though. Sam's whole family wanted to see James's killer dead. "If it helps, I think I broke his jaw."

"No shit? Good for you. I hope it hurts."

He made a fist, testing his bruised knuckles. He hadn't even noticed them when he was using the flogger, but a full fist was a little sore. "Me too. A lot. I hope he thinks of me when they start poking at it. I'd be happy for Sam to get just close enough to break it twice."

All right. So he was still a little pissed off. It wasn't constructive though, so he took a breath and tried a laugh.

"Sam gets close enough to him, he'll never get up again. I know this to be true."

He understood that Bowie was far from home and hadn't been able to process James's death like they had. But true or not, Sam didn't need that kind of talk today. "Bowie. The important thing is that your little brother is safe now, right? No more chaos, no more nonsense. That's worth being happy about. That's our focus now."

"Good. No more attacks, right? None."

"No. No more. We've had enough." Sam sounded husky, but that was from him doctoring the amazing stripes on Sam's back.

"Tell Stephanie we're really fine. I know she's going to ask you." He grinned. "Tell her hello for me, too."

"I will. She called last night. I figured I'd let you two rest. No more druggings or head injuries. Sam needs all his brain cells."

"He does. I hope he regenerated a few common-sense ones. Did he tell you about our vacation? He took me to the rodeo in Austin and offered to ride." Because that would have been great for Sam's head.

"Huh. Impressive. Did you say yes?"

Sam began to laugh.

"I thought about it, and I decided I'd better stay on your good side." He laughed with them. "We had a great week, though."

"I'm glad. You two deserved that. Momma had nothing but good things to say about you. Congratulations."

"Thank you. I feel the same way. Your parents were very kind to me. How are you?" *How is war?* What a thing to ask.

"Tired. Real tired, man."

Sam lifted his head and frowned.

"It can't be easy, what you do." He tried to draw Bowie out a little, but he doubted the stoic brother in the family was the talking type.

"Eh. It's my job. No worries. Look, kids, I got to go. Love you, baby boy."

"Love you, Bowie."

"Take care of yourself, Bowie. Get some time off soon and come visit."

"I'd love that. I'll talk to y'all later. Take care of each other."

The call ended and he let the tension hang there, waiting for his boy to say whatever was on that busy mind, and went back to tending the boy's skin. "It was good to hear from him, hm?"

"It was. I feel like...I don't know if he's disappointed in me. I think I would have thought that in the fall. I would have just assumed."

"I didn't get that from him. I think he'd rather that monster were dead and I get that, but he's more worried about you than anything else." He'd heard Bowie's concern —no more drugs, no more beatings—Sam's big brother just wanted the boy safe.

"We're okay. I can't quite believe it, you know? That it was...him."

"It's going to take me some time to reconcile that. I thought I knew him." He sighed. He needed to check on Clint today. "You and I are solid, though. And safe."

"Solid and safe." Sam nodded. "God, yes. We need to make sure everyone is okay. People might need to decompress."

He smiled. He and Sam had come to the same place, they had this, and they had people they needed to take care of. "I think you're right. We'll make some calls today."

"Yeah, we probably ought to. I know Mister Clint needs a friend."

"Clint hired him. He'd been working behind that bar for...years. Clint trusted him." And Clint had been there for Thomas, over and over again. It was his turn to listen. "I'd bet Angel's pacing too."

"I know he is. Everyone's going to be fucked up for a while."

"I don't know, maybe if they know we're all right, that will help. They don't have to worry." They could lead that charge. He put the salve on the nightstand and leaned back in the pillows. "We're not...fucked up."

"No, Mister. You and me, we've explored all fucked up can teach us."

That was the truth. "I can think of better things to explore. Like...coffee. And breakfast. And...this curve right here. Under your jaw. I like this one."

Sam smiled for him, lifting his chin. "I like how you explore, Mister. I like it a lot."

The things he would do for that smile.

He hunkered down where he could look easily into Sam's eyes and kissed his boy, tucking a finger into that curve he liked so much.

29

Sam opened the door, blinking at Angel, who stood in the hall with three coffees and a bag. "How long have you been out here?"

He'd called the giant butthead, startled as fuck to hear Angel's phone ringing outside the front door. His friend looked a little tired. A little fried.

"Good morning. Been keeping an eye on things for you. I just ran out for coffee and food. I got hungry, you know? Are you hungry?" Angel balanced a cardboard cup holder in one hand and held out a brown paper bag toward him with the other. "Breakfast."

"Come in. Dork." God, he did love the crazy guy.

"Thanks. I'll uh...just put these in the kitchen?" Angel sauntered in, the big man making their entry hall feel small.

"Yeah, that's perfect." Sam waited for Angel to put the stuff down before he pushed into his friend's arms. "Hey."

"Oh." Angel froze for half a second, then hugged him hard, squeezing the breath out of him. "Hey. I know I'm a lunkhead, but I worry."

Sam grunted, because *ow*. His Mister had proved in no uncertain terms whose he was last night.

"Whoa. You okay?" Angel let go suddenly. "Oh. Whoa. Wow. Turn around, let me see." The frown of concern turned into a toothy smile.

"Perv." Sam turned though, happy to show off. He'd earned those marks. Every one.

"Not. Just admiring." Angel whistled. "I haven't seen Tommy's work up close in a long time. You're a lucky boy. You look fantastic."

Sam felt his cheeks burn, but he just nodded his head. "Thank you. I needed him."

"I bet he needed you too, man. Are you okay? Is Tommy?" Angel moved back to the counter, handed him a coffee and opened the bag, taking out muffins and bagels.

"I'm okay. Never getting drugged again, please, God. Mister seems solid. He found me."

"Right. Clint told me that asshole drugged you. And that Tommy laid him out. I wish I'd seen that—Tommy doesn't hit people." Angel laughed, but it didn't quite have the man's usual energy. Angel grabbed a bagel and leaned against the counter. "I just can't believe any of this, Sammy. I really can't."

"Me either. I mean, I knew he didn't like me, and I know he wanted Thomas, but...he killed James. Cut him into pieces." Sam stared at Angel, and he felt his cracks start to show. "Man, James was a good man. A real good one."

"He was, Sammy. We all knew it. Don't you worry there." Angel gave his shoulder a squeeze. "I'm just...shit, I'm glad Tommy found you. Mike was worried after Tommy texted him. I should have come down to the club right then."

"I think..." He thought that maybe Thomas had deserved to be the one to find him, save him.

Angel caught his eye. "You think...what? You think it's time to come back to Mike's soon, right? People miss you over there."

"Soon. I'm taking a few days to process. I need to talk to Thomas."

"Oh. Sure. Of course." Angel picked up his coffee and took a sip. "So I guess you guys do scenes at home a lot?"

"There you go stirring up trouble again." Thomas walked past Sam and gave Angel a hug, and the scent of his lover's aftershave washed over him.

"Is that weird? Seems like the most natural thing in the world, loving on each other here." Sam still thought some of the trappings were smoke and mirrors.

"It's not that unusual, if the Dom has somewhere safe and private enough to work. Oh, is this for me?" Thomas picked up a coffee. "It lends itself well to intimacy during or following a scene."

"Lalalala." Angel covered his ears, grinning.

Sam let himself smile. "That's one of the best bits, right Mister?"

"I think so." Thomas tangled their fingers and smiled at him. "Oh! Did you see his back, Angel?" Mister puffed up proudly.

"After I stopped staring at his abs, yes. You did some very nice work." Angel clapped Thomas on the shoulder and Thomas grimaced, but just for a second. He doubted Angel even noticed.

"Thank you. Sam wears it well."

Oh, didn't that sound good? He beamed a little bit as he went to make Mister a plate.

"You don't show off at the club anymore, Tommy," Angel said, which made him wonder how often Mister and James would do that. "You should. Bring him floating sometime."

He looked over at Thomas, curious as all hell. Was that even a thing?

Thomas returned the look, one eyebrow raised. "Like Master Darren's boy, Kynan. You remember? He was floating from his new ink."

"Oh. Yeah. He totally was. It was...beautiful." That he understood, all the way.

Thomas looked at Angel. "My boy and I will discuss it. Sam has taught me an appreciation for keeping certain things...personal things, between us. If it proves to be something Sam is interested in, we'll try it."

Angel's brow furrowed, and he straightened up, mocking Thomas. "I look forward to enjoying any such...display of...*personalness*, should your boy find it of interest."

Okay, there was a weird dynamic there that Sam didn't understand. He found himself gravitating to Thomas, searching for comfort instinctively, and Thomas hooked an arm around him, seemingly without a conscious thought.

Mister smiled, though. "I do it better than you do."

"Christ, yes. Teacher's pet."

Thomas snorted, Angel chuckled, and they both started to laugh. "Angel is teasing me about the etiquette classes that Clint made us take when we were training."

Angel nodded. "I failed."

"Spectacularly."

"Oh, I am not surprised on either count. You're exceptional at doing the right thing, Mister." Sam winked at Angel. "You though...man..."

"Little shit." Angel's laugh filled the air. "Fuck, guys. You two scared the hell out of me."

"I'm sure. I'm sorry. But we're okay, Angel. Better than before, really, because he's behind bars, and that puts an

end to all the mystery. We have answers and we're safe."
Thomas ran a hand down Angel's arm. "Are you all right?"

"How the fuck do we go back? How do we trust anyone?
We trust members, staff, with so much. This sucks."

Thomas shrugged, the gesture easy, relaxed. "We just do.
Getting on the subway is an act of trust these days, and we
do that. We get in cabs with strangers driving, we go into
stores and libraries. The members need each other. So we
just...go home."

"Yeah. I suppose so. Maybe I'll just go to Mike's. I'm
trying to get Little Sammy to agree to that."

"Give us some time, Angel. We haven't talked about
Mike's yet."

Angel looked disappointed but shook his head and
grinned. "That's exactly what Sammy said."

Mister looked at him and winked.

"I know Mike is going to want to hear from you at least."

"Oh, sure. He's on my list to call today. I know he's
concerned."

"He thought he was doing the right thing too, Sammy.
Everybody did."

Thomas put a hand on the big man's arm. "Angel."

Sam sighed and caught Angel's eyes. "It's not about that.
Okay? I'm going to come back. I just need...I need a little
time to figure out how to be Thomas's boy without this
hanging over us. I really need to learn how to stop running
on adrenaline and shit." He looked to his Mister. "Am I
making sense?"

Thomas blinked at him. "Perfect sense, boy." Sir looked
at Angel. "You understand, don't you?"

"Yeah. Of course. Sorry, Sammy. I get it. I guess I'm
anxious to put this away."

"I get that. Me too. But it's a big deal." He'd learned a long time ago that adrenaline was a bitch of a mistress and it was hard to learn to live without it driving you. Him and Thomas? Shit, they'd had to fight hard for every second without someone trying to...well, kill them.

Thomas hugged Sam carefully, one hand on the back of his neck. "There are worse things than having to get used to no one chasing you."

"You think so?" Sam was all over that shit. He lifted his head, begging a kiss, and Thomas gave it up, grinning against his lips.

"Amen to that." Angel pushed off the counter. "I'm sure you're both uh...tired. I just needed hugs in person. I'll check on you in a couple of days, okay?"

"He's really squeamish about personalness, isn't he?" Sam had to tease. Had to.

"I am not squeamish." Angel protested, but he saw a little blush in his friend's face. "I just don't...want...oh, shut up." Angel grinned. "He's naughty, Tommy. Spank him."

"Mmm. That might be fun." Jesus, Mister looked like he was serious.

"Me? Naughty?" Sam pursed his lips and shook his head. "Nonsense. I'm as pure as the driven snow."

Angel laughed and headed for the door. "You don't know from driven snow, Texas."

He and Thomas followed, Thomas laughing along. Then Angel opened the front door, just opened it right up without a thought. Didn't check the peephole, didn't keep the chain on, just wide open to the hallway.

His breath caught in his chest for a second, but he forced himself to keep breathing, stay relaxed. He could handle this. He could learn to trust in this.

He heard Thomas puff out a breath beside him, and he knew they both had a little work to do.

"Thanks for the coffee, Angel. That was very kind. I don't mean to sound melodramatic, but we're lucky to have you."

Angel smiled. Sam knew his friend was more sentimental than most. "I'm glad I could help."

"Me too." He went to hug Angel once more. "Maybe we can all have pizza in a few days?"

"Perfect. Just get in touch." Angel went easy on the hug this time, then shook Thomas's hand. "Be good, you two." Angel laughed all the way to the elevator.

Thomas closed the door, turned the lock, and took a breath. "My coffee." He got a quick kiss on the cheek, and Mister headed to the kitchen.

Sam nodded and wandered, ending up on the wee balcony, face turned toward the sun. He had to wonder what James thought about all this—if he was at peace, if he was pissed.

"Sun is nice, hm?" Mister stepped up behind him and rested a hand on his hip, standing so close, without actually touching his back. "It was nice of Angel to stop by. Did you know he was coming over?"

"No, I called him, and his phone rang in the hallway. God knows how long he'd been waiting. He was wigged."

"God. That's...do you think he's serious about not going to the club anymore?"

"I don't know. Y'all have some bad shit to deal with. I never did like him, so I don't have so much." Although the bastard had tried to kill him...

"Dealing with him is one thing." Thomas's fingers dug into his hip. "We can't let him take the club from us. Any of us."

"Okay. I'll help. You know I will." He would go fetch the moon if Thomas asked.

"I'll talk to Clint, help him call the members if he wants me to. Angel's been there too long for this to keep him away." Thomas sighed. "It's a beautiful day."

"It is. It's gorgeous." Sam leaned, real careful. "I can make phone calls too, send emails, whatever y'all need."

"If I know Clint, he's already working on something. I'm sure we'll all know his plans before long." Mister reached around and pulled him in a little tighter, just enough to make his nerves light up as bright as the sun.

The sound that escaped him was a little raw, a little needy, a lot happy. "Mister, that's...fine."

Lord have mercy, he was in all the way.

"Mmm. I do love your sounds, boy. I don't think you'll have much trouble learning to live without the adrenaline. I can always find you some."

"Thank God for that. You make me fly, Mister." And they had so much more to learn together—ink and wax, things he hadn't imagined yet.

"So..." Thomas stepped back and let the cool breeze blow over his skin. "You will let me know when you feel ready to talk about Mike's?"

"I can talk to you about it. I loved it there. It was the first place I felt like I started to understand."

"That was a wonderful evening we spent there, it's true. I think our last evening at the club was good too—it certainly ended well." Thomas chuckled. "But there was something about Mike's, wasn't there?"

"Yes. I felt like I could be..." Sam tried to find words to explain, but he couldn't figure them. "It was easy to breathe, to get it. I think the club is...it's different, but we had a great night. Wild." Sam blinked, then began to laugh. "Oh, Mister!

How great is that? The formal club is all wild, and the biker bar is the place to cuddle?"

He got a laugh in return and a smile full of fondness. "That's quite an observation. The contradictions are a lot of what make us make sense, right? Less now than at first, perhaps, but we're still all about little negotiations. I enjoyed Mike's because I felt like you were able to truly relax. It's such a joy to spend time with you that way."

Sam blushed dark. "I felt like I belonged. Like that was natural. And when I sat in your lap..."

Mister leaned close to his ear and whispered, "Tell me. Can you find words?"

"I felt ten feet tall and bulletproof. I felt like all I had to do was be there with you."

"I felt like we were being rewarded. I was completely confident in us. So...we'll go there first when we're ready to go out again. What about the club? I think we need to make ourselves do it. Maybe on a totally quiet weekday afternoon or something. Sometime soon. I don't want to let a lot of emotion build up around it, you know?"

Sam thought about what Thomas said, and it made good sense. "I think you're right. It'll be weird, but it won't get less weird if we don't go. No ghosts, right?"

"No ghosts. I waited too long after James died, and the idea of going in got more stressful by the day. I don't want to do that again."

Listen to them, communicating, talking, loving each other.

"I'm ready when you are. Well, today is not really a 'put on a shirt' day..."

His Mister laughed and turned him around, letting the sun warm his sore back for a moment. "Oh no, my boy. We're not going anywhere today. It's definitely not a shirt day. It might not even be a pants day." He got a kiss, deep and slow, like they had all day to stand right where they were.

Sam melted into Thomas with a soft, happy sigh and gave thanks. He was home. For real. All the way home.

END

WANT to know what happened to Bowie and Angel?

Interested in learning more about BA's cowboys and Jodi's gentlemen? Want free fiction and news? Join our newsletters!

What's Up with Jodi
https://readerlinks.com/l/2317334

Spurs and Shifters
https://lp.constantcontact.com/su/A9CRUzp/baandjulia

Hey, y'all!

We want to thank you for giving No Ghosts a try. We hope you enjoyed the story. We recommend you move on to the next book in the series, a spin-off about Bowie and Gabe, called The Soldier and the Angel.

If you can spare a few minutes to post a review at the retail website where you made your purchase, we'd very much appreciate it!

Don't forget to "like" our Facebook pages and groups to keep up with all the news--new releases, sales announcements, giveaways, sneak peeks-- and of course the rodeo pictures, coffee memes and just general fun. We'd love to have all y'all!

Yeehaw and thanks for reading!

BA & Jodi

The Soldier and the Angel

In this companion story to The Cowboy and the Dom Series, Sam's only remaining brother, Army Ranger and EOD Specialist, Jim Bowie O'Reilly, suffers an injury in the line of duty, and is sent home to the family ranch in Texas to recuperate.

But sometimes you can't go home again.

Thomas and Sam welcome Bowie for a visit in New York, but their lifestyle doesn't easily lend itself to long-term house guests. Enter Thomas's trusted friend, EMT and former combat medic Gabriel "Angel" Rogers. The two men met once before when Bowie visited Sam for his birthday, and it doesn't take the men long to admit they'd had an instant attraction. They soon discover their kinks overlap as well and they set each other on fire.

But two big men need space and, as neither is in love with the city, Bowie invites Angel back to Texas to vacation in one of the beach houses he's flipped. On the eve of their departure though, Angel's coworker and friend is gravely injured in an accident leaving his ambulance crew shorthanded, and Angel stays behind for a week or two to help.

The distance might be more than either man can handle. With a whole country between them, they manage to screw up what was going so well and it takes a risky intervention to stop them from ruining the best thing they've ever had.

Read The Solider and the Angel!

ABOUT JODI

JODI takes herself way too seriously and has been known to randomly break out in song. Her MCs are imperfect but genuine, stubborn but likable, often kinky, and frequently their own worst enemies. They are characters you can't help but fall in love with while they stumble along the path to their happily ever after. For those looking to get on her good side, Jodi's addictions include nonfat lattes, Malbec and tequila any way you pour it.

Website: jodipayne.net
Newsletter: https://readerlinks.com/l/2317334
All Jodi's Social Links: linktr.ee/jodipayne

ABOUT BA

Texan to the bone and an unrepentant Daddy's Girl, BA Tortuga spends her days with her basset hounds, getting tattooed, texting her grandbabies, and eating Mexican food. When she's not doing that, she's writing. She spends her days off watching rodeo, knitting and surfing Pinterest in the name of research. BA's personal saviors include her wife, Julia Talbot, her best friends, and coffee. Lots of coffee. Really good coffee.

Having written everything from fist-fighting rednecks to hard-core cowboys to werewolves, BA does her damnedest to tell the stories of her heart, which was raised in Northeast Texas, but has heard the call of the high desert and lives in the Sandias. With books ranging from hard-hitting GLBT romance, to fiery ménages, to the most traditional of love stories, BA refuses to be pigeon-holed by anyone but the voices in her head.

BA loves to talk to her readers and can be found at http://batortuga.com/ and her newsletter signup link is http://bit.ly/BAJulianews

AVAILABLE FROM JODI & BA

The Cowboy and the Dom Trilogy

First Rodeo, Book One

Razor's Edge, Book Two

No Ghosts, Book Three

The Soldier and the Angel, a Cowboy and Dom Novel

Sin Deep, a Cowboy and Dom Novel

East Meets Westerns

(single titles)

Wrecked

Flying Blind

Special Delivery, A Wrecked Holiday Novel

Temptation Ranch

The Merry Everything Series

Window Dressing

Cowboy Protection

The Higher Elevation Series

Heart of a Cowboy

Land of Enchantment

Keeping Promises

Bigger Than Us

The Triskelion Series

Breaking the Rules

Making a Mark

Making the Rules

Les's Bar Series

Just Dex

Hide Bound

Wholly Trinity

The Lone Star Series

Tending Tyler

Roped In

The Collaborations Series

Refraction

Syncopation

Puzzles Series

Cryptic